MONTANA GRIT

BEAR GRASS SPRINGS, BOOK TWO

RAMONA FLIGHTNER

GRIZZLY DAMSEL PUBLISHING

COPYRIGHT

Cover design by Jennifer Quinlan.

This is for you, dear reader.
Thank you for your enthusiasm for the
stories I create.

ABOUT RAMONA FLIGHTNER AND MONTANA GRIT!

Want Bonus Epilogues, sneak peeks, early cover reveals and other special bonuses? **Join my newsletter!**

Follow Ramona On Social Media!
Newsletter
Facebook
Bookbub
GoodReads
Instagram

Montana Grit (BGS, #2)
An interrupted wedding. A deceitful bride. A devastated groom. Will they forgive each other and allow their love to rekindle?

After fleeing her past and settling in Bear Grass Springs as the schoolteacher, Leticia Browne has no intention of falling in love with the charming liveryman, Alistair MacKinnon. The pioneer town was to be her refuge. Survival and peace were her goals, not love. She never thought to marry. Never again.

Alistair MacKinnon is a patient man, slow to anger and quick to forgive. He's waited three years to marry Leticia and his wedding day is upon him. When the door to the church bursts open, interrupting his wedding, he realizes nothing is as it appears. Now, he must face his worst fears , the town's ridicule, and his hardest challenge yet.

Battling despair at her treachery, Alistair must fight to regain his trust in Leticia while fending off the courtship of a desperate woman. Leticia, now a shunned woman in town, must find a way to survive by her wits alone while evading an unwanted suitor. Will Alistair allow the interloper to destroy his dreams or will he fight for Leticia and their love?

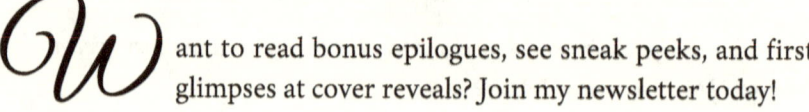

*W*ant to read bonus epilogues, see sneak peeks, and first glimpses at cover reveals? Join my newsletter today!

CHAPTER 1

Montana Territory, June 1885

*N*o one expected the wedding to be a disaster. In fact, it had been heralded by many in Bear Grass Springs, Montana Territory, as the wedding of the season. Another MacKinnon brother was to wed, to the dismay of the mothers in the town who had hoped for more than a wandering miner for their daughters. As for the bachelors of Bear Grass Springs, few eligible women lived in town; thus many of the men were equally disappointed to see the beautiful teacher marry the livery owner.

Alistair MacKinnon paced in front of the altar on a bright Saturday afternoon in early June. He wore his best suit and had polished his rarely worn dress shoes three times, although he fought grimacing with each step because they pinched his toes. He longed for his boots.

"Stop fidgeting and sit down. You'll give yourself blisters," ordered Cailean, the eldest MacKinnon sibling by three years at thirty seven. He shook his head in amusement as he watched Alistair.

"Ye were no' any better," Alistair grumbled.

Cailean chuckled as he thought about his own wedding to the

town baker, Annabelle Evans, the previous June. Although the two eldest MacKinnon siblings had left the Isle of Skye together over a decade ago, Cailean had worked to hide his accent, while Alistair had never lost his. "I know. But I was always the more emotional sibling. I never thought to see you pacing at your age."

"I'm only thirty-four," Alistair said as his brother smiled.

Ewan, the youngest MacKinnon brother at thirty, approached with a flask. "Take a wee nip," he urged the anxious groom-to-be and rolled his eyes as Alistair waved away the offered libation. "Ye dinna ken how much longer she'll keep ye waitin', an' this will calm yer nerves."

Alistair glared at his youngest brother. "I willna meet my bride on our weddin' day through a haze of whiskey." He allowed his brothers to push him onto the front pew.

"Ignore Ewan. You know Sorcha is with Leticia, and our sister will ensure they are not too late." Cailean rapped his fingers on the pew's back as time seemed to crawl. He looked toward the front of the church. "Guests are arriving, and Ewan and I should welcome them." Cailean placed a firm hand on Alistair's shoulder. "Stay here. Think about your bride-to-be, about what's to come." He gave his brother a pat on the shoulder and marched down the aisle with Ewan behind him.

Alistair sat in a daze on the bench as he thought about the last few days leading up to the wedding, his mind filled with images of his fiancée, Leticia Browne.

As spring would soon give way to summer, and the bear grass that gave the town its name verged on the point of blooming, Alistair breathed a sigh of relief that his long courtship with Leticia was almost at an end. As he squired his fiancée through the newly constructed home they would share in two days' time, he smiled with contentment. The new home had been built on the opposite side of Main Street from where the MacKinnon Livery stood, on a large empty plot near the alley that abutted the rear door of Annabelle's bakery.

"Dinna Ewan create a lovely home for us?" he asked, the hint of Scotland stronger in his voice as he beheld Leticia standing amid the early evening rays in their living room area on the ground floor. Although smaller than the home he shared with his siblings, the basic design for their new home was the same with the kitchen and dining area separated from the living room on the other side by a long hallway. Upstairs were three bedrooms, rather than four.

She smiled at him and sat on the secondhand settee given to them by Irene and Harold Tompkins—a couple who acted as doting aunt and uncle to the MacKinnons and ran the local Sunflower Café. "I love it."

"An' ye dinna mind that the kitchen is small?" Alistair stood over six feet tall, and his brown hair was virtually black in the dimming evening light. He watched Leticia with warmth in his brown eyes.

She laughed. "Do you know what it will be like to have a home that is mine? To decorate as I want, without worrying I'll offend the owner? To build a home with you?" She rose, smiling broadly as she wrapped her arms around his waist. Her thick blond hair, pulled back in a bun, loosened as his fingers tugged at the pins holding it in place.

"I'm fighting my impatience," he whispered as he pulled her close. "Two days seems an eternity."

She shivered and squeezed her arms tight around him. "It will pass faster than you imagine."

He sniffed her lilac scent and smiled. "Aye, I know. After waiting years to marry, I fear ye'll find another reason we should wait."

"No," she whispered as she traced a pattern over his lower back. "No more waiting, not after two days from now."

He groaned, bending his head to kiss her. She sighed softly, arching up to meet his impassioned kiss. After only a few moments, he broke their embrace, wandering the room. "I canna be trusted to touch ye just now." He shared a rueful smile with her, his smile broadening as he saw her pleased blush. He broke his gaze from her delighted blue eyes and looked around the room. "Ewan did a good job."

She chuckled as she ran a hand over her light-blue dress that nearly matched her eyes. "He did a masterful job, as you knew he would. He was determined to build a beautiful home for his brother." She traced the fine trim on the sill around a side window. "I can envision a vase of flowers here, with curtains blowing in the breeze."

He sat on a windowsill at the front of the house, maintaining his distance from her. "I can see us curled on that settee, warming each other on a cold winter day while Hortence plays on the floor."

She laughed as she thought about her six-year-old daughter. "You'll be on the floor playing with her."

"Aye, I probably will. Although 'twill be a tough choice. Canoodle with my wife or play with my daughter?" He frowned as he saw Leticia fight tears. "What is it, darling?"

She watched him through eyes drenched with adoration, love, and wonder. "I will always be humbled by how you have accepted Hortence as your own."

"She's an easy lass to love." He rose and outstretched his hand to Leticia. "Come. Let's explore our home." He laced their hands together as they wandered to the sparsely furnished kitchen and dining area, although it had a top-of-the-line Great Majestic stove. They continued upstairs, poking their heads into the three rooms before returning downstairs. "I ken I'm supposed to wait until after the ceremony to give you my wedding present, but this is all I can offer."

She fought a mixture of laughter and tears as she threw herself into his arms. "Oh, Alistair. I could want for nothing more than to marry you in two days' time and to live here with you and Hortence."

"An' ye dinna mind that wee Hortence will spend a few days with Cailean and Anna?" he whispered into Leticia's ear, provoking a shiver.

"I'll miss her. I've never spent a day apart from my daughter." She arched away, meeting his worried gaze. "But I want time with you, Alistair. Time for the two of us."

He moved as though to swoop forward and kiss her but then

backed up with such speed he bumped into a door. "Aye, 'tis good to know." He cleared his throat. "I dinna think we should linger here alone for much longer."

"Yes, you might damage the schoolteacher's reputation," she teased.

"I'm sorry ye had to leave your position, love," he whispered.

"I know," she said. "But I will marry you, and have a wonderful life with you. I will never regret that." Her latent anger at being forced to give up her teaching position at only twenty-eight eased as her wedding day approached. She followed him outside, looping her arm through his elbow.

"'Tis a good thing the schoolteacher taught her final class last week," he murmured. He breathed a sigh of relief as she chuckled at his teasing her.

They walked the short distance to the house he shared with his siblings, where his sister, Sorcha, helped mind the house with his sister-in-law, Annabelle. As the town baker, Annabelle did the majority of the cooking for the family, while Sorcha preferred to embroider, mend the clothes, and spin wool. The MacKinnon house sat next to a large livery and the nearby paddock where Alistair worked with his eldest brother, Cailean.

While Alistair and Leticia walked arm-in-arm through town, they smiled, nodded, and spoke to all they passed. As co-owner of the local livery established four years ago, Alistair knew most men in town, and, as the former schoolteacher, Leticia knew all those with children. The engaged couple ambled up the boardwalk, past the bakery, the bustling café, and the Odd Fellows Hall.

Bear Grass Springs sat toward the apex of a large valley with the Obsidian mining camp in the tall granite-peaked mountains above it, while a creek gurgled past the edge of town. Down the rolling hills, a broad valley opened up for as far as the eye could see, providing the perfect habitat for large herds of cattle. The green hills heralded a wet spring, although summer's heat would soon turn them a golden brown.

The couple turned as gunshots sounded, and raised voices floated on the wind from the opposite side of town. "Seems the good times have already begun at the Stumble-Out," Alistair said wryly as he looked at the saloon down the street that sat across from Betty's Boudoir, the town brothel.

"There's nothing to worry about as I'm sure Ewan is home," Leticia soothed.

Alistair squeezed her arm and turned for the family home. "For now." He inhaled deeply, then shook his head. "Stay for supper with us. Annabelle's cookin' tonight, so I know we'll eat well," he said with a wink. When they arrived at the MacKinnon home, they found his sister, Sorcha, the youngest MacKinnon sibling at twenty-four, on the parlor floor, playing with Hortence.

Hortence saw her mother and rose, hugging her around the waist. After her warm welcome, she ignored her mother, dropping to her knees to play with Sorcha again. "I have an aunt!" she proclaimed with a triumphant thrust of her fist upward, as though she had won something.

"Aye, in two days ye'll have two aunts and two uncles," Alistair said as he sat on the floor near her. "Ye're a lucky girl." He smiled as she giggled.

Her giggles faded as she ducked her head a bit and smiled at him. "I'll have a papa too."

He tugged her to his lap and held her tight. "Aye, technically ye will." When she stiffened in his arms, he stroked a hand over her head. "I already consider ye mine, Little Bug. The weddin' just makes it official." He grunted as she flung her arms around his neck and gave a small whoop of joy. He laughed as she kissed him on his cheek. Another grunt followed when she scampered off his lap, her knees and feet digging into his legs. He rose and joined Leticia on the settee, content to watch his sister and his daughter play.

"I love your nickname for her," Leticia murmured.

He smiled as he watched Hortence's exuberant play. "We found a ladybug on one of our rambles, an' she proclaimed it her favorite bug because it was part red and pretty." He shared a long look with Leticia. "I told her that she was my Little Ladybug, but that's a long name, ye

8

ken?" His gaze softened further as he continued to focus on Hortence. "So she's my Little Bug."

"She's been teased terribly about her red hair."

Alistair tensed next to her. "I hate the cruelty of others but especially when directed at children."

She kissed him on the cheek. "And I love how you want to protect her."

He held his fiancée's hand and sighed with satisfaction as she rested her head on his shoulder. When Annabelle called out that dinner was almost ready, they rose, washing their hands before sitting at the round table set for seven with a small bouquet of wildflowers at its center.

"Who brought you the flowers?" Cailean asked Annabelle.

She flushed. "One of the miners has a sweet tooth but can't afford a cookie. I gave him a few of the cookie pieces a couple days ago, and he brought the flowers today as a thank-you."

"And you gave him more sweets today," Cailean said matter-of-factly. He laughed as his wife blushed. He raised her hand and kissed it as she paused by his side in her movements about the kitchen. "I'm glad you're soft hearted, Belle. Not everything can be about profits."

She served them all large bowls of venison stew and set a plate of sliced bread on the table. After pulling a small slab of butter from the icebox and placing it alongside their meal, she sat next to Cailean.

"Did ye hear what Mrs. Jameson has proposed?" Ewan asked as he paused in wolfing down his supper. At their curious stares, he set aside his spoon. "She read a story about rules for schoolteachers and is intent on enacting them for the next one."

"What sort of rules?" Leticia asked.

"Ones to prevent *illicit behavior*." Her soon-to-be brother-in-law wiggled his eyebrows at her.

"Illicit behavior? When did I ever do anything illicit?" She shot a worried glance at her daughter, Hortence, but everyone appeared as confused as Leticia was.

"Seems she wants to forbid the walking out with gentlemen and to enact curfews. Female teachers should be home each night by eight, should refrain from wearing any form of scent or any provocative clothing."

Annabelle choked back a laugh. "Is she serious?" At Ewan's nod, she shook her head. "This is her petty way of declaring that Leticia was an unfit teacher, simply because she was courted by an honorable man while she taught."

"'Tis more than that," Alistair murmured. "Mrs. Jameson wants to strike out at us because she's bitter that her daughter willna be Mrs. Alistair MacKinnon." He leveled an intense gaze at his youngest brother who had just turned thirty. "I'd be careful, Ewan. She's intent for Helen to be a MacKinnon, an' ye better have yer wits about ye so that ye dinna get trapped by one of her schemes."

Cailean chuckled as he played with a ruffle on his wife's collar. "That's one of the reasons she was irate that Annabelle had *lured* me into marriage." He winked at his wife as she rolled her eyes. "After Mrs. Jameson overcame her delight in spreading gossip about us, she realized she'd lost me for her daughter."

His siblings laughed. "Helen wouldna have had ye!" Ewan said. "Not after ye told her that she looked worse than an overripe raspberry about to burst at the previous Founders' Day party. She couldna stand the sight of ye."

"The same could never be said for her mother." Cailean frowned. "All Mrs. Jameson cared about was that I had a good business and a large house."

"Now that she sees ye happily wed, it only makes her envy greater," Sorcha murmured. "An' she's delusional enough to believe her daughter would have been equal to Annabelle."

Cailean squeezed his wife's hand. "For me, Annabelle is incomparable. As Leticia is for Alistair." He raised his glass of water in a toast. "To the lucky couple, who, in two days' time, will end the longest courtship in town history."

They raised their cups before *clink*ing them.

Annabelle giggled. "Yes, this family will have the longest and one of the shortest in town history."

"As long as we are wed, I dinna care how many years it took us to arrive at this place," Alistair said with a loving gaze into Leticia's eyes.

~

A warm ray of early evening sunlight illuminated the kitchen of the bakery the next day. The butcher's block countertop was scrubbed clean, and four stools surrounded the counter peninsula, three currently occupied. Annabelle pulled a lopsided cake with a thick layer of frosting from a cupboard and cut thick slabs. She slid a piece of cake to Leticia, her daughter, and another to Sorcha who groaned as she picked up her fork. "How do ye expect me to fit into my dress tomorrow if ye continue to feed me such delicious sweets?"

Leticia laughed. "Imagine working here full time! That always posed a challenge." She took a bite of the white cake lightly flavored with almond and sighed with pleasure. "Tell me again why we are eating this now and not tomorrow?"

Annabelle smiled as she saw Hortence dig into her piece. "This was the cake that fell apart. It's only held together by a thick layer of icing." She cut a sliver for herself. "I couldn't celebrate my family's upcoming wedding with such a shoddy cake."

Sorcha grinned. "Just like ye to be a perfectionist." She ignored Annabelle as she shrugged and then turned to Leticia. "Now, tell us what ye have planned for my brother."

Leticia flushed, glancing at her daughter. "I have a small gift for him, but it's a surprise." She met Sorcha's mutinous glower. "I won't tell you what it is before I give it to him, Sorcha."

Sorcha grumbled. "Well, I ken ye have a few surprises waitin' for ye at the new house." She could not hide her snicker when Leticia blanched in alarm. "I have a feelin' ye'll be delighted."

Leticia's blush intensified, and she nodded at Hortence. Annabelle shook her head at Sorcha, and Sorcha grumbled under her breath about having to behave.

"I wonder what the men are doing tonight?" Annabelle asked in an attempt to change the subject.

"Uncle Ewan wanted to have Papa drink like a skunk, but that made Papa mad," Hortence said. She crinkled her nose. "Why? I thought skunks drank water."

Leticia laughed and ran a hand over her daughter's head. "They do, my little love. I think your uncle Ewan was interested in mischief."

Hortence smiled. "He's always interested in mischief. He said that's his middle name! And mine is *imp*." She finished her cake and jumped down from her stool, moving to the bakery's back room to play with the few dolls and toys stored in a box for her there.

Leticia watched her go, swallowing a lump in her throat as she watched her daughter. "You can't know what it means to have a family for Hortence." She blinked away tears as she looked at the two women who were her friends and who would become her sisters-in-law tomorrow.

Sorcha frowned. "If I didn't ken ye loved my brother, I'd be worried ye only wanted him for yer daughter."

Leticia choked on a laugh. "Heavens, no. I can't imagine life without Alistair. He's ..." She broke off, unable to form the words.

Annabelle nodded. "I know what you mean, Leticia. And I hope you do too one day, Sorcha."

Sorcha's shy smile slowly bloomed.

"As for what the men are doing tonight," Annabelle added, "I think Ewan has the misguided idea of insisting Alistair enjoy his last night of freedom. However, Cailean wanted to talk about the joys and responsibilities of marriage."

Sorcha gaped at Annabelle. "That's rich, considerin' what a horrible job he did after the first few months of yer marriage."

Annabelle shrugged. "Yes, but now things are wonderful."

Leticia sighed as she pushed away her half-eaten piece of cake. "And all Alistair wanted was a bit of peace. That's what he told me. He wanted time to think about Hortence and me, and what tomorrow would mean."

Sorcha swiped at her eyes. "Ye're not makin' me cry tomorrow," she rasped.

Annabelle pulled her prickly sister-in-law close. "Yes, she is. The moment they are together in front of the preacher, we'll be sniffling into our handkerchiefs."

Sorcha smiled as she saw the resplendent glow around Leticia. "Aye, ye're right. I canna wait to see Alistair's joy tomorrow. To watch ye dance with him and to know the happiness ye'll have together."

Leticia nodded, her eyes closed for a moment as though envisioning the scenes they described. "Although I'm certain I won't sleep a wink tonight, I must return home. Hortence needs her rest."

Annabelle rose, quickly washing the dishes and placing them on a drying rack. "We'll be by early to help you prepare. Don't worry, Leticia. Nothing will go wrong. You've waited and planned for this day for so long. It will be perfect." She hugged her friend close before following the trio to the back door and locking it behind them.

CHAPTER 2

The following morning, the early June day dawned sunny and cool, with a hint of the warmth to come later in the day. Birds swooped and chased insects in the slight breeze; children played outside, and a sense of quiet expectation thrummed through the town.

Alistair MacKinnon, dressed in his Sunday-best suit with shoes polished to a shine, paced the parlor in his family's home. He now considered his home to be the one he would share with Leticia and Hortence. His long strides ate up the confined space, and he spun every few steps to turn in the opposite direction. He had been forbidden from venturing outside for fear he would dirty his suit or shoes in the dust. "Are ye sure she'll be there?"

Cailean laughed as he sprawled on the settee. "As sure as a man can be. Belle's at Leticia's house now, helping her change and prepare. Sorcha will arrive there soon with flowers. They'll ensure your bride-to-be is at the church on time—or soon afterward." As the eldest MacKinnon brother, Cailean did not bother to hide his amusement at his middle brother's antics, as Cailean had been subjected to the same treatment the previous June when he had married Annabelle.

Ewan propped his shoulder on the parlor doorjamb and grinned as he watched Alistair. "Seems as though ye're keen on purchasin' a new carpet before ye move out. Ye'll have that one threadbare in no time, the way ye're pacin'." He winked at Cailean and smiled at Alistair. "'Twill be fine. She's as eager as ye are to move into that fine house I built ye."

"An' I paid for," Alistair grumbled. He paused and heaved out a breath before collapsing onto a chair across from Cailean. "Thank ye, Ewan, for the fine craftsmanship. I ken ye had many other projects to work on."

Ewan shrugged. "Only one was for my brother." His smile bloomed. "A wee surprise is waitin' for ye in the bedroom."

Cailean laughed and Alistair paled. "Thank God," Cailean said, "Belle and I honeymooned far away from the likes of you. I'd hate to see what antics you would have come up with."

Ewan laughed. "The only reason ye were saved from my mischief waiting for ye at home was because of Alistair."

Cailean cringed and looked at his brother with whom he shared the livery business. "Forgive me for not protecting you from him."

"As long as it's nothing permanent?" Alistair relaxed as Ewan shook his head no. "Then I'll forgive ye."

"What's the house like now that it's finished?" Cailean asked. "I haven't been there for too long."

Alistair half smiled before speaking. "Ewan did a wonderful job with the finish work. It's smaller than this home, aye?"

Cailean nodded at the memory of the plans and the short tour he had taken weeks before as it was being built.

"But it's more finely wrought. The windows will no' leak like the ones here, and the three bedrooms are a good size."

"Dinna give yerself much room for the bairns who will come," Ewan teased. He laughed as Alistair threw a pillow at him.

"Dinna think I've forgiven ye for wantin' me as drunk as a skunk last night," he said, the effect of his glower diminished by the glimmer of humor in his eyes. "Why ye thought I'd want to go to my wedding service with a hangover I'll never ken."

Ewan sighed. "If I were to wed, I'd need liquid courage."

Cailean rolled his eyes. "As though you will ever wed. No woman is foolish enough to take you on." He shared a smile with Alistair. "All will be well, once the ceremony starts. It's the waiting that drives a man insane."

Alistair grumbled and rose to continue his pacing. He looked up with trepidation as the front door opened. "Warren," he muttered.

Warren Clark, the town's lawyer and a good friend to Cailean, entered. He too was dressed in his Sunday best and looked as though he were about to venture soon to the church. "Hello," he said, his keen blue eyes taking in the two relaxed brothers and the pacing groom-to-be. "Alistair, I would like to speak with you a moment."

Alistair motioned for Warren to continue. "Anything ye have to say, ye can say in front of my brothers."

Warren nodded. "In that case, I wanted to reassure you that all the formal documents are prepared and only need to be signed after the ceremony."

Alistair nodded and strode toward Warren who stood hovering in the parlor doorway. Alistair held out his hand to shake Warren's. "Thank ye, Warren. I ken ye can do many other things with yer time than write up marriage contracts."

Warren smiled. "I added the portion you asked me to." He watched Alistair closely. "I still believe you should have discussed it with Miss Browne before the wedding. Those sorts of things can take a woman by surprise, and you never know how she'll react."

"Or interpret what ye meant," Alistair said. "I understand yer concern, but I know she'll be delighted."

Warren shrugged. "It's your decision if and when you want the second document to become public knowledge." He nodded to the other MacKinnon brothers. "I'll see you at the church." He waved to them and left as quickly as he arrived. Ewan followed Warren out, and Alistair ignored the flutter of nerves as he considered what Ewan could be planning for later in the day.

A tense silence descended over the room. "What the devil was that about?" Cailean demanded.

Alistair made a deep sound in the back of his throat. "I respect that ye and Annabelle have yer secrets. Ye must have the same respect for Leticia and me. When ye need to know, then I'll tell ye." He shared a long look with his brother, and Cailean nodded his head in agreement.

"I understand, Alistair." Cailean stood and gripped his brother's shoulder. "I have to adjust to not acting like your eldest brother."

Alistair smiled. "Ye'll always be the eldest. Carin' for us is ingrained in ye. An' knowin' ye are there if I need help is a relief. But Leticia will be my family now. My first loyalty must be to her."

Cailean squeezed his brother's shoulder, and his accent reappeared. "Aye, as it should be. I wish ye joy, brother."

They clapped each other on the back and then called for Ewan as they departed for the church.

~

S orcha placed another pin in the gentle upswept style Leticia had chosen for her wedding day. Sorcha held the mirror to Leticia and beamed. "There. Don't ye look lovely."

Leticia tilted her head from one side to the other before smiling, examining her blond hair in its fancy updo. "Beautiful. Demure ... yet with a touch of sophistication. He's never seen my hair this way."

Annabelle laughed as she ran a hand over the short veil Leticia would soon don. "I don't know as he cares how your hair is styled. All he's concerned about is whether or not you show up at the church."

Leticia frowned before grinning abashedly at her soon-to-be sisters-in-law. "Of course I'll be there. Nothing would prevent me from marrying him today."

"The townsfolk are looking forward to the celebration. They've been waiting for your marriage for years," Annabelle teased. "I'm glad you waited until I arrived and became a part of the family."

"Soon ye'll celebrate yer own first wedding anniversary," Sorcha said to Annabelle while fussing with Leticia's hair and dress.

Leticia waited for Sorcha's finishing touches before standing and walking to the mirror standing in one corner. This time Leticia focused on her cream-colored dress with buttons down the front. The well-defined bodice and cinched waist flowed to a full skirt and had a small bustle. "I've never worn anything so elegant. Thank you, Sorcha."

"'Twas nothing once I convinced Annabelle how I'd be much better off if she desisted in her attempts to aid me." Sorcha laughed as Annabelle blushed. "She's a menace with a pair of scissors."

"I've never proclaimed to be proficient in anything but baking." Annabelle fought happy tears as Leticia turned to them with her arms wide. "You're stunning." She frowned when she saw Leticia fiddling with the sleeve of her dress. "Hortence is fine."

Leticia gave her friend a weak smile as she sat with care on the edge of a chair. "Of that, I have no doubt. She's with Irene who's making her feel like a princess."

Annabelle sat while Sorcha continued to tidy the room. "Irene never had a daughter or a granddaughter. She's enjoying having a girl about to dress up and help prepare for the wedding." Annabelle glanced at the small watch pinned to her dress. "They have a few minutes to arrive before we need to leave for the church."

"Are ye thinking about yer husband? Yer dead husband?" Sorcha blurted out. She flushed as Leticia gasped, and Annabelle glared at her. "Beg yer pardon."

Leticia laced her hands together and met Sorcha's curious stare. "I rarely think about him. Our wedding day was a rushed affair, with him barely waiting for the preacher to finish his words before he dragged me down the aisle and away from all that was familiar." She closed her eyes. "I try not to remember those times."

"Oh, Leticia," Sorcha wailed as she dragged a chair to her side. "Forgive me. Ye never talk about him, and I wondered."

Leticia gave a weak smile. "Of course you do. As does Alistair. Unlike you Scots who relish in reliving the past and retelling your stories, I prefer to leave mine buried."

Annabelle raised an eyebrow. "Let's hope it agrees to stay unearthed. Too often, that which I would rather forget has a way of resurrecting itself." She smiled reassuringly, yet Leticia shivered.

Hortence burst into the room, her forward momentum stopped only by Irene's quick grab of her wrist. "Young lady, you are not to touch your mother. She is dressed in her wedding finery, and you want her to look her best."

Hortence bit her trembling lip. "I'm sorry, Mama."

Leticia exchanged a severe stare with Irene who released her daughter before she spoke. "Look how beautiful you are, Hortence." Leticia traced a finger down Hortence's cheek, frowning as the trembling lip turned into a quiver. "I love you, little one. You know I'll still love you after I've married Alistair. I'll always love you." She waited a moment until Hortence nodded.

"He'll be a good papa. I want him as my papa, Mama." Hortence giggled as her mother pulled her into a hug. When Hortence leaned away from her mother, she smiled at Sorcha as she swiped away a tear. "Aunt Sorcha made me a new dress." She held her arms wide to show off her light-pink dress with a ruffle at midcalf.

"And you polished your shoes," Annabelle teased as she saw the black shoes shining in the early afternoon ray of sunlight.

"Mr. Harold did that!" Hortence giggled. "It was s'posed to be a secret. But he thought it was unfair Miss Irene got to play dress up, and he didn't."

Leticia laughed. "I wouldn't say that to too many others, my little angel." She ran a hand down her daughter's silky red hair pulled in a braid. "Thank you, Irene, for helping Hortence prepare for today." Leticia shared a smile of understanding with her good friend.

"I fear we must leave," Annabelle said after another quick glance at her watch. "Or Ewan will be sent to search for us." She held out a hand to Leticia. "I'm so happy for you, dear friend," she whispered, then squeezed Leticia's hand before following Irene outside in the direction of the church.

~

L eticia stood at the rear of the church, hidden in a small alcove, as Sorcha and then Annabelle walked down the aisle to take their seats before the wedding. Sorcha sat and then her shoulders shook with laughter at something Ewan had whispered to her. Leticia smiled at Cailean's covetous, loving stare as he watched his wife coming to sit beside him.

Leticia's smile faded as her turn to walk down the aisle approached. She fought memories of her first marriage as she attempted to focus on the present. However, the bewilderment at what had occurred during that ceremony, the disillusionment of her wedding night, and the despair in the ensuing months of her marriage flickered through her memory. Her hands tightened at her waist in front of her, and she took a deep breath. She jumped as the man next to her nudged her.

"Are you ready then?" Harold asked as he winged his arm out to her. He patted her hand as she slipped it through his. "No need to be nervous. You're marrying a good man." He led her to the doorway, in full view of all present.

Leticia nodded, her gaze darting forward as she met Alistair's and saw a wondrous smile bloom. "Thank you, Harold, for walking me down the aisle."

He grinned. "I was delighted to be chosen over one of the brothers. Thought for sure you'd choose that young whippersnapper, Ewan."

She shook her head. "No, I wanted someone not from his family. Someone I've known since I arrived here." Her grip on his arm tightened a moment. "Thank you."

The off-key piano music started, and Leticia moved forward. Her gaze locked with Alistair's, and she barely noticed those who stood, gathered to celebrate her day with her. When she reached the front of the church, she took Alistair's hand to stand next to him.

A contented sigh escaped as her husband-to-be squeezed her hand. "Finally, my love," he whispered. He traced a finger over her gloved palm, and his smile reached his eyes as he felt her shiver.

"Finally," she murmured before focusing on the pastor.

CHAPTER 3

"*T*his wedding cannot continue!" a man bellowed in a deep voice from the back of the church as the doors ricocheted against the walls with such force it seemed the wood would split.

The pastor glared at the man striding down the aisle, while Alistair glowered over his shoulder.

"We aren't at that part yet, young man," the pastor intoned. "Sit down."

Alistair swallowed a chuckle at the pastor's indignant tone. However, when Alistair realized how tense Leticia was as she stood next to him, he squeezed her hand. "It's all right, love. I'm certain he is confused. Or he's a drunken miner intent on mischief." He frowned as she refused to meet his reassuring gaze before he focused on the indignant, yet triumphant man, coming to an abrupt halt behind them.

"This woman is a liar and an attempted murderess!" the man shouted as he pointed at Leticia.

A shocked gasp moved through the crowd, and the pastor closed his Bible and canted forward with curiosity as the dust-covered man made his proclamations. His brown hair was slicked back, greasy from days without a wash, and his unkempt beard held splotches of gray mixed with the brown. His dungarees were nearing their last wash, while any color in his calico shirt had long faded.

"She should be in jail!"

Cailean leaped to the front of the altar, wrapping an arm around Alistair's chest and shoulder. Cailean pulled his brother away from the man interrupting his wedding and then dragged him a few feet from his bride-to-be and the pastor. "Easy, Alistair," he murmured. "You don't want violence today or to end up in jail, rather than with your bride on your wedding day."

Alistair grunted and squirmed in his attempt to free himself from Cailean's hold, only stilling when he focused on the horrified, yet enthralled looks on the faces of his wedding guests. He took a deep breath before nodding. "Let me go, Cail." When he'd been released, he tugged on his jacket and waistcoat, remaining near his brother, to address the stranger. "Who are ye? And how dare ye interrupt my—our—wedding."

The man gloated as his gaze moved from a distraught Leticia in a demure cream-colored dress with its small bustle and train to an irate Alistair. "Did the harlot tell you that she was a widow?" He laughed. "She's married to me. Has been for nearly eight years." He moved toward Leticia who screeched and backed up a step. "You miscalculated, darling."

Leticia ignored the man calling himself her husband as any color in her cheeks faded, and she became as pale as the finest porcelain. She focused on Alistair, his posture more rigid with each moment, while his expression was more impenetrable.

"Is this true?" he whispered to Leticia, the pain and anguish glinting in his gaze like shards of glass.

"Yes, I married him." She held up her hand to Alistair. "Let me explain," she whispered as he remained standing next to his brother, rather than with her.

"Ye had three years, Lettie, to do that," he rasped as he watched her with growing agony. He nodded as he watched her swallow and fight tears but remained mute. "Why would ye no' tell me before?" He leaned forward to touch her, frowning when she flinched at his touch.

Tears coursed down her cheeks as she paled to match her wedding dress. "I can explain."

"Why wait until now? Now that yer deceased husband has reappeared on the day of our weddin'?" Alistair asked, waving to the avid onlookers crowding the church, many of whom had not been invited but had snuck in at the first sign of a disruption in the ceremony. "Is he yer husband?" Any hope in his eyes dimmed as he saw the truth in her gaze. "Ye're a liar," he murmured, his gaze filled with disillusionment and pain.

"Yes, but no. Let me explain," she wailed. She looked for an ally but found confusion and distress among the MacKinnon clan seated in the front pew.

The man calling himself Leticia's husband held a hand to his missing waistcoat and addressed Alistair and the pastor, speaking in a loud-enough voice to carry through the entire church. "I am Josiah Fry. This woman"—he pointed at Leticia—"is my errant wife, Mrs. Lorena Fry. I've been searching for her for years."

Leticia began to shake, fighting her tears. However, when she saw Josiah approach her daughter, Hortence, Leticia leaped toward him and pushed him away. "Stay away from her!"

"You know it's a crime to separate a man from his child." His brown eyes gleamed with devilry and triumph. "I'll leave you now, as no wedding will take place today. But I'll see you soon, dear wife."

He turned to meet Alistair's frozen gaze and smiled with sardonic joy. "You were as much a fool as she is." His grin became even more triumphant as Alistair frowned in confusion.

Every gaze in the church followed Josiah's lanky form as he sauntered down the aisle, whistling a triumphant tune. The door slammed shut behind him, as though tolling the end to Leticia's dream with Alistair.

And Alistair's dream with Leticia and Hortence.

Leticia fell to her knees, holding Hortence close. "It's all right, darling. You're safe." She rose on unsteady legs, gripping Hortence's hand. "Come. We must return home." Hortence walked beside her mother dutifully, Leticia's head ducked in an attempt to ignore the glowers from the townsfolk.

As Leticia walked down the aisle, the owner of the Bear Grass Springs General Store, Tobias Sutton, stood and blocked her path. "You're a liar and a hussy and who knows what else." He vibrated with righteous indignation. "And to think we welcomed you!"

Mrs. Jameson, the woman vying with Tobias for the worst town gossip, emerged from a rear pew and shrieked, "You are barely worthy of the Boudoir! How dare you sully our children's minds all these years when you are nothing more than filth?"

As more townsfolk stood, blocking Leticia's and Hortence's path, Annabelle hurried down the aisle and put an arm around Leticia's shoulder. "I would think you would show a bit of decency and charity, especially since you are standing in a church. Please, allow us to pass." She glared at Tobias and Mrs. Jameson and pushed forward, past those who no longer celebrated, but ridiculed, Leticia.

When they had emerged from the church and moved a ways down the street, Annabelle paused. "I will leave you, Leticia. I'm afraid I won't accustom myself to calling you Lorena."

"Annabelle," Leticia whispered, "please listen."

Annabelle glanced toward the church and saw her husband leaving with his siblings. She shook her head as she said, "I can't right now. Sometime soon I'll find a way to speak with you." She shook her head again. "I don't know when I've been more shocked. Or hurt." She glanced down at the tug on her hand.

"Will we still get cake?" Hortence whispered.

Annabelle's startled laugh eased a small amount of tension between the women. "I will try to save you some, my little darling." She ran a hand over Hortence's head before looking at Leticia. "Good luck."

Leticia watched as Annabelle spun to follow her family as they returned home. Leticia shivered at the realization she might never be welcomed in the MacKinnon home again before she dropped her head once more and trudged down the road to the small rented home she had planned to vacate today after her wedding to Alistair.

~

Alistair pushed his way out of the church, past the gleeful Mrs. Jameson and the other townsfolk who watched him with abject curiosity and pity. He ignored his brothers' calls and raced to the livery. The large barn had a door at each end of the long center walkway, a larger opening on the side that faced the paddock to the rear, and a hayloft above. Stalls for animals were along either side of the long central hallway, with a separate room for tack, another for feed, and a tiny office tucked in the rear. Small trapdoors above each stall from the hayloft allowed for hay to be dropped inside each one after they were mucked out. Once inside the livery, Alistair fell against one of the large support beams and shuddered. When he heard the livery door open quietly, he rasped, "Don't touch me!"

Soft footfalls entered, and he swiped at his face. He spun, glaring at the intruder, the fight leaving as he saw his brother Cailean. "I thought ye were ... her."

Cailean shook his head. "She has to attend to Hortence. And we wouldn't allow her near you just now." Cailean pulled out two stools, setting one near Alistair and claiming the other. Cailean sat as though in contented silence while Alistair punched at a wall and remained turned away from Cailean.

After many minutes, Alistair collapsed onto his stool, abject desolation emanating from him. "Where are the others?" Alistair asked.

"The family is in the kitchen. I imagine they salvaged some of the food, although I doubt you're hungry."

Alistair grunted his agreement to that.

"The townsfolk will be at the Odd Fellows Hall. Musicians were paid for, and they'll find an excuse for a dance." He watched as Alistair stared into space.

"What am I to do?" he whispered.

"Take a few days to understand what happened, Al. Then determine what it is you want to do," Cailean coaxed.

Alistair sat in stupefied silence a few minutes. "She never loved me enough." He rubbed at his face. "Never trusted me enough."

Cailean flushed red, unable to hide his anger from his brother. "I can't be impartial, Alistair. Not today. Not as I sit here and watch as you suffer." He sighed. "What do you need to do?"

Alistair huffed out a laugh. "I need to feel like a man again." He sniffled. "I ken ye wouldna understand that. Ye have Annabelle."

Cailean snorted. "I know very well what you mean. Most men would."

Alistair ran a hand over his face. "I hate that man. I hate that he … touched her. That he has the right to destroy what I most dream of. That he's not dead as he should be." Alistair shivered. "I never thought to be confronted with the man. Fighting his ghost was difficult enough."

Cailean frowned. "I don't know what to say, Al. I'm so sorry."

Alistair swiped at his cheeks and then rose as anger filled him again. He kicked at a stall, damaging one of the boards. "I treated her with kindness, patience, and respect, an' the entire time she played me false."

Cailean nodded. "Aye."

Alistair looked at his brother, meeting his concerned gaze. "I … I need …"

Cailean let out a long sigh. "Aye," he breathed as he rose. "I understand. Although it may cause more problems than it will ease."

Alistair pushed away from the stall and was caught in a bear hug from his brother. "I'll be back in the morning to fix the stall." He rushed past his brother, out the livery door, through town, thankful the townsfolk were engrossed in gossiping about the botched wedding inside the Hall. Strains of music filtered outside as he stalked past it toward his destination.

Alistair pushed open the door to the Boudoir, and the scent of cheap perfume, whiskey, and sin enveloped him. The lights were lowered to enhance the shadows in the corners and to induce indiscretion. The faint lighting also hid fading red paint on the walls and scuffed, worn carpets on the floors. Alistair watched as the whores draped themselves over men in the lower room, whispering in their ears, caressing shoulders and legs. Some took advantage of the armless chairs, sprawling astride their intended target as though he were a horse. Bawdy music played in the corner on a piano, giving the room a carnival atmosphere. A small bar served watered-downed drinks to the thirsty horde. He saw men following women upstairs and others descending. The dozen women who worked for the Madam moved from downstairs to above stairs, depending on the desires of their clients.

The large brute, Ezekial, who was the Madam's shadow, stood near the rear door to the main room, his silver gaze ever watchful for men who were forceful or out of control with the women. After accepting a glass of watered-down whiskey that cost twice as much as a regular glass at the Stumble-Out Saloon, Alistair sat in a chair. Soon a black-haired woman approached. He waved her away.

After he had dismissed a few more girls, the Madam sauntered up to him. She wore a shiny sapphire-colored dress with a demure cut to enhance her aging but attractive figure. Her makeup was tastefully done, unlike the garish, glaring rouge, kohl, and lipstick utilized by her girls. "Mr. MacKinnon. Such a surprise to see you here tonight." Her eyes held a mocking glint. "Although I'm uncertain if it truly is a shock that one as virile as you should seek us out after such a trying day."

He glared at her obsequiousness and her callousness. "Madam."

"You seem quite particular in what you desire," she said as she looked around at her girls. The majority were engaged with gentlemen, although a few hovered along a wall, smiling engagingly at those who seemed unconvinced. "What might tempt you tonight?" At his long pause, she pouted. "I'd hate to think you'll be like your younger brother. Here for my whiskey and music and little else."

The tic of Alistair's jaw further evidenced his anger. "Nae," he rasped. "I desire a light-haired lass."

The Madam's smile bloomed. "Of course." She motioned for a woman to approach. "I believe you'll find Divinity to your liking." The blond-haired woman with brown eyes and a large bosom approached.

He drank the rest of his whiskey and rose. "Aye, she'll do." He motioned with his head for Divinity to precede him up the stairs and followed her. As they walked down the narrow hallway, he ignored the sounds emerging from the other rooms. Just as he was about to turn into Divinity's crib, someone grabbed his arm.

"What do you think you're doing?" Annabelle's sister, Fidelia, known as Charity at the Boudoir, glared at him.

"I'm doin' what any man with sense would do," he snapped, freeing his arm from her grasp.

"You're a fool," she hissed. "You'll regret this." She shot a look down the hall to the retreating back of her latest customer. After another glare at Alistair, she rushed to catch up with her patron to follow him downstairs.

Alistair ignored her and followed Divinity into the small room, closing the door on his despair and anger as he pulled her into his arms, attempting and failing to forget the day's anguish.

When Annabelle returned home, she entered the kitchen to find Ewan staring at the cake, Sorcha slamming a kettle onto the stove, and her husband and Alistair missing. "Where are they?"

"In the livery. I'd let them be. Alistair looked worse than a rabid wolverine," Ewan said.

"An' when have ye seen a wolverine? Rabid or otherwise?" Sorcha asked.

Ewan rolled his eyes and attempted a smile for Annabelle. "At least we salvaged the cake from the horde who still insisted on descending on the reception hall."

"They can't expect a party after such a disaster," Annabelle breathed, slipping into a chair across from her brother-in-law.

"Seems they can. *Any excuse for a party*, one of 'em said," Sorcha snorted with a glower. "When they complained that I was takin' the cake, I told them how they disgusted me, an' I hoped to dance on their graves."

"You never," Annabelle breathed.

"'Twas Tobias and Mrs. Jameson. An' I don't regret sayin' it."

Sorcha swiped at her reddish-brown hair, stuffing it back into the loose chignon she had worn for the wedding ceremony.

Ewan grunted as Annabelle giggled. "Oh, I feel guilty laughing today. And I imagine much worse has been said to those two gossip-mongers."

"An' they wouldna be missed," Ewan grumbled. He set his hands over his belly. "Although I dinna ken as though Alistair will want to see that cake." He nodded to the elaborately decorated confection with the letters *A* and *L* interwoven atop.

Annabelle stared at the cake. "I can scrape that off, and then it will just be a pretty cake for us to devour." She rubbed at her stomach. "I hate to admit it, but I'm starving."

Sorcha chuckled. "I am too but did no' want to be the first to say it." She paused as she stared at her brother and sister-in-law. "'Tis it normal to be filled with such rage?"

Ewan nodded. "Aye, 'tis." He sighed. "I dinna ken how we can help him. His life has been shattered, and there's nothin' to be done."

Annabelle shook her head as she blinked away tears. "I thought I knew her. I trusted her. I can't imagine how much worse this is for Alistair." She grimaced as she swiped at her cheeks.

Their conversation came to an abrupt halt as Cailean entered through the back door to the kitchen. He swiped at his boots before entering, his intense gaze moving from his siblings to his wife. After sitting next to Annabelle, he slung an arm over her shoulder and let out a deep breath as some of his tension eased.

"How is Alistair?" Annabelle asked as she leaned into her husband's side.

Cailean shook his head as he met his siblings' worried gazes. "Irate. I've never seen him this angry." He swiped at his forehead with his free hand. "Or this devastated."

"Should I bring him some food in a little while?" Sorcha asked.

Cailean flushed. "He's not in the livery." He cleared his throat and thrummed his fingers on the table. "He's gone to the Boudoir."

Annabelle gasped, and Ewan rolled his eyes. "Won't solve anything," Ewan muttered. "He will no' be with the woman he wants."

"Men and their pride," Annabelle muttered, earning a warning squeeze from her husband.

Sorcha set a loaf of bread to be sliced and a crock of butter on the table with a *thunk* as she glared at Annabelle. "Don't go takin' her side. No' yet."

Annabelle leaned forward. "I'm not. I can't remember the last time I was so disappointed in someone." She frowned as she thought of her elder sister, Fidelia, who Annabelle had not seen or spoken to in months. "And I told Leticia as much when we walked out of the church." She met her husband's and then her sister-in-law's glares. "But now that I've had a little while to think about what happened, don't you think there's more to this story than what that man proclaimed in church?"

Cailean released her to place his forearms on the table. "Of course there is. But the fact remains that she lied to all of us. She misled Al for years, allowing him to dream and to think they had a future together. I don't know as he'll get past that."

Sorcha sat with a thud in her chair. "He built her a house, and she let him, all the while knowin' she was a married woman. How could she do something like that? She had to ken she'd get caught."

Annabelle shrugged. "You read stories of men starting over all the time. Why couldn't a woman attempt the same?"

Ewan rolled his eyes. "Because she's a woman. That's not how things are done." He grunted as Sorcha smacked him on his head.

Cailean grunted, although it was impossible to tell if in agreement with Ewan's words or Sorcha's actions.

Annabelle glared at her brother-in-law. "If you desire a future with a woman other than infrequent visits to a Boudoir beauty, I'd suggest you alter your way of thinking." She relaxed as Cailean gripped her hand. "As for Alistair, visiting the Boudoir won't help him."

Cailean sighed. "He'll feel more like a man again. I can't imagine how he felt, standing there with the town as his witness while his entire future was destroyed by that man and knowing that the woman he loved could have prevented it. The townsfolk will be chewing this over for weeks."

Sorcha shuddered. "An', if there's one thing Alistair hates, it's gossip. Especially when it has to do with him."

∽

L eticia stood in the small living area where she and her daughter had lived for the last five years. The windows were open, allowing the gentle breeze to move through the room. Hortence had changed from her special gown and now played with dolls in the bedroom they shared. Leticia stared into space as she relived the wedding scene over and over again. A pounding on the front door jerked her from her silent misery, and she answered it. "Hello, Mr. Barclay."

His displeased glare met her stare. "I'm upset to find you remain in this house. I want you gone, Miss ... Missus Fry." He sputtered to a stop as his ears turned red with irritation. "When I think that we welcomed you here. Gave you a job. Offered you shelter in a home for the mere pittance the school board was willing to pay because you were to be the town's schoolteacher!" He leaned forward. "And, all this time, you were no better than a two-bit whore."

He sniffed with indignation. "When I think how you rebuffed my advances. A woman like you! You should have been thankful for my attention."

Leticia kept her gaze lowered, although her cheeks flushed with irritation. "I thank you for the years you allowed Hortence and me to live here."

"And your daughter! You aren't a fit mother! Separating her from her father. I'd be surprised to find one person in this town to support you if you desire to keep her with you."

Her hand tightened on the door, turning her fingers white. "I will no longer reside in your home as of tomorrow." She jerked away as he stroked a hand down her cheek. "Although your opinion of me has lowered due to that man's arrival in town today, I would remind you that you have yet to hear my side of the story. You have listened to him yell his version of the truth without considering mine."

33

He snickered. "A woman who leaves her husband for dead is a woman who should know better. You've yet to learn your place, missus." He grunted as she jerked the door into his shoulder, forcing him back a step.

"The answer is still no," she rasped. "I will not join you in your bed." She slammed the door shut and flipped the lock. When she remembered he had a key, as the landlord, she slipped a chair under the handle to keep it closed.

"Who was that angry man, Mama?" Hortence whispered from the doorway to their small bedroom. She held a stuffed bear Alistair had given her for Christmas.

Leticia forced a smile for her daughter as she hastily swiped away a tear. "He owns this house. We will move tomorrow."

"Will we still live with 'Stair? With Papa?" Hortence's vibrant voice was filled with youthful naiveté and optimism. "Can we live in the house he built us?"

Leticia swallowed a sob as she pulled Hortence to her and kissed her daughter's head. "Not right away, love. But hopefully someday soon we will be together."

She glared at the knock on the door but firmed her shoulders as she peeked out the side window. Leticia gave Hortence, who hovered near the bedroom door, a reassuring smile as she unlatched the door and moved aside the chair.

She met the older woman's disappointed gaze with one of acceptance and resignation. "Why are you here, Irene?"

"Will you allow me in?" The older woman had a basket looped over her arm and waited with feigned patience for Leticia to allow her to pass. When Leticia stepped aside, Irene entered the home she had departed a few hours ago with such hope and joy.

"Mrs. T!" Hortence exclaimed, jumping forward and into the woman's arms. Due to her inability to pronounce Irene's last name, Hortence had shortened it to *T*. "Will my new papa come soon?"

Irene grimaced and shook her head. "I don't believe so, child. He … he seems to have other plans for the evening." She set her basket on the table and sat, pulling Hortence onto her lap. "I feared you would go hungry tonight since you didn't expect to be here. I cobbled together some of the food from the reception." She flushed. "Well, from what was to be your reception."

"Is there cake?" Hortence asked, giggling when Irene gave her fingers a slight tap as she attempted to peek into the basket.

"There is no cake. Ewan and Sorcha took that away before the townsfolk could carve it up. I imagine they have quite a bit at the house." Irene pulled Hortence close. "And you shouldn't pester your mama about going there tonight for cake. They are upset, and you don't want to cause them more distress."

"But Alistair always says I bring him joy. How could I make them sad?" Hortence scrunched up her face as though deciphering a challenging puzzle.

"I fear they are having a grown-up tantrum. You know what that's like." She brushed at strands of red hair that had come free from Hortence's braid.

"I get a tummy ache and need a hug from Mama before I feel better." She snuggled into Irene's lap.

Irene laughed. "Precious child, I fear adults aren't as sensible as you are, and it may take a while before they are over their tantrum." She met Hortence's confused gaze. "Sometimes hurts go deep enough that it takes a while for the other person to accept that we are sorry."

"But they will. It's what you do. You make a 'stake and say you're sorry. Then you can play again."

Irene shared a smile with Leticia as she swiped away a tear. "I sure hope so, dear child." Hortence hopped down and moved to the back room to play with her doll. "She doesn't understand, does she?"

Leticia shook her head. "Of course not. How could she?" She firmed her shoulders. "Thank you for the food. I had resigned us to hunger."

Irene tapped her fingers on the tabletop. "You aren't bustling me out of this house without answering some questions. Not when the whole town is buzzing worse than a hive of hornets about you. Is what that man said true?"

"On the surface, yes. I did marry him seven and a half years ago. It would be eight years in November." She met Irene's implacable stare. "I'm no murderer, Mrs. Tompkins."

The older woman frowned as she studied Leticia's absolute still-ness, as though awaiting condemnation. "No, I agree. That's not who you are." She sighed. "But this is a muddle, and you must set it to rights. That man you were to marry is devastated and undertaking activities better shared with a wife." She nodded as Leticia shivered.

"He went to the … ?" Leticia's voice faded at the confirmation in her friend's eyes that her fiancée was at the Boudoir. "Rather than seek me out to learn the truth, he shames himself and me."

"Oh, I don't know as there is much shame in visiting the Boudoir under these circumstances. His pride was sorely dented today by the interruption of your Mr. Fry. Imagine how he must have felt. Waiting patiently for you to agree to marry him, then waiting again as you insisted on a long engagement. Why would he be inclined to seek you out after your deception and failure to disclose the truth?" She raised her eyebrows. "For I won't call them lies. Not while you've been here in Bear Grass Springs. I see no mischief or malice intended by your failure to convey the whole truth about your past."

Leticia's laughter emerged as a choked sob. "I can't believe you'd be so charitable. A lie is a lie, Mrs. Tompkins."

"Hogwash. No two lies are the same, and that preacher man knows I don't agree with him and his Bible-thumping ways." She waited a moment. "I hope someday you'll come to tell me the truth. For now, have supper with your daughter." She rose and set her hand on Leti-cia's shoulder. "You've a hard road in front of you, but I hope you come through it relatively unscathed."

"Thank you," Leticia whispered and followed her friend to the door, locking and barring it after her exit. She looked around the barren room before moving into the bedroom to sort through their meager clothes that remained in the house. The majority of their wardrobe was already at the new home she was to share with Alistair. She packed essentials for her and Hortence into a travel bag, before encouraging Hortence to eat supper.

"When is Papa coming?" Hortence asked.

"Not tonight, darling," Leticia whispered around tears. "Something … came up, and he won't be here tonight."

"Who was that man yelling at the church?" Hortence attempted to dodge her mother as Leticia dabbed at Hortence's cheek. When Hortence realized it was futile to fight her mother, she stilled and allowed her to swipe her cheek so she could eat in peace.

"A man I once knew." She ran a hand over her daughter's shoulders. "He won't bother us."

"He made Papa very angry." Hortence tapped the tines of the fork on her plate. "The wedding was different from Aunt Annabelle's."

Leticia nodded as she rose, picking up Hortence's plate and turning her back to hide swiping at her cheek. "Yes. In fact, we must complete the ceremony on another day." When she turned to face her daughter again, she frowned to see Hortence biting her lip and her face scrunched up as she often did when she worked on difficult school projects. "What is it, darling?"

"Does that mean Papa isn't my papa yet? That I'm not his Little Bug?" Her lower lip trembled, and she bit her lip harder.

"No, you'll always be his Little Bug," Leticia soothed, running a hand down her daughter's back. When she sat, Hortence clambered onto her lap.

"But he won't be my papa?"

"I hope he will be. … I pray he will be. But I can't make you promises. Not today."

Hortence patted her mother's cheeks. "Don't cry, Mama. We'll find a way for him to love us again." She snuggled into her mother's arms.

Leticia let out a stuttering breath and held her daughter close, praying for some of her daughter's confidence in regaining Alistair's love and trust.

CHAPTER 4

The following morning, Alistair stood outside the livery with his arms slung over the wooden rails of the paddock as he watched the sky lighten in the minutes before the sun rose. A dusky pink lit the sky, and wisps of clouds similar to a mare's tail hugged the mountains. A soft breeze blew, although it was still cool in early June. He shivered as his hair was damp after a quick dousing in the icy water from the livery pump since he had decided not to enter the still-slumbering house.

"Thought you might appreciate this," Harold muttered, offering a cup of coffee as he snuck up from behind. "No one's up yet to grouse 'bout you gettin' a cup from the likes of the café."

Alistair nodded to the older man and took a big swallow of the black coffee. He smiled with appreciation. "Thanks. I fear Annabelle will sleep in today, and I'll have to make do with Sorcha's coffee."

"You could always make it yourself," Harold muttered. "Nothing wrong with a man making coffee." He raised an eyebrow at Alistair as he met the younger man's glare with a chuckle. "Seems you've still got quite a bit o' ire stuck in that craw of yours. Your time at the Boudoir did little to settle you."

Alistair snorted. "I was a fool." He speared Harold with a glare. "Dinna go repeatin' that." He relaxed when Harold nodded.

"Seems we generally are when our dander's up. And you had cause to be mighty upset."

"Aye, but not to act like a wounded bear with no thought to who I'd hurt." Alistair glanced at the house, but it remained darkened with no evidence of life stirring. "That woman last night deserved better than a man intent on another who had no regard for her." He ducked his head as though in shame. "I've never seen a more irate woman than Annabelle's sister when she saw me walk down the hall in the Boudoir."

Harold whistled. "Now ain't that interesting? I've always wondered about her story since Miss Annabelle arrived." He flushed. "Embarrassed to admit, I'd never given much consideration to the beauties at the Boudoir before then."

Alistair winced. "If the Madam hadna been present and expectin' her downstairs, I think Fidelia would have lashed into me. With great pleasure." He shook his head. "At the time I was affronted she was angry at me."

Harold snorted. "Anger has a way of coloring our perceptions." He watched Alistair as the younger man continued to study the sky change colors as dawn broke. "Have they changed toward your lady?"

He gripped the wooden paddock rail with his free hand until his knuckles whitened. "The fact remains that she isna mine. She never was. She never will be." He stiffened when Harold made a noncommittal noise in his throat. Alistair turned his head and glared at the old man he had come to consider an uncle. "She's married to another."

"Were you present at that ceremony yesterday?" When Alistair flushed red, Harold nodded. "Did you see her jump away from him, not wanting to be touched by him? Pushing her child away so he had no contact with her?" He frowned as Alistair's glower failed to diminish. "I understand heartache. I understand betrayal. I understand a need for time to lick one's wounds." He poked Alistair in his shoulder. "But one day you may come to realize you betrayed her as much as she ever did you."

Alistair watched as the old man stormed away, his gaze clouded with anger, guilt, and confusion. Alistair took another sip of coffee. After crossing his wrists over the top post, he rested his head against it, his mind replaying the previous day's scene. "Not yet," he muttered, unwilling and unable to think through all that had transpired since he had left for the church yesterday to be married.

~

Two days after the interrupted wedding, Annabelle sighed as she heard the bell twinkle at the front of her store and swiped at her hands. Sorcha had not arrived to help yet, and Annabelle imagined her sister-in-law immersed in her own work, spinning yarn. She also suspected Sorcha was intent on avoiding the probing questions that Annabelle had fended off all morning. The townsfolk's curiosity was growing, rather than abating, as time passed. She pasted on a smile as she emerged from the kitchen to the front room of her bakery where she sold her sweets and breads. Her smile faded when she saw the man in front of her.

"I'm sorry," she said as her smile transformed into a frown. "I have nothing for you today."

"Oh, don't be such a sour woman. You've never denied giving me scraps of goodies before today." He gave her an engaging smile.

She glared at him. "That was before I realized who you were. The man who slunk into this town, who is not a miner as you proclaimed, but a man intent on destroying my brother-in-law's future."

His brown eyes shone with shock and then delight at her words. "You're married to that bastard's brother?" He clapped his hands in delight. "I thought there was a connection between you all, but I couldn't be certain."

Annabelle stiffened as he rested his arms on top of her polished glass cabinets. "I'd like you to leave, sir, and not return. Your business, or whatever you'd like to call it, isn't welcome here."

. . .

41

J osiah Fry slapped a coin onto the counter. "I have money now."
He jingled a pocketful of change. "I no longer need to depend on
your charity."

Her gaze flicked to his coin and then back to him. "I'd suggest you
use your coin somewhere else. For you won't purchase anything in
this shop." Her derisive stare took in his disheveled state, oily brown
hair, and unkempt beard. "Perhaps you should consider a visit to the
barber."

His smile spread. "Always does a man good when a fine-looking
woman like yourself is concerned about his appearance." Josiah tipped
at his nonexistent hat and picked up his coin. "Although I will take
your advice. Should make the courtin' of my wife go a bit easier if I'm
cleaned up." He nodded as he winked at her, whistling as he shut the
door behind him.

Annabelle leaned against the wall behind her, wrapping shaking
fingers around her waist. "I gave him food and accepted flowers from
him," she whispered. "I welcomed him." She slammed her hand against
the wall behind her in anger and pushed herself away to return to the
kitchen to continue baking for her customers.

L eticia gripped Hortence with one hand and the bag stuffed full
of their clothes with the other. She firmed her shoulders before
urging Hortence to follow her up the steps into the Grand Hotel. The
door clicked shut behind her, and she tiptoed down the hallway past
the parlor on one side and smoking room for men on the other, then
the staircase along the wall to the desk area. It was located at the
entrance to the dining room, which was empty as it was midmorning.
She waited as she heard voices in the kitchen area.

Mr. Atkins, a heretofore pleasant man, frowned at the sight of her.
"I can't imagine why one such as you would deign enter here," he
snapped as he rushed toward her from the kitchen. He puffed out his
chest in an attempt to give more substance to his beanpole frame.

"I require a room for a few evenings." Leticia stroked a hand over her daughter's head.

The hotel proprietor flushed red before shaking his head. "When I think of how welcoming this town was …" His eyes flashed with contempt. "And, all the while, you've played us for fools." He pointed down the hallway to the front door. "I'll not rent rooms to a woman like you."

She grabbed his arm, flushing as he jerked away from her touch as though singed by a branding iron. "I don't ask solely for my sake." She looked down at her daughter.

He shook his head, sniffing in displeasure. "It is unfortunate that those among us will suffer due to your actions. However, I am unwilling to risk the reputation, the standing of my fine hotel, due to your presence. Please leave, *madam*."

She flinched as he said her name like the woman who ran the Boudoir, with a slight French accent. "Of course. Please forgive my presumption." She hefted her bag and grabbed Hortence's hand as she walked with her head high out of the hotel. Once again on the board-walk, she stood for a moment with little idea where to go.

"Mama, I'm hungry," Hortence whispered.

Leticia nodded. "Come. I defy her to deny me." She walked with renewed vigor, cutting down a back alley. She nodded to those she passed, meeting the glares and stares with an impersonal smile. When she reached her destination, she knocked on the door. She took a deep breath as footsteps approached, and the door was inched open. "Hello, Annabelle. Hortence is hungry."

Annabelle stared at Leticia a moment before nodding and opening wide the rear door to her bakery. Annabelle frowned as she saw the large satchel clutched in Leticia's hand. "I just took sweet buns out of the oven, and I have a glass of cold milk for both of you." Annabelle ruffled Hortence's hair and kissed her forehead. "I've missed you, Hortence."

"Mama stayed one day longer than she was s'posed to at our house, and Mr. Barclay threw us out today," Hortence muttered as she leaned against Annabelle's side for her hug.

Leticia met Annabelle's shocked stare and nodded her agreement. "We are looking for housing currently. It seems it will be harder to come by than I had hoped."

Annabelle scooped out a roll for each of them and poured glasses of milk, motioning for them to sit on stools across from her as she continued to work on her baked goods for the day. She sighed as a customer came in. After attending her customer, she returned.

"I should pay you for the rolls," Leticia mumbled, fumbling in her small purse.

"Nonsense," Annabelle said. "We're virtually family." She shared a long look with Leticia. "I hope someday we will be family."

"We should leave. When the townsfolk realize I'm here, they will boycott your bakery because of me." Her fingers gripped and ungripped her fork as she fought her anxiety.

Annabelle's amused smile eased her tension. "If there's one thing I'm not worried about, it's the esteem of the townsfolk. They already judge me for my support of my sister." She shrugged. "If I lose business, then I lose business." She watched as Hortence moved into the small office area where a cot remained.

Leticia also tracked her daughter's movement, her shoulders stooping as her daughter left the kitchen. "She's exhausted. Since Saturday she's clung to me like a bur and hasn't slept well. I imagine she'll curl up on your cot and be asleep in a matter of minutes."

Annabelle nodded as she swiped her hands on a towel. She scooped bread dough from a bowl and onto a floured area to knead it. "Where will you stay?"

"I have no idea," Leticia whispered. "If I could, I'd leave and never look back."

Annabelle punched her hands into the dough and glared at her friend. "I never thought you were so spineless. How can you say such a thing? Don't you know what that would do to Alistair?"

Leticia swiped at her cheeks, scrubbing away a few tears. "He doesn't want me. He's already visiting the whores!" She flushed, unable to meet Annabelle's gaze. "Irene told me where he went on the night of our wedding ceremony. I never thought ... I always thought

..." She blinked away tears as she met Annabelle's stare. "He'll never want me again. I misled him."

Annabelle snorted, earning a glare from Leticia. "Call it what it is. You lied. You failed to tell the truth."

"When you are on your own, with a baby on the way, you'll do whatever you have to do in order to survive," Leticia whispered. "Do you know how close I was to suffering the fate your sister has lived?" She met Annabelle's shocked gaze. "By the grace of God, I found another way. Yes, I lied. Yes, I deceived, but I found another way. Hate me for being clever. Hate me for keeping some part of my self-respect. But don't judge me."

Annabelle sighed, rubbing her forehead and smearing it with flour. "I never considered ..." She looked at her friend with newfound understanding and the rebirth of respect. "Someday will you tell me the whole story?"

Leticia nodded.

"I'd prefer it if you told Alistair first."

"If he'll listen to me," she whispered. "I've never wanted anything more than to be his wife. To know I'd have such a man in my life, helping to raise Hortence." She shook her head. "I hate that, if I'd been honest, if I'd had the courage to confront my past, we would have been safe to marry."

Annabelle frowned at that statement. "I can't say I'm a proponent of divorce. But considering I contemplated one with Cailean last year, I can't judge." Her brow furrowed more as she thought through the wedding ceremony scene. "That husband of yours seems intent on securing you as his wife again. He sounded quite intent on finding you." Her perceptive glance roved over Leticia's blond hair pulled in a tight bun and her church-best cornflower-blue dress. "Where will you and Hortence stay?"

"I wanted to rent a room at the Grand Hotel for a few nights." Her lips pursed. "But Mr. Atkins was unwilling to risk the reputation of his fine establishment to house one such as I, even though the hotel is three-quarters empty at the moment."

Annabelle set the dough in a greased bowl and placed a clean towel over it so that the bread would rise. She pulled out another bowl to start a quick batch of cookies for the early afternoon crowd that would come. "You have nowhere to go, do you?"

At Leticia's quick shake of her head, she bowed her head as though in shame.

Annabelle cracked an egg so hard that bits of the shell fell into the bowl. "Cailean may never forgive me." She scrubbed her hands on her apron and pinched the bridge of her nose. "I failed to help Fidelia. I refuse to fail you." She met Leticia's guarded gaze. "You may stay in my back room. For as long as you need to."

Leticia bent forward, placing her head on her crossed arms. "I should say no," she whispered. "I should refuse to be the cause of any rift between you and your MacKinnon family. But I don't want Hortence living on the streets. Living on scraps of garbage." She shuddered. "I can't do that to her."

Her friend gripped her arm. "I don't want you at the mercy of that man who calls himself your husband. You need a place where you can feel safe." She squeezed Leticia's arm once before releasing it. "I've braved the town's derision already over my sister. Don't fret about how they will react with you living here."

Leticia nodded and swiped at her cheeks. "Thank you. I thought I'd lost your friendship forever."

Annabelle smiled. "Give me a few days to break the news to Cailean and his siblings. Then you'll resume working out front again to earn your room and board." She smiled and winked at Leticia who fought a sob.

CHAPTER 5

That evening, Annabelle sat in one of the easy chairs in front of the windows in the bedroom she shared with Cailean. She waited for him, shifting in the chair in an attempt to stay awake. However, she drifted to sleep before he joined her upstairs. A tickling to her nose and a soft kiss to her shoulder woke her. She smiled before she opened her eyes, recognizing her husband's scent.

"What are you doing out of bed, love?" he whispered. "You need your rest." He eased her up, helping her from her wrapper and then into bed. He shucked his clothes and settled behind her, tugging her against him.

As she stroked his hand over her belly, she began to tumble into sleep before she jerked awake. "No," she gasped. "We must talk."

"Hush," he soothed, easing her back to her side and into his arms. "Whatever it is will keep until tomorrow."

She pushed and turned until she faced him. "No, it won't. And I refuse for you to hear about what I need to tell you from anyone but me." She looked into his eyes with a pleading gaze, sobering as he chuckled. "Please listen."

"You have to know there is little I would deny you. No need to look so worried." He brushed hair from her cheek to kiss it. "Say what you must and then let me enjoy holding my wife."

She traced circles on his chest. "First, I discovered that the man who I thought was a miner who gave me flowers for free food was really her husband." She felt Cailean stiffen underneath her as she alluded to Leticia but did not say her name. "I swear I didn't know."

"Hush," Cailean murmured. "Of course you didn't. None of us did, and why would you suspect he was anything but a prospector?" He sighed. "What did you do?"

"I barred him from my bakery." She swiped her face over his chest and breathed in his scent. "I feel like I betrayed Alistair."

He kissed her head. "You didn't. You were being kind, as you always are. I wouldn't want you to change now because such a man tricked you."

"I hope you mean what you say." She pushed until he was on his back, and she was balanced on his chest. "I saw Leticia today. She's been thrown out of her home. She has nowhere to live."

Cailean's jaw tightened at the mention of Leticia's name, and his eyes flashed with anger. "I don't see how that should concern us."

"Please don't let your anger misguide you." She cupped his cheeks with her palms. "More than we understand is at stake." She took a deep breath and met his wary gaze. "I've allowed her and Hortence to live in the spare room at the bakery." She pushed on him with all her might to keep him in place when he would have tossed her aside. "No! Stay and listen to me."

"How could you, Belle? How could you offer refuge to a woman who treated Alistair, our family, abominably?" His gaze was filled with confusion and hurt.

"I would never act to hurt you or Alistair or any MacKinnon. I need you to understand that." She waited until he gave a nearly imperceptible nod of his head. "However, Leticia is also my friend. She and Hortence are in need of help. There is much I don't understand, and I refuse to judge her before I know the entire story."

She met her husband's worried gaze. "I know this will hurt Alistair, and I can only imagine the choice words Sorcha will say." She ducked her head. "I couldn't throw Leticia and Hortence out when they stood on my doorstep, proud, hungry, and desperate. I betrayed myself six years ago when I failed to help Fidelia. I couldn't do the same today to Leticia."

Cailean nodded, the rigidity in his muscles easing as he listened to her arguments. "I know you meant well, but I fear you've only brought more pain to Alistair." He cocked his head and raised his gaze to lock on to hers. "However, the thought of Hortence homeless and hungry is …" He shook his head. After a moment, he ran a hand over the crown of her head before giving a subtle press to urge her to bend forward to kiss him. "I love you, Belle. I love how you care for all of us, better than we should be cared for."

She kissed him, easing to lie against him and snuggling into his side. "Thank you," she whispered.

"Once I overcome my rage, I'll try to understand." He kissed her head. "Be patient with me, my Belle."

"It's not as though I'm not angry too. I am. I just can't allow my anger to rule me and to hurt Leticia and Hortence. They are worth more than my rage."

Soft afternoon light entered the barn's open doors, dust motes dancing in the rays. The scent of fresh hay filled the air as a soft breeze entered, bringing a hint of pine forest. Alistair worked with a horse, his crooning not as soothing as usual. He sighed as the horse nickered and shifted from side to side as though sensing Alistair's personal turmoil. He ran a hand down the chestnut's neck, his soft caress calming the horse's nervous energy. "If only I could calm myself with such ease," he muttered. He spent a few more minutes with the horse before leaving the stall.

He stilled when he saw a figure in the open livery door, backlit in the shadows. His jaw tightened in recognition, and he moved with jerky movements farther into the barn to the room filled with tack. "No reason for ye to be here." He heard her deep inhale of breath at his snarl and then glared at the row of tack on the wall as her foot-steps followed his retreat into the barn. "Leave."

"No, I won't leave. Not until I've spoken with you." She stood close enough that he could smell the soft scent of lilacs she put on when-ever she knew she would see him. He remembered her saying she never wore it to school, as it was a waste of good scent and hard-earned money.

He kept his back to her as he blindly reached for a bridle. "Say what ye must an' go." When she softly traced a hand down his back, he spun to grasp her wrist. "Dinna touch me. Dinna think I need calming like one of the horses in a stall." He flung her hand away from him, yet he could not control the tic of his jaw.

"Alistair, please," she gasped as tears tracked down her cheeks. "You haven't attempted to speak with me. To hear my side."

"Ye lied! Ye lied to me!" he roared. "How could ye, after all we shared? After all the dreams I spun of us, for us, how could ye do that?"

"I never meant for this to happen. You must believe me." Her breath hitched as she fought a sob.

"An' why should I?" He cleared his voice of the gruffness, although his Scottish accent only thickened the longer he was in her presence. "Ye had years to tell me the truth, which ye never thought me worthy of. Why should I seek ye out now? Ye've had plenty of time to concoct yer lies."

"You can't believe I would willingly lie to you."

He leaned forward, his forehead almost touching hers as he nearly panted with his anger. "Don't, Leticia. Lorena. Whoever in God's name ye are. Do no'." He backed away until he brushed up against the tack. "For, aye, I do believe ye'd lie to me. Ye've given me nae reason to believe differently. For ye did deceive me. For years."

Leticia shook at the ridicule in his voice and gaze. "I know I've earned your mistrust. Please give me a chance to earn your trust again." She wrung her hands. "He wants me back. He says he wants his daughter, but..." Her wild, terrified gaze met Alistair's.

"He's yer husband. I canna see why that would surprise ye." His anger faded with his expression becoming more aloof the longer he beheld her standing before him.

She swiped at her cheeks and reached for him, only stilling her movements at the last second as he jerked his arm from her touch. "Hortence misses you." She paused at the anguish in his gaze at her mention of her daughter. "Why won't you help me?"

He shook his head. "I canna. Not now."

She stared at him, unable to control the fine trembling in her limbs. "Not *yet?*" she asked hopefully. When he merely stared at her with an implacable gaze, she nodded. "I won't bother you further today, Alistair. But I refuse to give up. Until you've heard my side of the story, I will never give up on us."

He watched as she spun on her heel and raced from the livery. He took a deep, shuddering breath before turning to the neatly hung tack and ripping it from the shelves. He heaved it over his shoulder, slamming it into a wall and onto the floor. When nothing was left to throw, he braced his arms on the barren wall, his shoulders heaving as he fought to calm his rage.

Alistair walked out of town, ignoring the interested stares and murmurings that erupted as he strode by. He ignored the few who attempted to engage him in conversation and continued his walk past the Merc, the café, and eventually the Boudoir. When he reached the edge of town, he veered toward a small path that would take him toward a place he had discovered after his arrival in Bear Grass Springs with Cailean four years ago. Although other townsfolk occasionally frequented the area, most continued up the main road to the mining town the locals had named Obsidian for its dark cliffs.

After a few minutes on the small trail, he heard the quiet babble of the creek, and a little of the tension in his shoulders eased. A scarlet-headed bird with yellow markings flitted in the brush, his colors brighter than usual as he called to a mate and ignored Alistair's presence. Alistair approached the creek—the air cooler, more humid, and mossy scented—and sat on a rock. Visions of Leticia danced in his brain, and he bowed his head.

Leticia laughing as she rang the bell for school. Leticia giving him an impish grin as she teased him. Her blue eyes, filled with wonder and joy after their first kiss. Her tremulous smile after she agreed to marry him. "No," he rasped, running his hands through his hair.

"Mr. MacKinnon?" a female asked, her soft voice emerging from the nearby cottonwoods.

He leaped to his feet and scanned the area.

In the shadows stood a woman nearly a foot shorter than his over-six-foot-tall frame. She clutched the edges of her shawl as she met his perusal.

"Miss Jameson." He nodded his head but did not attempt a smile. "I'm sorry to have bothered ye." He turned to leave, surprised when she rushed forward and grabbed his arm.

"No," Helen whispered. She met his startled gaze and seemed to accept the flush now spreading from her cheeks down her neck. "I wanted to speak with you."

He frowned as his gaze roved over her again. Where Leticia was lithe, Helen Jameson had a full figure, and he could not fail to notice the curve of her bosom or flare of her hips. She appeared to be wearing one of her Sunday-best dresses, the slightly faded royal blue enhancing the shine in her wheat-blond hair pulled in a bun. "We should no' be found alone together. We are no' courting."

She smiled while maintaining her hold on his arm. "That's just it. We could court. Now that you're no longer with Miss Browne, there are possibilities for us."

His confused gaze sharpened as he shook off her hold on him. "Ye were waitin' for me?" His frown turned into a glower at her nod of agreement. "Why?"

She clasped her hands together in front of her, as though hoping to exude a quiet confidence. Yet gripping and ungripping her fingers belied her nervousness. "I know how my mother is. I know how you and all the townsfolk talk about her." She ducked her head.

"Aye, 'tis no secret the majority consider yer mother a manipulative busybody," Alistair said with no trace of regret or apology in his voice. "I dinna ken how this affects ye bein' here this afternoon."

"If we were to court"—she swallowed—"and wed," she whispered, "I know I could convince Mother to cease in her plans for Miss Browne."

He shook his head as though she spoke a foreign language. "Yer mother's plans are rarely successful," he said with a roll of his eyes, "an' I dinna ken what she thinks she can do." He paused as he saw Helen flush. "Ye've never convinced yer mother of a single thing in yer life. Why would she listen to ye now?" His eyes gleamed with anger. "That woman would still ruin Le … her life an' gloat to the townsfolk about her new son-in-law while making my life a living hell."

Helen's hazel eyes flashed. "So I must be judged and condemned because of my mother? You don't believe I have the ability to do what I promise?"

Alistair heaved out a breath and pinched the bridge of his nose before taking a step farther from her. "Ye can speak as bravely as ye'd like. I ken what it is to face a bully and win. I doubt ye do." He nodded deferentially in her direction and turned to leave. "Ye need to find a smaller battle to start yer bid for freedom from yer mother. She's canny and fierce."

"Do you think I don't know what my mother is?" Helen asked. "Or how she treats those she deems less worthy than herself?" She fisted a hand on her hip, her shawl slipping unnoticed to the forest floor. "Don't you dare attempt to tell me what I know better than anyone else!"

Alistair fought a smile at her show of temper, his eyes gleaming with reluctant admiration. "Ye have no' had the chance to prove yerself yet, lass. Ye will. One day."

"I don't expect love," she said as she trotted after him. "I'd understand if you still loved someone else. Or if you needed to visit the Boudoir."

He spun to stare at her, his brown eyes lit with incredulity. "How can ye say such things and speak of marriage?" His gaze roved over her, quivering subtly as she stood with pride and determination in front of him. "I understand marryin' out of necessity. With good fortune, love will grow." He saw she understood he spoke of his brother, Cailean, and his wife, Annabelle.

He paused as he took a step toward her. "What a brave lass ye are." He stopped a pace away from her. "Whatever ye may want to do to spite yer mother—or to be free of her—dinna settle for a man who wouldna care for ye as ye deserve. Ye're worth more than that."

Her composure cracked, and she blinked as her eyes became shiny with tears. "You can't imagine what it is like, being judged to be just like her simply because she is my mother."

"Aye, I canna." His eyes shone with compassion.

She whirled away from him to pick up her shawl. After whacking it against a tree stump a few times to rid it of dirt, she lowered her head into a hand as she fought tears. "I have one dream. To be free of her."

Alistair sighed. "Ye have to want more from a man than the exchanging of vows. If ye dinna expect much from him, ye'll be sorely disappointed and willna ever receive what ye want. Or ye deserve."

Helen's shoulders stooped, and she clutched the shawl to her as her dress gaped with the change in her posture. "Why can't you agree? It would solve both of our problems."

He gave a mirthless chuckle. "Ye're smart enough to ken it would only triple them." He paused as he watched her battle for composure. "I thank ye for what ye offered to do for … her. It wouldna have worked, but I thank ye."

"You still love her," she breathed. "After what she's done and the lies and the humiliation in that church, you still love her."

Although he remained silent, his eyes gleamed in agreement with what she said. After a few moments of silence, where the only sounds were the breeze through the branches and the creek water falling against rocks, he murmured, "Love doesna end, or begin, easily, Miss Jameson. If it does, then it wasna love." He nodded to her before spinning on his heel and departing the place he had always considered a sanctuary.

CHAPTER 6

A week after the failed wedding, Alistair joined Warren Clark and Ambrose Finlay at the Sunflower Café for lunch. The three men formed the town's improvement committee. Alistair nodded to Harold as he entered the café and moved to the rear table, reserved for the meeting. Warren raised an eyebrow as he listened to Ambrose, the town's banker, drone on about bank security.

"I've read about improved safes that are much harder to rob. That way you don't have to rely on men to guard the bank."

Warren winked at Alistair as Ambrose puffed out his chest in dismay.

"That costs good money! As you know, I am not one to throw around my money after every new harebrained idea." He ran a hand over his expensive new waistcoat before hooking a finger into the gold loop of his pocket watch. "I believe in thrift at all times."

"Aye, of course ye do," Alistair said as he rolled his eyes. "Can we have a quick meetin' today? I've left Cail alone at the livery, and there's plenty of work to be done."

"Do you think the bank runs in an efficient manner when I'm not present?" Ambrose demanded. "Of course it doesn't. But the townsfolk saw fit to vote us onto this committee, and we must honor them and do our due diligence."

"They also expected us to do something other than argue about expenses!" Warren snapped, his blue eyes flashing before he took a deep breath. "Many pressing issues face our town, and we must find a way to meet them."

"The fact remains that we have no income. We have no town taxes. We have no revenue." Ambrose nodded in a regal manner as Harold *thunk*ed his plate of food in front of him.

Harold set down the other plates more gently in front of Alistair and Warren.

"There is little point discussing all we need until we find a revenue stream."

"If we are to become an incorporated town, we must show the legislature we can manage growth in a responsible manner," Warren said.

"I was not elected to impress the territorial legislature so that we could become incorporated. I was elected because I have sound business sense." Ambrose waved his fork at Warren. "There is no discussion until you find a revenue stream."

Alistair took a bite of the chicken fried steak covered in gravy and then swirled his fork in the mashed potatoes. "I'd eat up," he muttered to Warren.

Warren shook his head and ate slowly to savor the delicious meal in front of him. "You know that we need two teachers now that there are over forty children. We need a water tower, which means we need a way to get the water to the tower. A windmill would help power it." Warren continued to tick off ideas for improvement. "We should consider starting a volunteer fire department, but we need more than a bucket brigade. If we had an actual horse-drawn fire engine, that could induce men to join."

Ambrose set down his fork, having cleaned his plate in the short amount of time Warren had spoken. "We have no revenue. All these ideas will remain ideas until you have a way to fund them." He rose, nodding to Harold as he departed.

"I told ye to eat faster. Ambrose always leaves us with the bill," Alistair grumbled.

"It's impossible to eat as fast as that man unless you want to choke and die in the process." Warren glared at Ambrose's retreating back. "Is it possible to get him voted off the committee?" He sighed when Alistair shook his head. "And whose idiotic idea was it that we must be unanimous before we can act?"

Alistair half smiled. "That would be Tobias. He was irate not to be elected and wanted us to look like fools. I think we can change that provision."

Warren leaned back in his chair. "Things won't alter much for us until we obtain statehood. Congress denied our request this year, even though the voters overwhelmingly approved the idea last November."

Alistair shrugged. "Those in power dinna like sharin' it."

Warren rolled his eyes at Alistair's cynical opinion based on his experience as a Scotsman during the English's Clearances and changed the subject. "I'm surprised you decided to come to the meeting today."

"I'd always planned to come." Alistair ate a bite of mashed potatoes. "I had hoped to be a married man at today's meeting." He glared at the curious townsfolk who cast glances in his direction. He leaned toward Warren who swiped at his face as he finished his meal, acting as though he were in a deep discussion with the town lawyer. "I canna abide the town's pity."

"Have you spoken with her yet?" Warren murmured as he took a sip of water.

"Nae." He met Warren's gaze. "I ken I need to."

Warren watched him, compassion and understanding shining in his eyes. "She should be at the bakery now."

Alistair set down a few coins, enough to pay for his lunch and Ambrose's and rose. "Ye paid for the miserly bastard's lunch last time. It's my turn. I'll see ye soon." He nodded to Warren and left. When he exited the café, he turned to walk toward the livery but stopped after a few steps. He spun on his heel and approached the bakery.

The bell on the bakery door jingled as he entered, and he frowned as Leticia failed to come to the front area to serve him, although the shelves were virtually bare. After a moment he poked his head into the kitchen. "Hello, Annabelle," he said as he found his sister-in-law washing dishes. "Is she here?"

Annabelle failed to hide her surprise, and then a delighted smile bloomed. "No. She's making deliveries. I suspect she might be some time as Irene had a few things she wanted to discuss with her."

"I worked myself up to speak with her for nothing," he muttered.

"Are you ready to forgive her?" Annabelle asked in a low voice.

He shook his head and then shrugged. "I dinna ken. But I need to understand." He shared a tortured look with Annabelle. "I may be naive, but I canna base what I believe solely on what that man said in the church."

Annabelle nodded. "I agree. And, before you ask me, I don't know anything. I told her that I didn't want to know until after she had told you."

"Papa!" Hortence screeched as she raced from the back room. "'Stair!" She latched onto his long lean leg, hugging him.

"Oh, Little Bug," he breathed, tugging her free and pulling her into his arms. He hefted her until she rested her head on his shoulder. "How is my girl?"

She sighed with happiness a moment before she leaned away and glared at him. "Where have you been? I haven't seen you in a week! And I never did get cake."

He chuckled. "Yes, that is a shame. Ye should always get cake." The glance he sent Annabelle was filled with wry humor. "Although I'd think yer aunt Annabelle would fill yer belly with sweets every day."

Hortence let out a dramatic sigh and settled her head on his shoulder again. Her small fingers played with the dark-brown hair at his collar. "Mama says I should have sweets once a week." She groaned, and he chuckled. "How can Mama be so cruel when I'm finally living in a sweet shop?"

"I dinna know, my Little Bug. Ye'll have to ask her about it." He kissed her head.

She looked at him from under her eyelashes. "I thought you could speak with her. She never says no to you."

Alistair flinched and fought stiffening while holding her. "Yer mother an' I are no' friends right now, Hortence."

She pulled back a bit and patted his cheek, her brows creased with confusion. "Is your tummy still upset? I can hug you and help make it better." She wrapped her arms around his neck and squeezed tight.

"Oh, Bug," Alistair choked, gripping her to him. "I've missed you."

"And I miss you, Papa," she said as she began to cry. "Get over your mad. Please. Mama's so sad. She cries herself to sleep every night. And she hardly ever laughs, not like she used to. Nothing's good without you."

Alistair swiped at her cheeks and took a deep stuttering breath. "I wish it were so simple. It is no', my darling."

"You love my mama, and she loves you," Hortence proclaimed in the righteous voice of a six-year-old proclaiming a truth. "Why does it need to be *compicated*?"

He chuckled. "Life is complicated, Little Bug. Adults aren't sensible like you." He kissed her forehead and then set her down. "I should head back to the livery. I have work I must do."

Annabelle, who had remained quiet during his time with Hortence, spoke. "Won't you wait for Leticia?"

He shook his head. "No. Not today." He ran a hand over Hortence's red hair and chucked her under her chin. "I love you, Little Bug. Never doubt that." He frowned as he saw her chin quiver. He nodded to Annabelle and slipped out to leave through the front door.

A few hours later, Alistair entered the parlor of his family home to find both his brothers and Warren present. Although Cailean's age, Warren seemed older due to the air of responsibility that hovered around him. Unlike some in town, he was discreet and had an ability to show empathy where others were callous. Warren was also one of Cailean's closest friends in town. "I didna ken ye had a guest. I'll leave ye to it."

"Alistair, sit," Cailean demanded, motioning his brother to one of the empty chairs near the dormant stove. The open windows allowed the evening air to enter and cool the room after a hot June day. Cailean stared his brother down and gave a grunt of approval when Alistair acquiesced to his order.

"I won't take up more of your evening than is necessary," Warren began.

"Of course you're staying for dinner," Cailean said. "Annabelle would be upset if you ventured to the café instead of joining us."

"I wonder what she baked for dessert?" Warren shared a smile with Cailean and Ewan before sobering. "The reason I'm here is because I've received disturbing news about Leticia. While we are aware that she had another name, for the purpose of simplicity, I will continue to call her Leticia so there is no confusion."

He met Alistair's startled gaze. "I just received this information this afternoon. I did not have it before our meeting today with Ambrose." He waited until Alistair gave a jerk of his head in agreement. "I wired colleagues in Kansas in an attempt to determine if the accusations of Josiah Fry were credible. It seems he married a Miss Lorena Leticia Browning in November of 1877. Although quite a bit older than she was, I received no evidence that she was coerced into marrying him."

Warren rubbed at his temple, pushing hair out of the way. "In June 1878, he disappeared. Seems there was discord, and he wasn't seen again. Not until the day of your wedding ceremony."

Alistair nodded. "What date?" At his brothers' confused stares, he said, "What date in June did he disappear?"

"Late June. As far as can be determined, it was June 25, 1878." Warren scratched his head and said, "The story from Kansas neighbors is muddled. In one letter I received, she disappeared on a train before any indication of a struggle was found or any concern voiced about the husband. In another, she was served with a warrant for her arrest, and she evaded that issuance." Warren shook his head with a confused frown. "I'm inclined to believe she left town, and then a warrant was issued." He raised his gaze to look at Alistair sitting in a daze. "One thing I am certain of is that a warrant was taken out for her arrest. However, just as her husband disappeared, so did she."

Alistair dropped his head into his hands. "All this time, there's been a warrant for her arrest?" He groaned. "I've been engaged to a fugitive?"

Ewan spoke up. "Better than a murderess." He grunted as Cailean kicked him in his leg. "Sorry, Al."

Warren cleared his throat and shrugged before he continued to speak. "Seems she's been deemed a dangerous fugitive by the authorities. The home they were living in was a scene out of one of those gothic novels. Bed bathed in blood but no body. By the account I consider the most credible, they thought it was her doing as the stationmaster remembered her boarding a train, alive and well, but nervous and acting furtive. Thus the husband was deemed dead, although they never discovered the body."

"What truly happened?" Alistair asked.

"I don't know. I suspect only Leticia and her husband do." He stared at Alistair and then Cailean. "And I'm not traveling to Kansas in an attempt to unravel this muddle. Since they are both alive and well, I'm fairly certain that all warrants and charges will be dropped. We should be thankful no bounty hunters came searching for her."

Cailean waited a moment to see if his brother would speak. "At least her name was virtually her own."

Warren mumbled his agreement.

"What else worries ye, Warren?" Ewan asked. His cheerful countenance absent, he watched the lawyer with intense scrutiny.

After clearing his throat, Warren took a deep breath. "The old warrant should be easy to refute as the man she stood accused of murdering is alive and well. It makes you wonder why she would have felt inclined to murder the man." He shared a long look with Alistair who refused to comment. "The most pressing concern right now has to do with our townsfolk. Members on our esteemed school board are claiming that Leticia obtained her position as teacher to

the children in this town through deceit and malice. One in particular is calling for all her past salary to be repaid to the town as
damages."

"That's ridiculous!" Cailean sputtered out. "No matter the lies and
deception, she was a good teacher. She earned that salary."

"And ye ken who's makin' such a demand. That wretched Jameson
woman," Ewan snapped.

Warren nodded. "The demand is preposterous, but I can see the
reasoning behind it." He glared the brothers into silence. "How did she
obtain references? Was she truly a teacher in the past? Did she have
any formal training as she stated? It was her claim of such training
that convinced the school board to hire her and not wait for another
candidate. If the school board found the copy of references she gave
them and wrote to those listed, would they prove to be as false as the
story she peddled to the town these past five years?" Warren shook his
head. "You can understand the frustration from the townsfolk and the
desire for some sort of retribution."

Ewan snorted. "We've all been cheated by snake peddlers in the
past. Ye never demand repayment because ye ken the money lost was
payment for yer foolishness."

Warren shrugged. "Not all are as sanguine as you, Ewan. And most
snake peddlers have the sense to leave town before they are caught."
He watched the brothers for a few moments.

Ewan was filled with a restless energy, while Cailean attempted to
maintain his composure. Alistair sat in shocked silence.

Finally Warren motioned to Cailean and Ewan. "If you wouldn't
mind, I'd like a moment alone with Alistair. We'll join you in the
kitchen when we're done."

When Alistair did not protest their leaving, Cailean and Ewan
rose. Cailean gripped Alistair's shoulder as he walked past him, before
exiting and shutting the door behind him.

After his brothers left, Alistair met the lawyer's gaze. "Whatever ye
have to say, ye could have said in front of my brothers."

"Perhaps. However, I feel you should have the right to reveal what
you want at your own time." He paused and met Alistair's dispas-

sionate gaze. "No matter how you act or what you do or don't say, I know this isn't as easy as you are pretending."

Alistair motioned for him to speak as he clamped his jaw shut.

"Up to now, the townsfolk have focused their ire on Leticia. However, a growing group of people believes you were complicit in her deception and that you should also be held accountable."

"Ye can't be serious!" Alistair roared. "Ye saw me at that church. Anyone with eyes would ken I was as flummoxed as the rest of ye."

Warren nodded. "I agree with you. However, for the few pushing for some sort of monetary retribution, they know they will never recover the money from Leticia alone. Thus they are looking to you. You have a successful business. You have money."

"Greed wins out," Alistair rasped. He rose and paced to the window, gripping the sill as he stared blankly into the darkening sky.

"I'm afraid that is what it seems." Warren ran a hand through his brown hair.

"We have no money," Alistair whispered. "The fools have no notion that we have no money." He pinched the bridge of his nose. "They think because I built that house for Leticia that I'm a rich man. Instead of doing my share to pay down our arrears, Cail encouraged me to look to the future rather than be hindered by the past."

Warren sighed. "I must admit many are grumbling about your fine new home. And the fact your sister-in-law runs a successful business." He met Alistair's wild gaze. "There are always those who will want what another has."

Alistair sat as though poleaxed. "Why would ye no' tell me this in front of Cailean? The livery is half his. He stands to lose as much, or more, as I do. He's married."

"Nothing is certain. And I cannot discuss ... extenuating circumstances with you regarding Cailean." Warren raised his eyebrows and stood. "Shall we go to dinner?"

Alistair nodded and followed the lawyer to the kitchen and the round dining table to one side of the large room. He barely noticed the delicious stew Annabelle had prepared. Conversation flowed around him, and he absently listened as Sorcha teased Warren, and

Ewan roused Cailean's ire about his time at the Stumble-Out. After a few minutes, where Alistair had barely touched his food, he rose and fled the harmonious scene out the back door.

He stalked into the livery and stopped when he reached his horse's stall. The familiar earthy scents of hay, horse, and resin eased some of his tension, and he took a deep breath. He *click*ed for his horse, and she whinnied, poking her head over the edge of her stall as she sought a treat. She nickered in disappointment but turned her head into his hand as he rubbed behind her ears.

"There's my lovely lady," he murmured. Although he had curried her earlier, he pulled out a brush and moved into her stall, brushing her again. As he worked, he spoke to her, discussing his current dilemma and his anger at what transpired. "I dinna ken what to do, Brindle," he whispered, before chuckling out a mirthless laugh. "And I'm officially mad. Talkin' to my horse."

"You've always found solace talking with your horse," Cailean said as he slipped into the barn. "Are you all right, Al?"

Alistair gave Brindle a pat and moved out of her stall. "I dinna ken. Just when I feel as though I'm on the verge of movin' forward, somethin' happens to push me back." He set the brush down and moved to the pump, splashing water on his hands. He then sat on a stool. "I went to the bakery to speak with her today. To try to find a way through this morass." He slumped on his stool. "She wasna there."

Cailean's silence acted as though Alistair were in a confessional, encouraging him to continue his rambling thoughts.

"I held wee Hortence in my arms again," he whispered. "I'd refused to admit to myself how much I missed her. How the loss of her was nearly as painful as the loss of her mother."

He dropped his head forward and swiped at his wet cheeks. Anger laced his voice as he slapped a palm against his thigh. "And now to realize I kent nothin' about the woman I was to wed. A warrant was out for her arrest." He shuddered.

Cailean took a deep breath. "You still must hear her side of the story, Al. All we've heard are accusations and memories that could prove false."

"I now wonder if they'll prove any less false than she is."

After a few moments of silence, Cailean asked, "Why did Warren need to speak with you alone?"

"Dinna ask, Cail. Not tonight." He looked around the darkened interior of the barn. "It'll keep for tomorrow." He sensed Cailean's desire to pester him about Warren's private discussion, but he maintained his silence.

"Fine," Cailean said. "Tomorrow we talk."

"Aye," Alistair whispered. "Tomorrow we must talk."

CHAPTER 7

*B*y midmorning Cailean had mucked out stalls, fed horses, and filled water troughs. The promise of a warm late June day seeped into the barn on a dry breeze, and the doors at either end of the livery and to the paddock were thrown open. Horse flies pestered the horses, their tails swishing steadily in an attempt to swat them away.

As Cailean worked, he thought about his anniversary with Annabelle last week. He had hoped to sneak away for a few days with her, but had opted to remain in town and have a small, private celebration in their bedroom. He sighed, closing his eyes as he gave thanks for her understanding at his reluctance to leave Alistair at this time. As his mind wandered to his brother, he opened his eyes, his gaze darting around the livery as it searched for him.

"You're unusually silent today," Cailean said as he watched his brother and business partner work without whistling or making any noises to the horse he curried. "I've waited long enough to discover what Warren said that upset you."

Alistair brushed harder than intended along the horse's flank, earning a snort of reproof from the horse. He set aside the brush and rubbed the sore area, muttering a few words to the horse. "More of the same. Seems there are those determined to recover the money given to … her as salary."

"Why would he ask Ewan and me to leave the room?" Cailean shook his head.

"A few townsfolk are intent to prove a point at any cost. They are bandying it about that I knew of her lies. And, due to my knowledge, I should be held accountable."

Cailean furrowed his brows and slung his arms over the stall door as he watched his brother. "Anyone at that church saw your shock. You couldn't have feigned that."

Alistair's smile was rueful. "Memories have a way of shifting about to serve one's purpose." He met his brother's gaze. "They want me to pay what she owes."

Cailean squinted at his brother and tilted his head as though he were hard of hearing. "No one can be that obtuse."

"It seems some are, and I suspect 'tis that vengeful Jameson woman looking at any way possible to strike out at her and us. I should no' have doubted her meddlesome abilities when I spoke with her daughter a few days ago." Alistair patted the horse once more before moving out of the stall. Cailean backed up to allow his exit and plopped down on a stool. Alistair joined him, picking up a piece of hay to twirl with his fingers. "An' no, I will no' be trapped by that woman," he said, answering Cailean's unspoken question about Helen Jameson.

"What do you have set aside?" Cailean asked.

"Very little. I put most of what I'd saved into the house Ewan and his men built for us." His jaw tightened as he thought about the house sitting empty behind the bakery on a slight hill with a view of the mountains from the front.

Cailean sighed as he massaged his forehead. "As it was, they under-paid her."

Alistair gave a soft grunt. "Thank God they did. Can ye imagine comin' up with more than the $1,000 they'll be demanding if this lunacy is allowed to continue?" He looked around the livery. "We'll lose the business." His bleak gaze met his brother's.

Cailean glowered. "Don't. Don't you dare apologize. You've done nothing wrong. As far as I can see, neither has Leticia." He waved his hand as though in a conciliatory manner. "She lied, but she taught those children, better than any teacher they've had to date."

"I dinna have the money to hire Warren as my lawyer, and I refuse to ask him to work for me without payin' him." Alistair ducked his head.

"Aye. 'Tis a sound plan. The family will hire him," Cailean said, anger causing his accent to thicken. "We must hire him now afore the lunatics on the school board agree to their course of action." He patted Alistair on the leg. "Never forget. We stick together. When they attack you, they attack us." He watched Alistair a moment before he rose. "I'll go speak with him."

He left his brother deep in thought and walked to see his friend. When he entered, Warren raised an eyebrow and motioned to follow him into a back room he used as a private office and storeroom. He shut the door, granting them more privacy.

"I wondered when you'd visit me," Warren said as he watched his friend. He sat in a swivel chair behind a large desk covered in neat stacks of paper.

"We need to hire you. To help Alistair," Cailean said. "I only hope you haven't been hired yet by those opposing him."

Warren shook his head. "They're busy working on strategy and haven't yet realized they will need a lawyer." He shrugged. "Or they underestimate you."

"I hope they continue to underestimate us so that we outmaneuver them." He met his friend's somber gaze. "We want to pay you what is properly owed you, Warren."

He shared a long look with Cailean. "It may be expensive."

Cailean took a deep breath. "How binding is that agreement I made with Belle before our wedding?"

Warren eased back into his chair and steepled his fingers. "Extremely. She will have to agree to break it." He watched as his friend swore under his breath. "And I refuse to help you undermine her so that it is easier for you to manipulate the terms."

Cailean nodded, respect shining in his eyes as he beheld his friend. "I wouldn't want you to. I should never have asked such a question."

Warren fought a rueful smile. "Desperate measures and all that."

Cailean held out his hand, gripped Warren's, and shook it. "As long as we are agreed, we will find a way to pay you whatever you are owed. Thank you, Warren." He slapped his hat back on his head and left, his boots sounding on the floor.

~

That afternoon Cailean entered the back door to his wife's bakery and frowned when he saw Leticia washing dishes. He looked into the spare room where Hortence sat at the small desk, drawing. He winked at Hortence and then turned to meet Leticia's guarded gaze.

"Why are you here, Mr. MacKinnon?" Leticia asked.

His eyebrows rose at the formal address. "I'm Mr. MacKinnon to you? *Hmm*, times have changed." He set his hat on a stool and sat on another. "I wanted to see my wife."

Leticia waved a hand around, unintentionally spraying him with sudsy water. "As you can see, she's not here."

Cailean nodded as he looked around the tidy small kitchen. The butcher-block countertops were wiped clean, the ovens were off and slowly cooling after a day's worth of baking, while only a few bowls remained to be washed. "You're like a cat, aren't you? Always landing on your feet."

Leticia dried the bowl before setting it aside. She kept the towel in her hands as though to keep her hands busy. "I fear we have little to say to each other."

He leaned across the countertop. "Do you even care what you've done to him?" He glared at her as she backed up a step, her expression guarded and blue eyes unfathomable. "He has always had the tendency to be serious, but now he's lost all ability to appreciate joy. To laugh." Cailean shook his head. "He only half smiles when it is at something ironic or disappointing. Not joyful."

"I don't see why you are concerned about our relationship. I've been informed, by numerous sources, that he has overcome whatever meager passion he had for me by frequent visits to the Boudoir." She flushed at her words.

Cailean scratched at his head and bit his lip as though embarrassed to discuss such a topic with her. "One visit, Leticia." They shared a long look. "You unmanned him in front of the entire town. With your deceit and lies. He spent years, true to you, and then to not marry you?" Cailean shook his head.

"I didn't go running off with another man!" Leticia snapped, her hands on her hips.

"It may seem irrational and nonsensical to you, but it was what he needed."

Leticia snorted with scorn. "Men and their need to feel manly."

Cailean stood, the stool scraping as he rose with alacrity. "Don't tell me that isn't part of the reason you were attracted to Alistair. That he was strong, capable, and manly enough to protect you and your daughter and to provide for you?" He glared at Leticia. "You can't have it both ways, Lettie."

She blinked away tears and wrapped an arm around her. "I'm so disappointed in him. In me. In everything."

His anger seeped away as he saw her tears, and he nodded. "You've created quite a mess, and only you can clean it up." He watched as she swiped at her cheeks. His voice gentled as though against his will. "Keep trying to reach him. He's angry and hurt, aye, but, underneath it all, there's love for you." He flushed as though he had said too much. "I should go."

"Please spend a few moments with Hortence first. She's missed all of you so much and doesn't understand why we can't go to the livery anymore." Leticia sighed with apparent relief as Cailean turned toward the small room rather than the rear door.

Cailean entered the tiny room his wife had used as her living area —when she had first opened her bakery the previous year after her arrival in Bear Grass Springs. He ran a hand over Hortence's head, her silky red hair slipping past his fingers. "Hello, Hortence. I've missed you."

She looked up at him with serious eyes. "You're mad at my mama. And you didn't want to see me."

He crouched next to her. "Of course I want to see you. Sometimes adults can be hardheaded and not realize how they are hurting those they care about."

"Like 'Stair with Mama?" She doodled on her paper, her gaze downcast.

"Yes, and like your mama to us."

Hortence dropped her pencil and threw herself into his arms as he fell on his bottom.

"*Shh*, little one. It'll be all right." He held her and scooted on the floor until he leaned against the small cot Leticia and Hortence shared as their bed.

"You don't hate me?" she croaked out.

He kissed her head and rocked her. "Of course not. You're our Little Bug," he murmured, calling her by the nickname Alistair had given her this spring.

"My mama's so sad."

Cailean heaved out a breath as her tears continued to fall. "I know. So are we."

"We should have ice cream and cake and make it all better."

He chuckled at her suggestion and held her closer. "I wish it were so simple. Although, in many ways, I think you're right." He heard the back door open and attempted to tease Hortence. "You don't want Miss Annabelle to think I've made you cry, do you?"

She giggled into his shoulder but snuggled in tighter, refusing to ease out of his embrace.

He stilled when he heard a low voice, rather than his wife's higher-pitched tones. He felt Hortence stiffen in his arms. "What is it?"

"It's that bad man again," she whispered. "Make him go away."

Cailean rose, setting Hortence on the cot. He swiped at her cheeks and gave her a gentle pat to her head before he tiptoed to the doorway. He saw the man called Josiah Fry backing Leticia into a corner.

His voice sounded as a low rumble, and Cailean could not make out the words.

"What are you doing here?" Cailean demanded. He smiled with grim satisfaction as the lanky man spun to face him. "Were you hoping to gang up on her while you thought she was alone?" Cailean pushed away from the doorjamb, entering the room. He stood at least three inches taller than Josiah Fry, and his hazel eyes glowed with anger.

"As she's my wife, I can do as I please with her," Josiah said, his deep voice ringing throughout the room.

Cailean nodded. "Aye." He flicked a glance at Leticia as she gasped at Cailean's easy acquiescence to Josiah's proclamations. "That's what many would say, and much of the law agrees with you." He took another step into the room. "However, I don't agree. The woman wants nothing to do with you. Leave her be, or you'll have the MacKinnons to answer to."

Josiah laughed, his hand lashing out to grab Leticia's arm to hold her close before she could scurry away to safety. "She's nothing to you. She's not family. Why concern yourself with her or her br ... child?"

Cailean took another step forward, stilling as Leticia gasped when Josiah's grip tightened. He bit his jaw, biting back what he would say before speaking in a low tone. "You're not helping your case, Mr. Fry. Let her go. Let her soothe her daughter. If you are to gain what you wish, you'll need the support of townsfolk. Antics like this will hardly help you."

Josiah laughed, thrusting Leticia's arm away and shaking his head in disgust as Leticia stumbled. "She'll come around. When she sees she has no option but me, she'll understand I'm better than what will otherwise befall her."

He met Cailean's intense gaze filled with warning before he sidled from the room, slamming the back door of the bakery behind him. Cailean waited a moment to ensure Josiah had truly left before facing Leticia. "Are you all right?"

"I'm fine," she gasped out. "He doesn't like being interrupted. Not by someone from your family."

Cailean frowned as she massaged her forearm and walked behind the counter. "You should lock both doors when you are here alone, Lettie." He waited until she nodded. "What did he say that upset you?"

She took a deep breath before meeting Cailean's gaze with a panic-struck expression. "He wants me back. Wants the life we used to have. Says that nothing has gone right for him since ... we've been apart and that only I can turn things around for him." She swiped at the corner of one eye.

Cailean shook his head. "I don't understand, Leticia. None of us do. Won't you explain it to Alistair and then to us?"

"No use speaking to a man who won't listen," she snapped. "And I refuse to beg. I've done enough of that in my lifetime." She spun away as the back door opened again.

Annabelle entered, her joyous smile at the sight of her husband dimming as the tension in the room enveloped her. "Is it too much to hope that you aren't bickering?" she murmured as she gave her husband a scolding look.

"Hello, love," he said. "We need to talk."

"I had a lovely day. Thank you for asking. We sold out of every-thing, and Leticia has been a wonderful help since she began working here again. I don't know how I survived without her aid." She smiled at Leticia's shuddering back before glowering at her husband. "I'll find you at home where I will look forward to our discussion."

He lost this battle with a smile and earned a startled shriek from her as he yanked her close for a quick kiss. "See you soon, love." He stroked a hand down her cheek before casting a glance at Leticia's back. He frowned. "Be sure to look in on Hortence," he whispered to Annabelle before he departed.

~

Leticia accepted Annabelle's offer to watch Hortence for a short while and slipped out the back door to go on a walk. The previous days had teased of the warm summer weather to come, and

the afternoon approached a stifling heat. She walked the heavily traveled road that led to the miners' camp, pausing after a few minutes as
she left town and the incessant racket of a multitude forging their
lives. She cut off the main road and approached a creek that leaked
from the mountain, its stream of water a little less each day, and sat on
a rock in the shade.

The rippling, gurgling sound of the water soothed her while the
fresh scent of an in-bloom honeysuckle bush wafted in the air. She
breathed deeply, dipping her hand into the water and shivering at the
cold temperature. Long stalks of grass waved in the subtle shift of the
wind, while a white and black butterfly flitted around her. She pulled
out her handkerchief, dropping it in the water before wringing it out
to scrub at her face. A goldfinch flew back and forth across the creek
as it hunted insects.

"Do you shiver because you've been found out?"

Leticia jerked, turning on her rock to face Fidelia Evans,
Annabelle's sister who worked at the Boudoir. "The water is cold."

"I imagine you've become quite adept at manipulating a story to
suit your needs." Fidelia's kohl-darkened eyes were filled with scorn.

Leticia rose and stumbled over a few rocks before she stood on
firm ground to face Fidelia. "I've done nothing to earn your contempt.
You have little right to judge me."

An angry flush overshadowed the liberal coating of rouge, causing
Fidelia to look like an overripe tomato. "You have no idea how much
right I have to judge you." She took a step toward Leticia. "You, who
obtained a respectable position by lies and deceit, when you had no
right to it."

Leticia squared her shoulders and met Fidelia's derisive glare. "It is
a common practice to presume someone dead after a seven-year
absence. Our separation was the same as a death."

Fidelia snorted. "You can justify it any way you want, but you
know you lied. You deceived. You took a position deserving of respect
in town, denying someone worthy of the post." She shook her head as
though mystified. "You entangled yourself with a decent man and
then caused heartbreak and embarrassment."

"I had my daughter to consider."

That statement earned no sympathy from Fidelia, and her expression hardened further. "Don't expect that to earn any compassion. Annabelle would tell you that I have none." Fidelia paused a moment. "It will be interesting working with you as a colleague."

Leticia's breath emerged as an *oof* as she shook her head. "I'm not working at the Boudoir. I'll never work there."

Fidelia shrugged her shoulder, the loose sleeve slipping down to bare her upper arm. "So you say. So said every woman and girl working there. But we'll see." She backed away, disappearing down the short trail to the road that led to the brothel.

Leticia moved a few steps to collapse on the rock. The bucolic scene no longer offered succor, and she wrapped her arms around her waist. Her body trembled slightly again when she heard more footsteps. "Please leave. There can be nothing more for you to say to me today."

"I hadna realized I'd yet said anything to ye today," Alistair said.

She jerked to her feet. "I beg your pardon. I spoke with … someone earlier, and it wasn't a pleasant conversation." Her gaze roved over him, and she frowned at the despair in his eyes. His clothes hung on him, and she feared he had not been eating.

Alistair watched her with a yearning and yet anger-filled gaze. "Why are ye here?"

"This is where we always came. To talk. To … be alone." She flushed and shrugged.

"Aye. This is *my* place." He glared at her. "Can ye no' leave me in peace?"

Her eyes flared with anger. "I never thought you a coward!" She slapped a hand over her mouth as the words popped out.

"I'd be careful what I said," he rasped. His brown eyes were lit with hurt and disappointment.

"In all the time I knew you, you fought for what you wanted. You cajoled and you persisted. You weren't charming like Ewan, but you were steadfast." She shook her head in confusion and disappointment.

"Now that you're faced with adversity, you slink away, as though a wounded animal to lick your wounds."

"Ye have no right to be disappointed in me," he whispered. "Not when ye had every opportunity to tell me the truth! To spare me the infamy of accusations that ye are a liar and a murderess—at my own ceremony no less!"

"When was I to do that, Alistair? After you spoke of honor and truthfulness and your inability to esteem those who deceived? When would I have ever felt I could tell you my greatest fear? My greatest shame?"

"So this is my fault?" His brows furrowed as he beheld her blond hair falling from pins and her hat askew.

"Why can't you accept that we both are at fault?" she whispered, reaching out a hand. A tear leaked down her cheek when he failed to raise his hand to meet hers, and she let her arm drop to her side.

"If I had spoken to ye yesterday when I stopped by the bakery, would ye have told me the whole truth?"

She looked down before she could hide her guilty look.

He shook his head in frustration. "Or would ye have prevaricated and told me more lies?"

"Alistair ..." she whispered as her voice faltered.

"Ye ken I learned from Warren last night ye were a fugitive? That ye had a warrant out for yer arrest?" He frowned as she did not feign a response but stared at him woodenly. "Ye already kent this?"

"I learned of it recently." She swallowed. "From ... him." They shared a tortured stare.

"Will ye return to him?" he asked, his gaze boring into hers.

She shrugged. "I don't know. He has ... conditions to returning to him that I find hard to accept." She gasped as Alistair breached the few steps separating them until he was close enough his coat brushed her dress.

"Do ye prefer him to me? Is that why ye tried to forestall the wedding? Because ye hoped he'd return and find ye?" His gaze burned with insecurity and embarrassment.

"Oh, Lord, no," she whispered. "Never."

"Then why consider returning to him?" The intensity of Alistair's gaze remained, although a reluctant concern replaced his other emotions.

She closed her eyes. "No one will acknowledge my existence in town. Except for Annabelle and Mr. and Mrs. Tompkins. I walk as though a ghost down the boardwalks and on the streets, when before they called out to me, doffed their hats, moved aside in deference." She sniffed. "Now I'm barreled over as though I were a speck of dust, with little concern when I stumble or fall."

She opened her eyes as he made a deep grunting noise in his throat as though in anger or agreement. She squinted as she studied him but could not decipher which. "I want more for me. For Hortence." In a small voice, she whispered as she looked at her feet. "I've been advised she won't be accepted to attend school here next year. That a child with such a mother should not associate with the deserving children of the town."

She heard him swear and felt him move away. Her gaze tracked his movement as he approached the creek and picked up small pebbles.

"The townsfolk hold a lot of anger against ye." After a long pause, he chucked a pebble upstream and then another. "They want me to pay for yer deception."

"What are you talking about?" Leticia whispered. She moved toward him, raising a hand to run down his back, remembering at the last moment his bellow to not touch him the last time she had attempted a soft caress. Her hand dropped as she awaited his response.

"I'm surprised the likes of Mrs. Jameson could hold back from spewin' her angry plan at ye." His mirthless chuckle melded with the babble of the creek.

"What's going on, Alistair?"

He stared at the water gurgling through the rocks. "She, and probably others on the school board, is determined to be repaid all the money they paid ye. An', seein' as ye're as poor as can be, they're lookin' to me to pay the perceived debt."

"I'm sorry," she whispered.

He spun to look at her. "For what? For causin' me financial ruin? For lyin' to me? For destroyin' my dreams for us?" His gaze filled with anguish. "For never truly trustin' me?"

She raised her eyebrows as though to keep from crying and pursed her lips. "All of it."

"Aye. I'm sorry too. Sorry I ever took a shine to ye. I could be wed now, to another, with a bairn or two already." He pushed past her, stopping as he heard her stutter in a breath as she stifled a sob. He paused as though waiting for her to say something and, when she failed to speak, stomped away.

She followed behind him, her pace slower and more erratic as her tears marred her vision. As she approached the outskirts of town, she swiped at her cheeks and tilted her head high. She passed the café, surprised when Harold looked up from sweeping the boardwalk.

"Miss Browne." He doffed his hat. "I'd be most pleased if you could come to the café tonight with Hortence."

She flushed. "What a generous offer, Mr. Tompkins, but I'm afraid we cannot tonight." She jumped when his broom slapped the board-walk in front of her, impeding her forward momentum.

"If you refuse to sit in the front, like a valued customer, come to the back. Irene and I want to talk with you." He pinned her with a severe stare, his rascally grin returning when she nodded her agreement.

She murmured her thanks before slipping away, ignoring the glares of a few townsfolk who pushed past her.

Annabelle sat outside on the back porch, breathing in the evening air as it cooled. The hills shone a brilliant gold as the early evening rays slanted across them. When the kitchen door slammed shut, she turned her head as her husband joined her.

"No welcoming smile for me?" he teased.

"Why were you rude to Leticia today?" she asked as she continued to frown at him. "She was so upset after your visit that she went for a walk."

Cailean tugged his wife into his embrace, holding her so that her back was to his front with her head tucked under his chin. "She wasn't upset with me. That man who claims to be her husband visited while you were away." His arms tightened around her waist as she gasped. "Thankfully I had agreed to spend time with Hortence, and I was still there."

"Why won't he leave her alone?"

"Do you mean he's bothered her before today?" He pushed on her shoulders until she turned to face him.

She leaned against the banister at her back. "Yes. He is there most days, badgering her. There's little I can do as he comes in as a paying customer." She flushed. "Although I told him that he was barred, he ignores me. Doesn't give much credence to what a 'silly woman with more beauty than sense' has to say." She glowered as she mimicked the man before she clasped Cailean's hand. "I've spoken to the sheriff, but he says I can't bar a paying customer who has done nothing worse than flirt with the staff."

"Why have you said nothing to me about it before now?" He traced his fingers down Annabelle's cheek before resting them on her shoulders.

"I know how upset you become when I attempt to talk about her. The MacKinnons feel betrayed by her, but I think she has been equally betrayed. Not by us," she said when he began to protest. "But by that man. By life." She shivered. "I can't help but have a sense of Fidelia about Leticia."

"Someday you must give up that guilt, love," Cailean whispered as he kissed her forehead.

She leaned forward, wrapping her arms around his waist as she rested her head on his shoulder. "When my sister is free of the Boudoir and that life, then I might let the guilt go. I'm afraid that, until then, I will always feel a sense of loss." She rubbed her face against his shoulder. "It's been four months since she left our care, and returned to her life at the Boudoir. I live in constant fear that the customer who nearly killed her in February will attack her again."

"Aye," he murmured, running a soothing hand over her back.

"I thought she'd seek me out before now." Her breath stuttered as though quelling a sob. "I've done what she asked though. Even as I wait in fear every day to be informed of her death, I've not pestered her at the Boudoir."

He *tsk*ed in her ear. "You've never been a pest. Instead you've shown her that you are willing to honor her wishes. And you are giving her time to realize how foolish she is to turn her back on family and your love."

After a few moments, he eased her away and grabbed her hand. They walked to the far end of the empty paddock next door. She fought a teasing smile. "This isn't the best place for a tryst, husband."

He flushed. "Don't tempt me." He let go of her hand and slung his forearms over the top rail of the paddock. "I need to talk with you, and I need privacy. I want to be outside and not stuck in our room. It's too nice an evening to be inside."

Any levity fled, and she sobered. "What is it?"

"Alistair is threatened with financial ruin due to his association with Leticia," Cailean said as he described the threat against his brother in a succinct summary. "Which means we could lose the livery."

"No one in town will stand for this," she stuttered.

"They can and they will. Someone is fueling their anger, and it's more than Mrs. Jameson. I don't yet know who it is." He took a deep breath as he looked out at the sky with clouds streaked in pink. "We need money, Belle, to fight the challenges coming our way."

"Surely the livery makes a good profit," she said with a frown.

"It does, for a life here in a small town in Montana. But I had to take out loans to pay for Ewan and then Sorcha to travel here, and I've not yet paid them off. Alistair used all his savings for the house he built Leticia." He looked at the livery. "We've a good business. We have a home, aye, and we won't be hungry. But we've no ready money." He looked at her expectantly.

She froze and backed up a step. "No. You can't ask me that. You agreed. You promised!"

He nodded. "I know what I promised. I signed the damn papers." He took a deep breath to calm his temper. "I had hoped you would consider aiding us."

"It's not my money, Cailean," she whispered.

He frowned as he watched her. "Of course it is. It's from your father. He wanted you to have it."

She shook her head. "I've always considered my inheritance from my parents to be the bakery in Maine. I used the money from that sale to start the bakery here. I've been fortunate that it's a success. I set aside almost everything else from my father for Fidelia. It wasn't right that she be left nothing. That she be ignored in his will as though she never existed. You can't expect me to treat her with such little regard."

He kicked at the post before bending over and resting his head on his arm on the paddock rail. "Dammit." He pushed away, pacing a few steps before returning.

She bit her lip. "I'd feel like I was stealing from her, when I already refused to help her once."

"Does she know you've set aside money for her?" He watched her as the tic in his jaw became more pronounced.

She nodded. "I told her about it when I first arrived. She has no interest in it. I remain hopeful she will someday." She shook her head in frustration. "I want to help, Cailean, but you can't ask me to betray Fidelia. Not again."

He nodded. "Aye, I understand." He studied her intently. "Why did you not tell me the truth when you had that agreement written up?"

She closed her eyes a moment before tilting her chin and meeting his gaze. "I knew you had little regard for the women in the Boudoir. And you barely knew me. I feared you would not have as much concern for my sister as you showed to me." She gripped his arm. "I'm sorry I didn't tell you before now. I never realized we were still in arrears."

The tension slowly eased as he let out a pent-up breath. "I understand, Belle. And I know Fidelia better now. I want her away from the

Boudoir because that will be good for her and because it will bring you peace." He stroked a hand over her cheek as respect lit his gaze. "I always knew you were smart, but I never realized how good at strategy you were until now." He kissed her quickly and pulled her close for a moment. "I thought you were saving the money for you, in case something happened to our marriage. Or I was a rascal and abandoned you. Or for our daughter so that she too had her own money. Instead, you were saving it for your sister." His eyes shone with pride as he looked at his wife before his gaze roved over the livery. "I'll make a list tomorrow of what we have in excess and see what we can sell."

"No!" she gasped as she grabbed his arm and pushed away to meet his gaze. "I make a nice profit at the bakery. I've a small sum saved at the bank, in an account I set up before we married."

"How much, Belle?"

"A little over $200." At Cailean's shocked expression, she smiled. "I don't pay for any of the household bills, and I make a decent profit most days." She sighed. "Besides I didn't use all the money from my bakery in Maine. I kept a little back in case the business floundered."

"I'll repay you when I can."

She stroked a hand over his cheek, her fingers rubbing over the stubble there. "No, my love. I want to give it to you, … to us, to help Alistair." She rose on her toes and kissed him softly. "Thank you for not pressuring me to use Fidelia's money."

He tugged her to him. "I admire your loyalty, and I don't wish to be the cause of any further misunderstanding between your sister and you." They stood together, holding each other for long minutes. "Come to bed, love. Tomorrow morning comes early."

Leticia knocked on the back door to the Sunflower Café, her hand on Hortence's shoulder. She followed Hortence inside after Irene opened the door and ushered them in. Set along one wall of the cramped kitchen, a small table stood with a clean tablecloth and plates. Wild daisies in the vase brightened the table, while a piece of paper and a pencil sat next to Hortence's seat.

"We thought you could draw us a picture," Irene said as she ran a hand over Hortence's head. "We haven't seen you in far too long and miss your drawings."

Hortence smiled and sat at the table, her face scrunched up in concentration as she considered what to draw. "I'll draw you a bear!" she said, her youthful triumphant voice ringing out.

"Wonderful," Harold said as he entered the kitchen.

Leticia sat at the chair across from Hortence so that Harold and Irene could move around the kitchen without her in the way. They worked in silent harmony, and she jerked back in surprise when a bowl of soup was set in front of her.

"Eat," Irene said. "You haven't been eating enough from the looks of you." A basket of freshly cut bread was placed on the table, and another smaller bowl of soup was set before Hortence.

Harold and Irene continued to work, making dinners, serving and clearing tables, while chatting with their customers. After Leticia and Hortence had eaten their fill of fried chicken and mashed potatoes, Leticia lingered over a cup of coffee.

"Don't even think of leaving," Harold barked. He nodded as Hortence crawled onto Leticia's lap and fell asleep.

After the evening rush had quieted, Harold and Irene joined them at the table. "I have some of Miss Annabelle's cake," Irene said. She smiled at Hortence when the mention of cake failed to rouse her. "Poor dear. She's tuckered out."

Leticia kissed her daughter's forehead as she tugged her more securely onto her lap. "She saw Cailean today."

"That's not the only one who visited you today," Harold said around a mouthful of cake. "That no-good husband of yours sniffed around again."

Leticia sighed. "He refuses to understand that, after so much time apart, we no longer suit."

Irene watched her intently. "Why didn't you divorce the man?"

"I worried he would find me when I had to divulge where Hortence and I were in order to process the divorce. I've come to realize he would have found me anyway, no matter where I was." She blinked away tears. "I was a fool to wait and waste any time I could have had with Alistair, and fools must pay the price." Her voice trembled, and she exhaled deeply.

Harold grunted in agreement before slurping down a sip of hot coffee. "The only foolish thing you did was not trust that man of yours. He deserved better, and so did you."

"There's little he could have done," Leticia whispered, as she buried her face in Hortence's hair.

"Hogwash," Irene snapped. "He could have helped you obtain a divorce. He and that Clark boy are bright and would have found a way to free you. Thataways you wouldn't have had to hope fate would continue to be kind."

Leticia sniffled. "Fate's rarely been kind, Mrs. Tompkins."

Harold took another sip of coffee and speared her with an intense look. "What did that husband of yours mean when he said at your wedding ceremony how you'd miscalculated?"

Leticia flushed, glancing at Hortence to reassure herself that she truly was asleep. "I was pregnant with Hortence. I knew I must flee to protect my baby. I mixed a sleeping draught in his whiskey and snuck away." She kissed her daughter's head. "He thought I meant to kill him."

Irene snorted. "He's even more of a fool than I realized. You're no murderer, although you were desperate." She tapped her fingers on the tabletop in agitation. "Since that time, you've hoped everything would turn out fine without any more work on your part. Seems to me the passive route didn't work for you. Now you must decide on what you want and be an active participant in your life. Stop wishing and waiting for things to turn out as you hope. Work for it, and you may yet obtain what you want."

Harold grunted, agreeing with his wife's words. "Unlike other places, divorce is easy to obtain here in Montana, Miss Leticia. I'm surprised you didn't know that."

"Not having a newspaper has decreased the news from around the state," Irene said. "Our grandson Frederick and his brothers keep us informed. Seems divorce is nearly as common as marriage in the big cities, like Helena and Butte."

"It would scandalize the people here," Leticia whispered.

Irene chuckled. "I wouldn't be so sure. Mrs. Jameson is divorced. As is our nephew, Tobias. And so is Mr. Barclay." She paused. "I'm sure I could think of many more. It's hard to keep a wife in the mining towns. And many women want the right to seek a better provider than the man they first married."

"I doubt Alistair would look fondly on a divorced woman," she whispered.

"Divorced or widowed," Harold said, "you've lived your life with dignity since you came to town. Ain't no reason to be ashamed for wanting a man like Alistair MacKinnon. That Mr. Fry seems a scoundrel."

Leticia shivered. "That's one way to describe him." Her arms tightened around her daughter. "I'm afraid I don't have as liberal a view on divorce as you do."

Harold watched Leticia with growing concern. "You were desperate to leave him seven years ago. Why do you believe you'll feel any differently this time?" He met her startled gaze and then growled with impatience as she remained quiet. "It's still not too late to seek a divorce. Many reasons would be acceptable to a judge."

"I fear parts of my story will shock you, as nothing is always as it appears." Leticia breathed in Hortence's scent as she slept on her lap. "Thank you for your counsel. Thank you for always being my friends."

Irene and Harold shared worried glances before Harold spoke. "No need for you to thank us. We stand by our friends. The townsfolk are feeding off your misfortune with Tobias fanning the fervor of their discontent, and I have to hope they'll soon find another scandal to entertain them. You've suffered enough."

She shared a watery smile with them. "I should get her home." She eased to stand with Hortence in her arms. When they waved away her offer to pay for dinner, she blushed. "Thank you for dinner. And your kindness."

CHAPTER 8

*B*efore the sun had yet risen, Cailean joined Alistair on the back porch, blowing on a steaming cup of coffee. "I'll have to remember to thank Belle for leaving the coffee ready for Sorcha to brew this morning."

"Ye should ask her to do it every day," Alistair said, his gaze raised as the sky lightened. Long wispy clouds changed from light pink to yellow to white as the sun rose over the mountains. Alistair ignored the back door opening and closing as Ewan joined them, sitting on an uncut piece of firewood. "I saw her yesterday," Alistair said.

Cailean hitched his hip onto the banister and leaned against the porch post. "What did she say?"

"She apologized." The words brought no visible comfort as Alistair continued to brood. "Seemed she thought that would make a difference."

Cailean took a sip of coffee and studied his distraught brother. "Did you give her the chance to explain?" When Alistair shrugged, Cailean sighed with frustration. "What more can she do than explain? You must hear the truth from her."

Alistair glared at Cailean but remained quiet.

Ewan yawned as he attempted to wake, slurping down a few sips of coffee as he listened to his brothers talk.

"Do you want her to become a social pariah? Because she's succeeded in that. Do you want her to be financially ruined?" Cailean waited for some emotion from his brother but frowned as Alistair continued to stare at the distant mountains. "For she's successful there too."

Alistair closed his eyes. "I ken what yer doin,' Cail. An' I can't say I wouldna do the same to ye." He let out a deep breath. "It's as though I'm gutted every time I see her. She didna trust me enough. Didna trust in us enough. An' I canna forgive her."

"Do ye want her to beg?" Ewan asked. He met Alistair's glower. "Do ye want to ruin any chance of reconcilin' by makin' her feel worse for actin' on her fears?" Ewan shrugged as he had an all-over body shake and stifled a yawn. "I kent she failed ye. She left ye open to ridicule and scorn and pity."

"Aye," Alistair said. "I don't ken if I'll ever forgive her."

"If ye can no', then one of ye should leave town. At least for a time. For while ye're both here, the townsfolk are speculatin' about ye." Ewan met Alistair's irate gaze. "The saloons are taking any number of bets." He raised his hand as he ticked them off. "How long until ye forgive her? How long until ye woo her? How long until ye ... bed her?" He raised his eyebrows at Cailean's incredulous laugh. "How long until ye move on to another?"

"Fools, the lot of 'em." Alistair snorted. "I'm sure ye heard worse bets, but ye're refusin' to tell me what they are." He frowned as his carefree brother remained serious.

"Ye spoke of Cail not holding on to his hurts too tightly last fall with Annabelle. The same is true for ye, Alistair." Ewan set his now-empty cup of coffee on the porch floor. "Ye are no' a bitter man, an', until ye understand why she acted as she did, ye willna have peace. Even if she's no longer in this town."

"He wants her back," Alistair rasped, his head dropping until his chin hit his chest. "He's her husband. I've no right to prevent their reunion."

"Horse dung," Cailean snapped. "The woman I saw yesterday had no wish to be with that man, husband or not." He met Alistair's glare. "I saw him with her. I saw him manhandle her, backing her into a corner with his taunts and jeers. If how he treats her now is any indication of her life with him then, I can't condemn her for doing whatever she had to do to start over. Especially with her bairn."

Alistair frowned as he listened to his brother. "Did he hurt her?"

"Aye. Bruised her arm." He watched as Alistair frowned and battled concern for her. "But more than that, he tried to destroy her spirit." He slapped Alistair on his back. "Find peace with your anger, Alistair, and talk with her. Truly talk with her." He reentered the kitchen for another cup of coffee, the door slamming shut as he retreated.

Ewan shifted, standing in the place Cailean had vacated. "She'll hear the rumors soon." When Alistair stared at him blankly, Ewan shrugged. "That ye are courtin' another."

"Who am I to be courtin'?" He shook his head in frustration. "Damn small town. Makes me want to leave an' become lost in a city."

"Don't leave, Al," Ewan said. "Not when we're all together again." His hand gripped the banister a moment, relaxing as he stared at the paddock and distant mountains.

Alistair heaved out a large sigh. "I won't. I might want to, but I willna. I promise." He nudged his youngest brother in the shoulder. "Now, who am I courtin'?" He took a sip of coffee after asking his question.

"Helen Jameson."

Alistair spewed his mouthful of coffee into the yard, coughing as he tried not to choke.

Ewan slapped his brother on the back a couple times to help. "Seems Mrs. Jameson is walking around like a stuffed pheasant, as pleased as could be about how things are progressin' for her daughter."

"Christ," Alistair swore. "I met her once, in the woods. I went to my thinkin' place, and she was waitin' for me. Ambushed me with crazy ideas." He paused until Ewan made a noise to continue. "She

89

wanted me to court her now that I was done with Le ... *her*. I declined."

Ewan shook his head. "Seems ye were no' as emphatic as ye needed to be. That mother is a menace and found out ye met. God help ye." He paused. "And God help Leticia when she hears the news."

Alistair shivered. "Aye. She'll have no reason to believe I havena started up with another." He bent his head forward. "I havena treated her as I should."

"Whatever ye do, speak to Leticia soon. Ensure she understands ye still care for her." Ewan met Alistair's defiant gaze. "Ye ken ye do. Stop actin' like an ass." He slapped his brother on his arm, leaving him to his thoughts.

~

Alistair entered Warren's office, his hat in his hands as he waited for Warren to emerge from the back room he used as a private office and file room. After a moment, Warren poked his head out and smiled.

"I thought I heard someone enter. You are as quiet as a cat." He motioned for Alistair to sit and then joined him, sitting across from him at his large desk. Warren's jacket was slung across the back of his seat, and he began to unroll his shirt sleeves.

"No need on my account," Alistair said with a humorous gleam in his eyes.

"The heat is stifling today, and there's no breeze," Warren muttered as he relaxed into his swivel chair. "What brings you by?"

"I dinna ken if Cailean spoke with ye?" Warren nodded and Alistair frowned. "Can ye aid me, even though I dinna have much money?"

Warren sighed. "Cailean is one of my best friends. Of course I will help you, Alistair. Besides, I hate to see an injustice perpetrated against someone who is most likely a victim." He watched as Alistair flushed with what seemed like shame. "As is what I imagine is the true situation with Miss Browne."

Alistair shrugged, and Warren pinched the bridge of his nose.

"God save me from stubborn Scotsmen," he muttered. "I take that to mean you still haven't spoken with her?" He rolled his eyes as Alistair shook his head. "If you want to defeat that man who claims to be her husband, you must convince her that you are on her side. Otherwise she'll have no reason to believe you. No reason to remain in this town. No reason not to leave with him. Legally she is wed to him. Not to you."

Alistair gripped his thighs with his hands as he fought escalating tension. "I ken what ye say is true. My brothers just told me the same thing." He paused a moment as though thinking through all he had learned since that disastrous wedding ceremony. "Do ye know any more than what ye've told me?"

Warren watched him. "I've made further inquiries, but I've yet to hear back from my colleagues." He speared Alistair with a severe stare. "I understand the desire to know the facts. The need to better understand what happened." He frowned as his gaze became haunted. "I know what it is to love and lose and to regret what I might have done."

He leaned forward, the chair squeaking with the movement. "All the evidence in the world shouldn't matter, Alistair. Either you believe her or you don't. Something in the future will cause you to doubt her. If you continue to hold on to these doubts, this bitterness, you will never be free of that one single day. That one hour in the church." He sighed. "Which isn't fair to you or to her."

Alistair sat as though poleaxed. "Ye're sayin' I need to have faith in her before ye have proof?"

Warren nodded. "Yes, and show her that. For, if you don't, the anger and disillusionment will not be all your own."

Alistair rubbed at his forehead. "Is this the advice ye give to all yer clients? Doesna seem very lawyerly to me."

Warren laughed. "No, this sort of meddling I save for friends." He watched Alistair with concern. "I understand you are confused by the report of the warrant for her arrest, but so far it is only a report." He raised an eyebrow. "Besides, you know she isn't a murderess as the man she purportedly killed is in town."

Alistair's gaze was filled with embarrassment. "She has every right to be as upset with me. When she hears the rumors about Helen Jameson and me ..." He frowned at the flash of anger and hurt in Warren's gaze.

"What rumors?" Warren choked out.

"Accordin' to her mother, I'm courtin' the lass." Alistair huffed out a frustrated breath. "God help me."

"Helen's not that bad." Warren's protest earned a confused stare from Alistair.

"No, but the mother is. I canna imagine takin' on the mother, even if I wanted the daughter, which I do no'." He shivered. "*Bluidy* small towns and their rumors."

Warren chuckled as he relaxed into his chair. "Seems like you have your hands full, Alistair. I don't envy you."

The noncommittal grunt sounded through the room. "So ye'll help me? I canna promise fast payment, but I will pay ye. The livery provides steady income, but it doesna mean I'm rich."

Warren nodded. "I'd already agreed to help you when I spoke with Cailean. And it's a good thing he came to visit me when he did. A few members of the school board arrived not long after his visit and were quite vocal in their disappointment when I refused to represent them."

Alistair canted forward, his eyes lit with curiosity. "Do ye ken if they intend to seek retribution from Leticia and me?"

Warren nodded. "Before I was able to inform them that I was already hired as your lawyer, your accusers reviewed their grievances against you with me." Warren shrugged, unable to hide an amused smile. "Their case has little substance. It's supposition and want. Nothing based on fact." He rolled his eyes again. "The entire idea shows their naiveté and lack of legal knowledge. They have no evidence, no facts that prove you had any prior knowledge of her deceit."

"How can ye prove that?"

"They admitted as much to me. The fools," Warren said with a sigh. "Besides, I've already interviewed a half-dozen witnesses at the wedding ceremony and have their testimony as to your shock and rage. It will only help prove your innocence, should it progress any further. I suspect it won't."

"Why? They seem determined." Alistair took a deep breath and released it as he battled the tension and worry in his gut.

Warren rested his forearms on his desk and chuckled. "Even after I told them twice how I could not represent them as I represented the MacKinnon family, they still thought to sway me to their side, wanting me to take on their case pro bono." At Alistair's confused expression, he explained, "They wanted me to work free of charge for the good of the community to rid it of those who would sully the reputations of the residents and the quality of life found here."

Alistair snorted. "If they truly believe that, they should focus on the Boudoir and the saloons, not on me and the former schoolteacher."

Warren nodded. "Even after declaring myself as your legal representative, by the time they'd spewed all this information, I had learned what I needed to." His eyes gleamed with satisfaction. "I always enjoy denying that Jameson woman."

"And Tobias," Alistair muttered.

"Yes. That was an added bonus," Warren said. "Thus I would not worry overmuch about a lawsuit. I think it is a lot of hot air and would be thrown out of court should it progress that far." He squinted as he smiled wryly. "I could always threaten them with a lawsuit for defamation of character." He chuckled. "I'd love to see them sweat."

"Do ye think that's necessary?"

"No, but, if they become more of a nuisance, it's something I can do."

Alistair sat in silence with his head bowed as he thought through all Warren had told him. "Will ye continue to be my lawyer? I have a sense I'll need more of yer aid afore this is all over. That husband of hers seems wily, an' I dinna trust him."

Warren nodded. "With pleasure. And we can work out a payment plan." He shook Alistair's hand and rose as Alistair stood to leave. "Think about what I said."

"Aye, I think of little else," he rasped. He slapped his hat on his head and nodded once before he slipped out the door.

~

Leticia heard the jingle of the bell and entered the storefront of Annabelle's bakery. A slight hitch in her step betrayed her displeasure at her next customer's identity, but she pasted on a bright smile. "May I help you, Mrs. Jameson?"

"Yes, I'd like a loaf of bread and three cookies."

Leticia placed the items in her basket and held her hand out for money. "These are not on credit, Mrs. Jameson. Miss Annabelle doesn't accept credit, as you well know." She wriggled her fingers of one hand while keeping her other hand firmly clasped around the handle of the basket. After a severe glare, Mrs. Jameson dug out the requisite coins.

"Here you are, smug and secure in your little world, living with your daughter in a back room off the charity of one who should despise you." Mrs. Jameson took as deep a breath as her corset would allow. "Have you no decency?"

"If that is all, Mrs. Jameson?" Leticia asked, whirling to return to the back of the store.

"Are you foolish enough to pine for a man who is already courting another?" She cackled as her comment caused Leticia to freeze. Mrs. Jameson's smile broadened as she saw the devastation and despair Leticia could not hide as she turned to face Mrs. Jameson again. "You are a fool to believe you wouldn't be found out for your deception. And even more so to believe a man would be constant." She leaned forward as though imparting a great secret. "They never are."

"If I may inquire, who is he courting?" She cleared her throat as it thickened, and she battled tears she refused to shed in front of Mrs. Jameson.

Mrs. Jameson thrust out her bosom and smiled with triumph. "My daughter. Yes, Helen has finally done something worthwhile with her life." A sigh of pleasure escaped. "When I think of that fine house we will live in ..."

"Are you certain Mr. MacKinnon is intent on your daughter?" Leticia whispered.

"They were seen alone in the woods." She speared Leticia with a knowing stare. "You know what that means. No man would conspire to meet with a young woman of good standing alone without having honorable intentions."

Leticia froze and then nodded. "Of course. How fortunate for them both."

Mrs. Jameson clapped her hands together. "It's almost too wondrous for words." Her gaiety faded as she glared at Leticia. "Don't believe for one moment that, by marrying my daughter, the town's desire to have a full restitution of funds from you has wavered. You are in arrears, missus."

"I am in no such thing until a judge declares it," Leticia snapped. "And, unlike your most fervent desire, you will never be judge and jury of those living in this town."

Mrs. Jameson reared back as though struck. "You have no right for righteous indignation. Not after the scandal and deception you perpetrated for years."

"Just as you have no right to judge when you do not understand the full story. But then we all know you only attend church for the social prestige you believe it brings you. Not because you actually heed the preacher's message to practice charity."

Mrs. Jameson turned as red as a raspberry and puffed up her chest. "If it is the last thing I do, I will ensure you and your brat are out of this town by the end of summer. With my daughter married to Alistair MacKinnon." She spun on her heel, slamming the door shut behind her.

Leticia collapsed, leaning against the wall behind her, her knees shaking so that she could barely hold herself up. As another customer entered the store, she pushed herself upright and forced a welcoming smile.

That afternoon, after the bakery had closed, she walked with Hortence to the schoolyard. As it was summer vacation, the yard was empty, but there was open space with a fence around it. "Go ahead and play, my darling, but stay within the fence."

She sat on the school steps, watching as Hortence ran around, playing with imaginary friends. Leticia stood as she saw Josiah Fry on the other side of the fence.

He watched Hortence with disinterest before focusing on Leticia.

"Why are you here?" She clamped her jaw shut as her voice quavered.

"Do you believe I would allow that man who is no relation of yours to prevent me from speaking to my own wife?" He walked through the entrance to the schoolyard, coming to a halt in front of her. "You are more beautiful than when we met."

"I have no interest in your useless attempts at flattery. We both know your words are meaningless." She jerked her head away when he attempted to stroke a finger down her cheek. "You have no right to touch me."

"Except for the rights of a husband. I've been too long without mine." He watched as she blushed but met his gaze. "I fear you've been far from chaste since last we were together."

"How dare you imply I have acted in such a manner. I have a daughter, and she will always come first." She faltered as she backed up one riser on the steps away from him, allowing her to almost meet his height and granting her a bit of distance from him.

He laughed. "I'm certain, if you had wanted to be with him, you would have found a way."

"He is an honorable man!"

"Ah, he's foolish then? Doesn't take what he wants?" He smiled as he leaned forward, his smile broadening as he saw trepidation in her gaze.

"Unlike you."

He chuckled. "I knew I wanted you, and I had you. You should be thankful I deigned to marry you." He sobered. "If you had stayed with me, we could have had tremendous success. Neither of us would be eking out a living in backwater towns. We would have mansions and servants to do our bidding."

She shook her head as her voice emerged laced with scorn. "You have always deluded yourself with your ideas of what you could do. What you would obtain. I am not obtainable. I am not yours."

He leaned forward, backing her up until she hit the door to the locked schoolhouse. "You will return with me. For, if you don't, I will ensure you never see your daughter again."

Her indignant flush faded as though she suffered a tremendous blood loss, and she gripped the door handle to remain standing. "Your threats will never come true." She paled further as he leaned forward and whispered in her ear.

"What will the townsfolk say when they learn about the warrant taken out for your arrest?"

She shivered at the blatant malice in his voice.

"Will they rally about you when they hear you left me for dead, covered in blood, or will they abandon you?" His triumphant gaze homed into her panicked eyes as she pushed against him to free herself from his touch.

"I never did anything to cause you to bleed!" She shoved again, and he backed up a step.

"You should know by now a woman's word is worth little. A woman who has been found out as a liar has even less credibility." He hooked his thumb in his suspenders as he rocked back on his heels. "Why would anyone believe you?"

She gasped and wrapped shaking arms around herself.

"You know what I want." His implacable gaze met hers. "Don't defy me, or you'll regret the consequences."

She jerked back, slamming her head against the closed school door in an unsuccessful attempt to avoid him stroking her neck. He gave her a jaunty salute before turning away and heading into town and the saloons.

She collapsed to her knees as tears coursed down her cheeks. After a few moments, she calmed enough to look for Hortence who was nowhere in sight. Leticia leaped to her feet, running down the schoolhouse steps as her frantic gaze darted around the area in front of the school. She raced around the entire building and searched inside the empty privy, but Hortence was nowhere in sight. "Oh, my darling, where are you?" Leticia ran from the yard, her gaze frantic as she searched for her daughter.

CHAPTER 9

*J*ack Renfrew entered the livery, his gait stooped, although with no hesitation as he approached Alistair and Cailean. Faded to a pale dun color, his buckskin pants and jacket were well-worn. A subtle scent of animal musk clung to him. Although he had spent years working as a trapper, he had settled down on a decent plot of land in the valley with mountain access nearly a decade before as the land filled with settlers and cattle. The townsfolk knew the change in seasons by Jack's visits to town. "Hello, boys," he said, spitting an amber-colored splat of saliva and chewing tobacco onto a pile of dirtied straw they had just mucked from the stalls.

Cailean smiled and shook his hand. "Good to see you, sir." He took a break from work and leaned on his pitchfork.

"No need for formalities between us," Jack said, clasping Alistair's hand now. "Heard about some trouble at the church last month."

Alistair stiffened before nodding. "Aye. The wedding ceremony was interrupted. I dinna ken when it will occur."

Jack pinned Alistair with a knowing gaze. "Well, I wouldn't let some interloper stand between me and my woman. It's how I won the affection of John's mother, God rest her soul." He paused as he met

Alistair's tormented gaze. "If called for, I'd meet mischief with mischief."

Alistair studied his friend before grunting, the sound noncommittal. "What brings ye in?" He looked behind Jack. "Where are yer horses and yer son?"

"He's tending them outside."

Alistair grunted again, this time in disgust and marched outside. Soon he reentered with a black stallion, an appaloosa, and two pack mules along with John Runs from Bears Renfrew, Jack's son. Alistair led each horse into a vacant stall, handing a bridle to John, and put the mules together in another.

Jack watched as Alistair and John each curried a horse and discussed their favorite techniques for caring for horses. His amber eyes shone with pride as he watched his son.

"What brings you to town?" Cailean asked. "I know you rarely like to leave your land, and I didn't think we'd see you until after trapping season."

Jack straightened his hunched shoulders. "I have a business proposition. I think your brother should be privy to what I'll say. John knows my thoughts and has come to agree with them."

Cailean flicked a glance to Alistair as he listened to their conversation and saw him nod in agreement. "This sounds serious."

"That's 'cause it is," Jack said. "John can keep an eye on things here while we talk. He'll come for you if the need arises."

Cailean squinted as he studied Jack. "Someday you'll have to tell me the story of how a learned man becomes a trapper in the wilds of the West and married to an Indian woman."

Jack laughed. "That's a story for another day."

Alistair joined them, leaving John with the horses, and followed them across the small yard to the house. They entered the kitchen, and he poured cups of coffee from the pot left on the stove before joining them at the table. He tilted his head and heard the soothing sound of Sorcha humming as she spun yarn upstairs in her room. "What's this business ye have for us? We are no' in a place to expand."

Jack blew on his coffee but refrained from taking a sip. "The bald truth is I'm dying. I've seen the doc here, and he confirmed what I know." He half smiled with appreciation as the MacKinnon brothers remained quiet. "I can't eat anymore, except for a few bites here and there. Doc thinks I have a mass in my stomach."

"How long do ye have?" Alistair asked, the coffee in front of him forgotten.

"Weeks maybe." His eyes gleamed with passionate rage. "I thought I'd live long enough to see things change. To see prejudice ease." He frowned as the brothers watched him with confusion. "You know what it's like to be thrown off your land. To lose everything."

Cailean shared a quick confused look with Alistair and nodded. "Aye, we do. We lost our land to the British during the Clearances. It's why we're here and not on the Isle of Skye in Scotland."

Jack's gaze gleamed with triumph. "I thought you'd understand. John will lose everything the minute I die. No matter that I am his father and a white man and that I would leave all I have to him. The law sees him as Native, and they can't own land."

Alistair frowned. "How do we have anything to do with this?"

"I'm selling my homestead, my land, everything. It's final in two days." He sighed. "Well, almost everything. I'm keeping a few horses and some of the trapping gear." He rubbed at his forehead. "John and I will live in a small cabin I've rented here in town, back near the lawyer's house."

"Seems ye have it all planned out," Alistair muttered. "What worries ye?"

"My fear is that John will still have difficulties inheriting the money I'd leave him." His lips turned up in a wry grimace. "You know what a miserly, prejudiced man Mr. Finlay is. He barely allows me entrance into his bank, never mind John. The money would rot, or worse, in there before John would ever see it again."

Cailean shook his head in confusion. "Just give it to him then."

Jack rolled his eyes as he tapped at the side of his coffee cup. "And leave him open to every fortune hunter? They'd try to rob him blind within a week, killing him if necessary, and I know the sheriff would do little to come to John's aid."

Alistair frowned as he shook his head again. "I beg yer pardon, but I dinna ken how we can help ye other than to stand by John as best we can."

Jack looked from Cailean and then to Alistair. "I want to buy him a share of the livery." He met the brothers' shocked gazes. "He's as good with horses as Alistair."

Alistair rose and began to pace. He ran a hand through his thick blackish-brown hair. "Ye dinna ken what ye ask, man. The livery is our dream. 'Tis our legacy."

Cailean quelled any further utterances by Alistair with a severe glance. "How much would you offer for John to be an equal partner, for one-third interest in the livery business?"

"Five thousand dollars."

Cailean's eyes bulged, and Alistair leaned against the kitchen counter as his breath came out in a *whoosh*. "Don't be daft. That's too much," Cailean sputtered.

"How do ye ken ye can trust us?" Alistair asked.

John rested his hands over his stomach. "You treat John with respect." He nodded at Alistair. "Not once, in all the times we've come into town, have you acted toward him in a different manner because he's mixed blood." He smiled as Alistair scowled. "How that comment angers you gives me added confidence in my proposal."

He nodded to Cailean. "You didn't hesitate to leave the livery, with all your animals and gear, under his care while we talked."

Cailean frowned. "Why would I? He's excellent with the animals, and I trust him."

Jack fought a glower, a tic in his cheek heralding his frustration. "Don't act disingenuous. You know what is said of John." He listed the offenses one by one as he spoke. "That he's a savage and that the townsfolk should lock up their children and womenfolk at night in case his wild inclinations emerge. That he will rob you blind given a chance. That he will rustle your cattle or horses if he's in your vicinity."

Alistair snorted. "Hogwash, all of it."

Jack's eyes gleamed with satisfaction. "Because you immediately discount the rumors and fearmongering, I know John can have a good life here. He'll be with horses, which are his true love. He can hunt and trap if he wants. I've taught him everything I know."

"If we agree—and we need time to think this over and discuss it— what does your partnership entail?" Cailean asked.

"When I die, Barclay won't rent the small cabin to John. I don't know anyone in town who'll rent to him. The landlords like my money, and some tolerate John, but few are brave enough to over-come their prejudice and face the town's displeasure." He looked at the MacKinnon brothers. "Yet you are brave enough to. You've faced the censure of this town numerous times and managed to keep the townsfolk's esteem."

Alistair rubbed at his head. "Where would John live? We dinna have much space here."

"If a cot is in the tack room, he'll be fine."

Alistair grunted with displeasure. "Maybe for the summer but no' in winter." He shared a long look with Cailean before addressing Jack. "Ye've given us a lot to consider, Renfrew." He rose and followed Cailean and Jack to the barn. When they arrived, John murmured to a cantankerous horse they had just accepted from a passing traveler. Alistair paused as he watched John soothe the horse, half smiling as the horse nudged John's shoulder for another pat.

John looked up, his long black hair loose down his back. His dark brown eyes appeared black and met Alistair's assessing gaze a moment before looking at his father. A deep sorrow, one of old grief and of loss yet to occur, shadowed his gaze. John blinked, schooling his expression, and walked to his father's side. "We need to board our horses here a few days." John's deep, scratchy voice emerged haltingly as though rarely used.

"Aye, shouldna be a problem." Alistair watched the pair leave before he turned to look at his brother. "What do ye think?"

Cailean sighed and pulled out a stool. "Some of what he says makes sense. We've seen how the townsfolk tolerate John, but few truly welcome him. The only business that accepts him without reservation is the café." He paused a moment. "And the bakery." He watched as his brother paced down the center aisle of the barn. "The money would be helpful."

"Aye, but I dinna want our only consideration to be based on money." Alistair ran a hand through his hair. "An' it seems an excessive amount of money."

Cailean nodded. "Yes, although I wonder if that's the only way Jack can see to set aside the money for John."

Alistair grunted once more and sat on an empty stool. "I dinna want us to go into arrears due to me."

Cailean rubbed at his head. "Why should we do any less for you than we did for Sorcha or Ewan?" He watched Alistair with a challenging gaze. "There is nothing I wouldn't do for you, Al."

Alistair nodded. "I'd want something formal drawn up. Even if the law doesna see it as necessary, I want there to be a written understanding between us."

Cailean played with a piece of hay. "You want to do this?" He looked around the livery. "You want to share what we have with another?"

Alistair followed his brother's gaze, over the stalls to the tack room and then to the ceiling, as though envisioning the hay stored above. "Aye. Ye ken as well as I do that we need the extra hands. We lost young Larry over a year ago to the promise of the mines in Butte, and I wouldna mind someone who has a keen understandin' of horses." He shook his head. "I ken we could hire a young lad to help, but it would mean more expenditures rather than a way to ease our debts. Plus more time to teach him the caring of horses."

Cailean twirled the hay between his fingers. "I should speak with Belle too. She has an astute sense for business." His gaze was troubled as he looked at Alistair. "I know I should feel grateful not to go further into debt, but I worry this is too easy. That we are being duped in some way."

Alistair rose. "I ken what ye mean. Talk with Warren this afternoon. See what he says as well. Tomorrow we can decide what we want to do afore we speak with Jack again."

~

Alistair stood, staring at the horses in the paddock, lost in thought as he considered the offer from Jack Renfrew, barely registering when another pair of arms draped over the paddock rails. After a few moments of silence, he glanced to his right and stiffened at the sight of Leticia's husband. "What're ye doin' here?"

"Thought I'd visit the man who thought he could marry my wife." Josiah chuckled as he followed Alistair's gaze. "That's a fine-looking chestnut filly you have there."

"Aye, although she isna mine. We're merely carin' for her." He continued to look ahead although his body was tense, as though awaiting battle.

Josiah spat to the side, a long line of chewing tobacco melting into the dirt near his feet. "Seems curious you'd know that horse isn't yours, but you were about to steal my wife."

Alistair's hands played with a piece of hay, tying it over and over again into small knots. "After nearly seven years apart, I'd think ye'd consider her free of ye, considering ye failed in yer husbandly duties to support her and yer child. It makes me wonder why ye'd finally find her now." He tipped his head forward and to the side to stare at Josiah out of the corner of his eye. "Makes me wonder what ye're about."

Josiah laughed. "You're either brave or stupid, MacKinnon. That wife of mine nearly killed me when she left."

Alistair squinted as he faced his nemesis. "Was it ye that had a warrant taken out against her? Or was it the sheriff's doing?"

Josiah shrugged. "Does it matter who took out the warrant? I'd be more concerned she'd plot the same fate for you." He spat into the dirt again. "No matter what she did or didn't do to me, a warrant was merited."

Alistair glared at the horse and clamped his jaw. "Are ye admittin' she didna leave ye a *bluidy* mess?"

Josiah laughed. "Oh, how quickly the rumors have spread. It's delightful to see that human nature is constant."

Alistair watched as the horse trotted around the paddock, answering Cailean's call. Alistair shook his head in a subtle manner, signaling Cailean not to join him. "I have difficulty believin' a woman such as Leticia would act in such a way."

"Ah, yes, the dutiful teacher with the pristine past."

His jeering laugh caused the hair on the back of Alistair's neck to stand on end.

"From the moment I met her, that woman lied, cheated, stole, and beggared everyone around her. I'm surprised she kept her penchant for larceny hidden all these years."

Alistair shook his head, his face reddening as the mocking laugh from her husband continued. "Ye describe yerself, not Leticia."

"That woman is better at deception than a chameleon to make her sound virtuous. She spins more tales than anyone I've ever met." He shifted as Alistair leaned on one arm and faced him. "I'm certain she's attempted to plead her case with you. About her difficult time with her horrible husband and how she was forced to act as she did." He squinted as Alistair met his gaze with blatant loathing.

"If she is all ye say she is, why do ye want her back?"

Josiah shrugged. "I have the ability to appreciate her talents. Not a gift you have as a man who clings to honor the way you do." His derisive smile broadened as Alistair strangled the wooden rail in front of him. "Dishonor can be so much more fun."

Alistair spun, gripping Josiah by his nearly threadbare shirtfront. "Leave her be! She's suffered enough from ye."

Josiah laughed. "She hasn't begun to understand the meaning of the word. Not if she disobeys me." He slapped away Alistair's hands and stood at his full height, although he remained a few inches shorter than Alistair. "I'm coming into money soon, and we'll leave town. My wife and I. Together."

"Another tall tale ye're spinning yerself. Ye've no money, and ye ken it." Alistair spit on the ground next to Josiah's boot.

Josiah laughed. "I'd talk to your brother." He pulled his hat forward and straightened out his shirt. "Forget you ever met her. She isn't worth your regard or your worry." He spun on his heel and walked away.

Alistair straightened, staring after Josiah as he shook with rage and battled doubts. "I will no' believe ye," he rasped to himself.

"Talking to yourself again?" Cailean asked as he slipped through the rails of the paddock and stood beside his brother. "Thought you might need my help a few moments ago."

"I could handle him."

Cailean's gaze focused on his brother. "Seems you can't handle what he said." He frowned. "Don't give anything he says credence, Al."

Alistair heaved out a sigh. "Who am I to believe? That lying bastard? Or the conniving woman I was to marry?" He shook his head. "There is no one to believe in."

Cailean grabbed his brother's shoulder. "Aye, there is. There is Leticia. You know you love her. You know you can forgive her any deceit. Just give it time, and don't do anything rash."

"Do ye have any dealings with the man?" Alistair sighed at Cailean's affronted expression. "It must be Ewan." He nodded in the direction of the departed Josiah. "He said I should speak to my brother about money he's about to come into."

"Dammit!" Cailean snapped. "If Ewan has lost money to that man …" He kicked at the post.

"If Ewan has, we can do nothing about it now." Alistair watched his eldest brother. "I want to talk with Ewan. Not ye." Alistair watched as Cailean gave a reluctant nod. "I've earned the right."

Alistair stormed into the livery, kicking at a few piles of hay before moving into an empty stall that needed mucking out. He relished the opportunity for hard physical labor to clear his mind and to work off his impotent rage. Cailean had left to speak with Warren, and Alistair appreciated his time alone. After he had cleaned two stalls, he paused in the hallway and frowned. Small pieces of hay fluttered from above where the hay was stored on the upper level of the barn. He tilted his head when he realized the trap door to the stall he had just cleaned was opened.

"I know I shut that," he muttered. He grabbed a wooden ladder and propped it against the opening, climbing up to latch it shut. He heard a snuffling sound as he reached for the wood cover and poked his head into the upper area filled with hay. He frowned when he saw Hortence laying in a pile of hay, crying.

He pulled himself into the loft and smiled as he met her startled gaze. "What's the matter, Little Bug? No reason for my Bug to cry."

Rather than reach for him to soothe her, she curled into herself as she sobbed. He sat next to her and pulled her to his lap. "Oh, sweetheart, I hate to see ye so sad," he murmured as he rocked her and ran a hand over her back. After a few minutes, her crying quieted.

"I hate him!" she cried.

"Who?" He kissed her forehead as she turned to rest her cheek against his chest.

"The bad man who continues to bother Mama. He was at the schoolhouse today." She shook. "He made Mama scared."

"Why did ye leave yer mother alone with him?" Alistair asked.

"He makes my tummy hurt. He scares me," she whispered. "Do you think he hurt Mama?"

Alistair took a deep breath to calm himself as he attempted to soothe the little girl he considered his daughter. "No. He was just here. He didna hurt yer mother."

"Will you come with me? Mama will be very mad at me." Hortence's lower lip trembled.

He brushed away strands of hair from her cheek, scrubbing away traces of tears at the same time. "Of course. An' she'll be so happy to find ye safe and well that she willna have time for anger." He kissed her on the forehead again and helped her stand. He held her hand as they walked to the trap door. "How did ye get up here?"

She flushed. "You showed me the other ladder." She pointed to the far end of the barn where another entrance to the loft had a permanent ladder built into that wall.

"Why did ye open this?" he asked.

"I wanted to see you and the horses." She flushed. "But there are no horses!"

He chuckled at her disgruntled tone. "No' in this stall, no." He helped her down the ladder, pulling the trap door shut behind him. When they were in the stall, he hefted the ladder and set it aside. "Come. Brindle has missed ye. We can spare a moment for ye to say hello, and then ye must return home to see yer mother."

Hortence brightened at the prospect of seeing her favorite horse and grabbed at his hand to drag him down the aisle. As she *clucked* at the horse in the way Alistair had taught her, Leticia burst into the entrance at the opposite end of the livery.

"Hortence!" she sobbed. When she saw her daughter well, stroking a horse, she fell to her knees.

"Leticia," Alistair breathed as he rushed to her. "Are ye all right?" He stroked a hand over her shoulder and pulled her close as she cried and tried to catch her breath. "*Shh,* ... lass, Hortence is safe."

"I thought I'd lost her. I thought ..." She shuddered as she tried to calm her panic. After a moment, she relaxed in his arms.

"She was hidin' in the loft. I only discovered her because I saw hay fallin' from the trap door." He looked over his shoulder to ensure her daughter was well, his eyes lighting with joy to see her giggle as Brindle gave her a small nudge with her large snout. "She's terrified of yer husband."

Leticia eased from his arms and accepted his aid as she stood. "She's a smart girl." She smoothed a hand over her skirts, brushing away dirt. "I'm sorry to have interrupted your day."

Alistair shook his head and bit back what he would have said as Hortence ran to them.

"Mama!" She threw herself against Leticia's legs and hugged her around her waist. "I was bad. I'm sorry."

"Why did you leave the schoolyard?" Leticia ran a hand over her daughter's head, shoulders, and back as though reassuring herself that Hortence was well and unscathed.

"I don't like him. He scares me, Mama," Hortence whispered. "I knew I'd be safe here."

Leticia shuddered and kissed her head. "You frightened me, little one. When I couldn't find you at the school or at the bakery ..." Her voice stuttered to a stop. "Thank God, you came here and had some time with Brindle."

"She missed me!" Hortence proclaimed.

"I'm sure she did," her mother said.

"'Stair told me that she did," Hortence said as though that were all the proof she needed. "When can I call him papa? When will you be over your mad?"

Alistair made a grunting sound and shared a long look with Leticia. "Soon, Little Bug. Soon."

"For now let's get you home and cleaned up," Leticia said. "Thank you, Alistair, for ensuring she was safe."

Alistair nodded and watched them leave. He gripped the doorframe to stop from running after them to walk beside Hortence. The dredges of his anger melted away as the vision he had cherished reformed.

CHAPTER 10

*L*eticia walked beside Hortence toward the café for dinner, pausing as Helen Jameson stepped in front of her. "I beg your pardon," Leticia murmured as she attempted to walk around her. Helen matched each of her evasive steps, and Leticia glowered at her as she was unable to pass. "Run along to see Mr. Harold," Leticia murmured to Hortence who skipped ahead into the nearby café. When certain Hortence had arrived safely, Leticia focused on Helen. "What do you want?"

"For once, my mother and I have a similar goal. I'd like you to leave town. Leave Mr. MacKinnon to me. I know I will make him happy in ways you never could."

Leticia straightened her shoulders, her gaze becoming even more severe. "What makes you say that?"

Helen's cajoling smile did little to ease Leticia's nerves. "I have never misled him. He can trust me." She shrugged and attempted to appear nonchalant, but her fierce blush revealed her embarrassment. "Besides, men find more pleasure with women who haven't had children. Everyone knows that."

Leticia laughed. "You are a child if you believe the nonsense your mother preaches." She took a deep breath and glanced around, grateful the other townsfolk were ignoring them. "I would hope you had enough self-respect to think for yourself and to not allow your mother to misguide you with her prejudices."

Helen's jaw firmed, and any attempt at friendly persuasion disappeared. "I refuse to spend my life living with my mother as the hopeless spinster." She bit her lip as though having revealed too much. "I will marry a man with high regard in this town, and I have chosen Mr. MacKinnon."

Leticia gripped her hands together in front of her. "It only works if he has chosen you too."

Helen shrugged. "He will. He must." Her show of bravado cracked. "We were seen in the woods, and he must act honorably."

"Honor is ingrained in his very being. You never have to worry that he will be honorable," Leticia said, a trace of bitterness in her voice. "If you will excuse me, I must join my daughter." She stopped as Helen gripped her arm when she attempted to slip past her.

"I have your word that you won't attempt to come between us?" Helen released her at Leticia's terse nod.

Leticia entered the café and found it mostly empty. She and Hortence had arrived after the supper rush. Hortence sat at a table with Harold, laughing at a tall tale he told her. He motioned for Leticia to go into the kitchen.

"You look ready for a fight," Irene said as she worked at the large stove.

"Did you know?" Leticia asked as she sat at the table and watched Irene cook. At Irene's frown, she said, "That he's been courting another?"

Irene laughed and shook her head. "Hold that thought." She sailed through the door, delivering plates of food before returning to sit with a sigh across from Leticia. "You must know better than to believe rumors. Especially when they come from the Jameson women." Her eyes sparkled with merriment.

Leticia failed to see any humor and slouched in her chair. "The last time I spoke with Alistair, he said he regretted ever knowing me. Ever courting me. That he could be married with children now if he hadn't wasted his time on me."

Irene grabbed Leticia's hand, stilling its tapping on the tabletop. "That's his male pride and anger speaking." She waited until Leticia nodded. "You know as well as I do that he hadn't spoken more than a 'Hello' to Helen Jameson in years. He has no interest in her."

Leticia sniffed. "But he won't want to ruin her reputation."

Irene huffed out a scoffing laugh. "He's not. Her mother is. Focus your anger on the correct target." Irene's eyes glinted with ire. "That woman will destroy everything in her path in her quest for money."

"I think she seeks security in her old age." Leticia blew her nose in her handkerchief.

"Perhaps. Although I think control and manipulation play an equal part." Harold entered with a new order so Irene rose to prepare another meal. "Don't allow yourself to be tricked into doubting him now. Not without just cause."

~

Helen walked away from speaking with Leticia and came to an abrupt halt as she nearly ran into Warren Clark. She frowned as he blocked her path. "Mr. Clark," she said in a deferential manner.

He glowered at her, his blue eyes bright with a deeply hidden fury. "What are you playing at, Helen?" he whispered. His gaze roved over her demure outfit of a light-brown dress, a slightly darker shawl, with her wheat-colored hair pulled in a loose bun.

"Unlike you, I have to find my way forward in life. It isn't handed to me on a platter," she snapped. "I'm doing what I must to survive."

"By destroying that woman's faith in her man?" he whispered, his voice low as they stood in a deserted part of the boardwalk as most had ventured inside their homes for the evening.

"He's not her man any longer. He's mine. Or he will be mine," Helen said with a triumphant lift of her chin. However, her eyes shone with trepidation before she masked it with false jubilation. She faltered as she saw the moment's worth of agony in his gaze before he glanced away.

"I don't think you know what you are doing, Helen. To them. To yourself." His gaze bore into hers again, his blue eyes shining with intensity. "To me."

Her breath was shaky as she took a deep inhale. "You're delusional if you believe I'd concern myself about you." She pushed past him and strode for home.

Warren raised a shaky hand and swiped at his brow as he watched Helen's retreat.

~

Cailean opened the door to the bedroom he shared with his wife and frowned. Rather than finding her in bed, she stood by the window, staring at the stars. "Why are you still awake?"

"It's Saturday evening. I don't have to bake tomorrow, and I can sleep in," she murmured, moaning with contentment as his arms wrapped around her waist and pulled her tight. "I wanted to wait for you before heading to bed."

"I know you are worried about Leticia and Alistair," he said, falling silent when she spun in his arms and burrowed into his chest.

"I am, but we must discuss something else." She sighed as his hands caressed her back. "Please, don't run away."

Any humor in his expression faded as he heard her plea. "I won't run from you, love." He cupped her cheeks as she tilted her face up to his. "You can tell me anything." He frowned as he felt her shiver in his arms. "There's no reason for fear."

He felt her take a deep breath. "There is. But I must overcome it." She grasped his hand and kissed his palm. Then she lowered it over her belly. "I am with child."

"Belle?" he whispered, his eyes widening and mouth dropping open as he finally understood what she said. His hand caressed her stomach before he dropped to his knees, pulling her close. He kissed her belly, and she felt the moisture through her clothes.

"Don't cry, darling," she whispered, threading her fingers through his hair.

"When?" he asked as he pressed his head against her belly.

"January or February. I've missed my second monthly," she whispered.

"Thank you," he said, raising a wondrous, joyful gaze to meet hers. "Thank you, my Belle." He rose in an instant, catching her as she stumbled from his sudden movement. He pulled her to him, kissing her deeply for a moment. "I feared we would never be given a second chance. Every month, I've prayed … I've prayed for you to tell me this news."

"Truly?" she whispered, her fingers stroking away his tears that continued to fall. Her joyous smile matched his.

"Truly, my Belle. I worried I'd never have the chance to know such joy with you. To share this with you." He pulled her close. "I won't lie and say I'm not scared to my bones, because I am. After what happened last time, I will be filled with fear until you are well, holding our bairn in your arms. But I promise to be there for you. No matter what happens."

"Oh, Cailean," she murmured, on her toes to kiss him again. "I have every hope that this time will be different. In fact, I know it will be. Because, this time, you will be beside me."

"Yes," he said. "You must take care. I think you should give up the bakery."

She laughed as she shook her head. "Now you speak nonsense. Plenty of women work and are in expectation of such an event. No reason I can't continue to do the work I love."

"They aren't my wife," he muttered. "At least consider cutting your hours or takin' an extra day off if needed or hiring more help."

She sobered as she settled on her side in bed, facing him. She could not stop caressing his face, her fingers running through the day's growth of whiskers. "The money from the bakery will also help pay off any arrears. I refuse to have debt play any part in our future."

Cailean raised and lowered his brows in an impish way a few times, easing her serious mood and causing her to laugh. He leaned into the palm she placed on his cheek. "As to that, Alistair and I had a very interesting offer today from Jack Renfrew." When she shook her head in confusion, he said, "Trapper Renfrew."

"What could he want that would ease our debt concerns?"

Cailean sobered. "The poor man's dying. He's terrified what will happen to his son, although he's a man grown. John must be close to thirty."

"He's wise enough to fear prejudice."

"Aye, especially when word leaks out John has quite an inheritance." Cailean met his wife's concerned gaze. "Renfrow wants John to be a partner with us. Wants to buy him a share of the livery."

Annabelle sat up and shook her head. "No, it's yours and Alistair's. You've worked for it."

He ran a hand over her shoulder before kissing it. "Aye, we did. But John's good with horses. He would be a real help." Cailean shrugged. "And we'd pay off our arrears and have money to pay Warren and still have a little saved for our bairn. Without having to touch the bakery money."

"You're too calm about allowing someone else into your partnership with Alistair. What don't I understand?"

"I love our partnership, our livery, aye, but, if I can help the family, help us, I'll do it. I spoke with Warren, and he'll write up a contract saying we each have a one-third ownership. It means the MacKinnons are still majority owners. And that two of the three must be in agreement before any major change can occur."

When he flushed and looked downward, she frowned. "What else is there?"

"Jack was willing to pay an extraordinary amount for John to have a part of the livery. Warren and I spoke, and only half is truly warranted." He took a deep breath. "With the excess money, we'll establish a trust in the MacKinnon name, but with a codicil stating it's truly for John."

He looked up and watched for his wife's reaction. He furrowed his brows as she merely shrugged her agreement. "Why aren't you angry?"

"Why should I be?" She ran a finger over his ruffled brows and smiled at him.

"I'm robbing you of riches."

She laughed and rolled her eyes. "They were never mine. Never ours." She patted her belly as her eyes filled. "I'm so proud you're my husband, that our baby will call you *Father*. That you will teach our baby what is right and wrong and honorable."

"Belle," Cailean rasped, kissing her. "And you shall be the most wondrous mother." He pulled her close. "When shall we tell the family?"

"Not too soon. I want this to be our secret for a while." She arched up to kiss him. "Besides, I fear Alistair would not welcome such news yet, and I would not want to cause him more pain."

Cailean tugged her into his arms. "I had hoped we'd have Alistair's room for a nursery."

"Perhaps, … if he isn't to use the house he built, we could buy it from him and live there."

Cailean relaxed with her settling along his side. "That's a discussion for another day. For now, let me enjoy this wondrous news." He sighed with contentment as she burrowed into his arms.

The pine door of the Stumble-Out Saloon creaked as Alistair pushed it open. He paused as his eyes adjusted to the darkened interior. Wide pine plank floors creaked under his weight, and his gaze darted from the long bar along one wall to the gambling tables in the back. A crowd of men stood in the area in front of the bar, discussing politics, ranching, and mining. Lanterns hung along the walls, although long shadows and darkened corners were common. A miasma of smoke clung to the ceiling of the saloon, while the stench of unwashed men permeated the air. Curtains were drawn on the front windows, dimming any late-evening light. He frowned in confusion as he saw a few of the Boudoir whores draped over the laps of finely dressed men sitting at tables as they paused in their card play.

He breathed a sigh of relief that Annabelle's sister was not among the women present.

He fought a glower and pasted on an impassive expression as he found Ewan at a table toward the rear of the saloon, focused on his hand as he matched wits with card sharks more skilled and with far fewer scruples than he had. Alistair shook off invitations to join tables and marched to his brother's side. He clamped his jaw shut to prevent interfering in the game as he noted Leticia's husband sitting across from Ewan.

At the end of the hand of five-card stud, he watched Ewan lose hard-earned coin. Alistair leaned forward and murmured in his brother's ear, "I must speak with ye now."

Ewan jerked, finally noting his brother's presence. He flushed at the summons, as though treated like a recalcitrant child, but pushed away from the table and followed Alistair to the long bar that occupied most of one wall of the building, its mahogany finish dulled from smoke and infrequent polishing. Casks of whiskey stood to either side of the mirrored area behind the bar.

After Alistair nodded to the barkeep for two whiskeys, he traced a groove in the wood before sipping at his drink. He feigned disinterest at his brother's impatient huff as Ewan stood next to him.

"What was so important that ye had to tear me away from my poker match?" Ewan whispered in his brother's ear. He took a swig of the whiskey, hissing as it burned his throat.

"Ye do ken that man sittin' across from ye is Leticia's husband?" At Ewan's shrug of indifference, Alistair growled with frustration. "An' that ye're fundin' whatever he has planned every time ye lose to him?"

"It's not like that, Al. I know I just lost, but I'll earn it back again when I win." His brown eyes shone with his sincere belief.

"When was the last time ye won?" Alistair glared at a man over his brother's shoulder to back away and give them privacy for their conversation. "When was the last time ye left here without beggaring yerself?" He swore as he saw the answer when Ewan remained mutinously quiet. "Cail is already in arrears after bringin' ye and Sorcha over. There's no more money if ye lose too much."

Ewan nodded. "I know. Cailean's already done enough. I'd never ask for more from him."

"And yet ye expect me to step aside as ye allow yerself to be fleeced by a man who would steal away the one woman I've ever loved?"

Ewan leaned forward until they were almost nose to nose. "It's no' as though ye want her. For, if ye did, ye would have done more than moon about yer bad fortune. Ye would have done somethin' to ensure she stayed yers."

Alistair reared back as though his brother had punched him, his hand instinctively guarding his belly as though awaiting a second sucker punch. "I'm askin' ye to no' sit at a table with him again. I ken it's too much to hope ye will no' play again." He shot back the rest of his drink and stormed past his brother.

When he reached the front porch of the saloon, he paused. He had no wish to return to his brother's home. He walked up the main street of town, his boot heels forming a resounding *clunk* on the boardwalk. When he reached the end of the boardwalk, he paused again before walking the short distance to the home he was to have shared with Leticia.

When he arrived, he sighed and glared at the empty, darkened house. "Damn fool," he muttered to himself. He jumped as a voice emerged from the shadows of the house.

"Why are you a fool?"

"Leticia? Where is Hortence? Why are ye here?"

Her shrug was barely visible in the long shadows. She tugged a shawl around her shoulders as she remained hidden. "Hortence is spending the night with the Tompkinses. She fell asleep there, and I didn't have the heart to wake her and force her back to the tiny room at the bakery."

Alistair frowned. "I ken there is more to that story than ye're sayin'."

She laughed, but it was filled with despair rather than joy. "How dare you believe you have any right to know about my life? After you shut me out without ever letting me explain?"

Alistair took a step before her but halted as she shifted away. "Lettie?" he whispered. "What are ye doin' here?"

"I wanted to remember the dream. One last time." She swiped at her cheek before turning to look at the dormant house. "I needed to rid myself of the dream of what could have been."

"No, Lettie. Dream. Always dare to dream."

He saw the nearly imperceptible shaking of her head. "You have no right to say such things to me. Not now. Not after ..." She sucked in a breath as she bit back impulsive words.

He grabbed her as she spun to race past him. "Don't go," he whispered, his breath teasing a shiver from her as it blew against her neck. "Don't do anythin' rash."

She shook as she crumpled into his arms, her arms hanging at her sides rather than clasping him close. "Don't ask me for promises."

He pushed at her until he held her head between his large palms, his thumbs tracing over her hairline. After a moment, where she refused to meet his gaze, he groaned and swooped forward, capturing her lips in a kiss. When she stiffened and then leaned into him, he groaned again and tugged her closer.

The kiss deepened, and he walked her backward until they were hidden in the shadow of the house. She made a small *thunk* sound as she backed into a wall of the house, and he pressed against her. "Feel me," he rasped. "Feel how much I want ye."

She kissed him with an intensity born of desperation and clasped him to her. She reached down to tug at her skirts, but his hands tangled with hers, dragging them away from her clothing. He held her hands pinned to the wall by her head, his kisses continuing to muddle her senses.

Finally he raised his head. "No, Leticia. I willna dishonor either of us more than I have tonight." He kissed her again. "I willna love ye as I want until ye are my wife."

"You still wish to wed me?" Her voice hitched as though fighting a sob or intense passion.

He pulled her hands to his lips and kissed each one. "I should beg yer pardon for those wild and rash kisses but canna." He backed up a step until a shaft of moonlight lit his face and allowed her to see his expression. "I canna lie to myself or to ye. Not any longer. I want ye. I'll always want ye." He released a hand and stroked it over her head, brushing at her silky hair. "Watchin' ye and Hortence leave today was one of the hardest things I've ever done. I wanted to be with ye. Walkin' beside ye. To have that right." He kissed her forehead.

"Even though I lied to you?" she whispered. "Even though I embarrassed you?"

"Aye." His gaze roved over her, no longer filled with disdain and disappointment but with wonder. He smiled as it elicited a shiver from her.

"What about the other woman you are courting?" At his frown, she breathed, "Helen?"

He shook his head and ran a soothing hand over her head. "Dinna worry about Helen, love. I fear she is misguided. I ken now is not the time, but I want to hear yer story. The real story." He bent forward and kissed her softly on her lips.

"What if you don't want me after you hear the truth?" she asked as a tear leaked out.

"If I learned one thing during this wretched time, it's that I'll always want ye. I promise ye this." He looked into her eyes with a fierce intensity. "I will listen. I will try to understand. And I will no' judge ye." He traced her cheek. "I can see how ye've suffered, an' I've no right to judge what ye did all those years ago."

"But I'm still married to him," she whispered.

"After we speak, we'll continue to work with Warren to free ye of that bastard ye married." He ran a finger over her cheek as she breathed in a stuttering breath. "Then I'm certain all will be right again." His eyes gleamed with reborn hope as he watched her.

She took a stuttering breath and then jumped as she heard someone walking down the street. "Don't take too long to come speak with me," she whispered before she slipped by him and raced away.

Alistair braced a hand against a wall of the house he dreamed of sharing with Leticia one day and took deep, restorative breaths. When he turned for home, hope filled him for the first time since his wedding ceremony had been interrupted.

As he slipped through the quiet streets, he paused, sensing he was being watched. He froze and moved into the moonlight when he saw Helen Jameson approach him. "What do ye want, miss? I believe ye've already caused enough mischief."

She shivered as she pulled her shawl tighter around her. "I wanted to speak with you, but we are never alone."

"An' ye're a fool to believe we're alone here. Any number of towns-folk could be witnessin' our conversation." He nodded to her in what he hoped looked deferential rather than dismissive and moved to walk past her.

"You really want her, don't you?" she whispered.

He paused and met Helen's wounded gaze. "Aye. As it should have been obvious to ye from the beginning. She's the one I will always want. Will always desire."

Anger and hurt warred in Helen's gaze before she backed away a step. "I will never understand you. You could have had a willing woman you could trust."

"When ye've felt what I've felt, then ye can talk to me. Then ye can dare judge me. Good evenin,' Miss Helen." He scooted past her, ignoring her sniffles. He breathed more fully when he arrived at his brother's home and closed the door behind him.

A warm breeze blew, easing the summer evening's stifling heat. Leticia scurried along the shadowed alleyway behind Main Street, intent on returning to her room at the bakery, her mind filled with Alistair. She tried to batten down her hopes for them, but her breath hitched at the thought of reconciling with him. She jolted as a shadowy figure emerged in front of the bakery's rear entrance. She froze at the voice.

"Did you have fun during your little interlude with your Scot?"

Josiah asked as he blocked her access to the door and her easy escape from him.

"You have no right to spy on me!" She gasped as he grabbed her and spun her around until she was backed against the door.

"You seem to like this position," he jeered.

"Let me go," she hissed.

"Scream or make a loud sound, and I will ensure you never see your daughter again." His gloating smile spread as she stilled in his arms. "Remember, I am in control. You aren't, and you never have been."

"She's your daughter too," Leticia protested. She lowered her voice to a barely discernible whisper as his hold on her tightened further.

"I highly doubt that. I know how you carried on with other men when you didn't think I was watching." He manacled her wrists with one of his hands, holding them behind her back and thrusting her chest out. "You always were a fine-looking woman, Lorena. I can't blame men for taking notice of you."

"That is not my name."

"It is the name I gave you. The name you accepted when you married me. It is the name you should use."

She shivered at the possessiveness in his tone. "I never cheated on you. It's insulting you would think I did."

He chuckled as he tugged her closer, ignoring her instinctive stiffening. "You tried to kill me. Why wouldn't you attempt to trick me with another man's bastard child?"

"I never tried to kill you. And I have never been unfaithful. That's not who I am."

"Oh, but you were a con artist. You seem to have forgotten that. It will be one of life's greatest pleasures to remind you of who you were and lead you down that path again." He breathed into her ear before nibbling on her earlobe. "Do you really believe he'd want you, when he could have a pristine woman like that Miss Jameson?"

"Let me go!" she said as she bucked against him.

"You know how I liked it when you struggled." His hold tightened as she pushed against him. He leaned forward and kissed her, growling at her when unable to deepen the kiss. "Dammit, kiss me back," he rasped.

She pushed against him, resolutely keeping her mouth shut as she evaded his kisses.

After a few more unsuccessful attempts, he leaned away. "You may think you've been successful this time. But I will have you again. As my wife and all that entails."

He chuckled as she shivered. "Don't for one moment believe my plans for you, for us, have changed. If you return to that worthless Scot, I will follow through with my plans for your brat. That is a promise." He met her devastated gaze. "And you know I always keep my promises." He ran a finger across the sensitive skin of her hairline in a mocking imitation of the way Alistair had touched her earlier, before Josiah released her with such swiftness that she collapsed to her knees. "Sleep well, darling wife."

She watched as he sauntered away before she rose on shaking legs to wrench open the bakery door and lock it behind her.

"What has you so quiet?" Cailean asked Ewan the next day as they worked side by side at the livery. Sunday was Ewan's day off as a carpenter, but he often helped out at the livery. "Are you angry with Alistair?" He glanced outside to watch his brother training a yearling in the paddock.

Ewan grunted. "I should be. He interrupted my play last night."

Cailean sighed as he speared hay with a pitchfork to spread out in a stall. "Do you ever consider he was right to interrupt you?"

"Don't start," Ewan snapped. "I'm having a small losing streak. It'll turn around soon enough." He glared at his brother's grunt of disapproval. "I dinna ken if I should talk about somethin' I saw last night or let it go."

"Would it hurt the person you told?" Cailean asked. He paused in his work as he saw his brother's tormented expression. "Aye, I can see it would. Well then, would it make a difference in how they acted or what they did?"

"Aye," Ewan said, staring at Alistair, crooning to a horse like he used to before his failed wedding. "I'd take away his newfound joy."

"Dammit," Cailean muttered as he heaved a pile of hay into another stall. After a few minutes of hard work, he paused, rasping for breath. "Tell him. He'll understand you did it out of concern as a brother. Not because you're angry about last night."

Ewan nodded before taking a deep breath and setting aside his pitchfork. He stood along the adjoining paddock fence as he watched his brother work. "Ye're in good spirits," Ewan said as Alistair joined him.

"Aye, I've worked that yearling hard enough today. He's spirited and a joy to work with. I just wish he were mine." He swiped at his forehead with the sleeve of his shirt. He met Ewan's gaze, his eyes lit with a deep joy. "An' I ken things will work out between Leticia and me. 'Tis a wondrous day." After a moment he sensed Ewan's discomfort. "I canna apologize for interrupting yer game last night."

Ewan shook his head. "I should be angry with ye. Not speak with ye for a week. But that's not why I'm standin' here, like a fool, havin' trouble speakin'." He continued to study the yearling. "Cailean believes I should tell ye what I saw. But I fear 'twill only bring ye pain."

Alistair stood facing his baby brother, fighting a frown. "What are ye sayin'? Ye're speakin' in riddles."

"I saw Leticia last night, kissing a man."

Alistair let out a relieved laugh. "That man was me. I rambled by our house, an' she was there. We ... enjoyed an embrace." He couldn't hide his broad smile.

"Nae." Ewan cleared his throat. "This wasna at yer house, Alistair. But at the back door to the bakery. An' she was in the man's embrace for quite some time." He waited as Alistair remained stock-still next to him and silent. "I was too far away to hear anything they said. And I left before they saw me. I think it was her husband."

Alistair shook his head as though attempting to make sense of the nonsensical. "I ... How could she? After what we shared an' what I promised?" He spun on his heel and strode into the barn.

Ewan grimaced as he heard a stall door slam. He followed Alistair, squinting as his gaze adjusted to the dimmer light in the barn. Cailean nodded to the far stall in the corner of the barn, and Ewan walked in that direction. "What will ye do?" he murmured, ignoring Cailean's arrival as both focused on Alistair.

"Leave this damn town and travel. There's naught keepin' me here!" He kicked the wall. "Burn the *bluidy* house!" He threw a pitchfork against the wall and leaned against his outstretched arms, his breath sawing in and out.

"I'd miss ye, were ye to leave, Al. Even if ye do interfere when a man plays cards." He frowned as Alistair failed to respond to his teasing.

"Belle and I will buy the house from you if you're interested in selling," Cailean said. He grunted when Ewan jammed an elbow in his waist.

Alistair's breathing calmed, although he remained with his back to his brothers. "I'm no' certain what I want to do with the house. If I do decide to sell, I'll sell it to ye for a fair price." He took another breath. "An' I'm no' leavin' town. No' when we're finally all together again."

Cailean made a grunt of agreement. "I never doubted that."

Alistair pounded a fist on the wall and spun, his eyelashes spiked with unshed tears. "I envy ye," he rasped. "I wish I could say I lived without doubt. That I had such trust in another." He rubbed at his face, clearing it of sweat and tears. "I thought I'd begun to regain it yesterday, but I've been played for a fool again."

"You can't know that," Cailean protested.

"When a woman leaves my arms to jump into another man's, I ken I'm a fool. Or not the man I thought I was." He flushed at the last admission.

Ewan huffed out a breath. "I think it means ye still are no' in full possession of all the facts. Speak with her, Alistair. Ye ken ye want her after last night. Discover why she acted like a shameless hussy."

Cailean choked on a laugh. "Leticia? A hussy?" He shook his head.

"There's no way you'll convince me that she'd rather be with the man she deserted seven years ago than with you, Alistair." He met his brother's irate gaze. "But I otherwise agree with Ewan. Talk with her. For once, talk with her and have it all out in the open."

Alistair sighed. "Aye, I will. But not today. Not while I'm so filled with rage that I'll say somethin' I'll regret." He relaxed as he picked up a pitchfork. "Tomorrow we will have our reckoning."

CHAPTER 11

*T*he next morning, Annabelle opened the back door to her bakery, creeping inside in an attempt not to waken Leticia. She smiled with success when the door to the small room remained closed, and she began to work on the breads and rolls for the morning. A few hours later, she glanced at the still-closed door and frowned. Leticia should have emerged to help as opening time neared. "Something's wrong," Annabelle muttered, swiping the back of her hand over her forehead.

She approached the door and tapped on it. When she heard no answer, she pushed it open. Upon initially seeing someone covered up on the bed, she instinctively backed away. However, she paused when she recognized the small figure all alone. "Hortence?" she whispered. She moved to the cot, noticing Hortence was alone and asleep.

Annabelle spun to scan the room. A note with *Annabelle* written in an elegant hand on the front rested on her small desk. She snatched it up, leaving Hortence in her ignorant sleep.

She ripped open the letter, scanning it in horror. Her gaze jerked to the door and Hortence and then back to the letter that she reread. After a moment's indecision, she raced out the back door to the livery.

"Cailean!" she gasped as she arrived a few minutes later. "Alistair," she breathed, holding on to a post as she caught her breath. She waved the letter, keeping it out of Cailean's hold and handing it to his brother.

Alistair studied her for a moment before reading the letter.

Annabelle,

I will always be thankful for the constancy of your friendship. During the most difficult times, you were my friend even though you were also a MacKinnon. I have one last selfish request. Please care for her as though your own.

Your friend,

Leticia

"No!" Alistair roared, racing from the livery and in the direction of Annabelle's bakery.

"I have to return to the bakery. Hortence," Annabelle whispered to her husband.

Cailean grabbed his wife's arm before she could pursue his brother. "What did her letter say?"

"Leticia left town." She shook her head in stupefaction. "But she left Hortence. She wanted me to care for Hortence as though she were my own."

"She went with that man?" Cailean rasped.

Annabelle shrugged as she fought tears. "For some reason, she left Hortence. I don't believe she has any intention of coming back." She rubbed at her belly. "She's abandoned her beloved daughter."

Cailean flinched, breaking his gaze from hers as an early morning customer entered the livery. "Go to Alistair. I must stay here."

Annabelle squeezed his arm and walked in a sedate manner to her bakery. She noticed a small crowd gathered outside and grimaced. When she entered the back, she found a piece of paper and scribbled on it CLOSED FOR THE DAY. After stuffing it in one of the window-panes, she ignored the groans of disappointment outside and returned to the rear rooms.

She crept into the back room to find Alistair on his knees, bent over Hortence as though in prayer. When Hortence woke, asking for her mother, tears coursed down Annabelle's cheeks.

"Yer mother has gone away for a few days," Alistair whispered, tugging her onto his lap as he moved to sit next to her on the bed. "She's asked us to care for ye while she is away."

"But she will come back?" Hortence asked, snuggling into Alistair's embrace. When Alistair nodded, the child relaxed. "I've missed you, 'Stair."

"Aye, as I've missed ye, Little Bug," he whispered, his voice thickened with tears. "Come. Let's have ye away home so we can care for ye properly. I know yer aunts have missed ye." He wrapped her in a blanket and hefted her into his arms. Her giggle eased the tension around his eyes, and she curled into his embrace.

"How long until you're my papa?" she asked.

"Too long." He shared an intense look with Annabelle.

"I must bake for the hotel, café, and Boudoir. Then I'll be home." She squeezed his arm and watched as he left through the back door.

Later when Annabelle arrived at the back door to the café, Irene grabbed her by the wrist and hauled her inside. "You are not simply dropping off the buns today and disappearing. You must stay for a chat."

Annabelle shook her head and released her wrist from Irene's tight grasp. "I don't have time today. At the house, we have ..."

"A child who's been abandoned, yes," Irene said as her eyes sparkled with fury. "We've heard."

"How?" Annabelle whispered. She set the basket on the kitchen table and sat at a chair. She absently nodded her thanks as Irene placed a cup of coffee in front of her and joined her. "We haven't told a soul."

"When Alistair is seen leaving with Hortence in his arms from the back of your shop, and you shut the bakery for the day, the townsfolk take notice and speculate. It didn't take long for the stationmaster to mention that Miss Browne had departed with that ne'er-do-well early this morning."

Annabelle leaned against the back of her chair. "Did he say where she was headed?" She shrugged at Irene's confused expression. "It would help narrow the search."

"You're serious about bringing her back?" The older woman ran a hand over her calico skirt as she sat at the table with Annabelle. "Why? Alistair wanted little to do with her."

"He was working through his anger. He never wanted her to leave. To never see her daughter again. Even if he wanted nothing to do with her, he would never wish that for her."

Irene's eyes gleamed with triumph. "Which means that cantankerous puff of hot air will be foiled again."

"I never realized you disliked Mrs. Jameson as much as you do," Annabelle murmured.

"Oh, I have my reasons." She tapped the table. "However, now that she thinks she has her claws into a man like Alistair MacKinnon, he'll have to be wily to free himself."

"Even if he has to be as blunt and rude as Cailean was famous for before he married me, I know Alistair would find a way to evade marriage to Helen. He doesn't want her, and he's feeling cornered by her. Something a man never likes to feel."

Irene's shrewd gaze met Annabelle's. "And he loves another." Her smile spread at her friend's nod of agreement. "Good. That's as it should be." She rose. "If he has any sense, he'll catch tomorrow's train. Have him stop by before he leaves, and I'll have a basket ready for him. You'll be busy with the bakery, and I don't want to add this chore to what you already have to do."

Annabelle swallowed her protest. "I will graciously accept your help." She rose, grabbed the handle to her now-empty basket, and headed back to the bakery to reload for another delivery.

Sorcha walked down the boardwalk, intent on completing her morning purchases early since she needed to care for Hortence so Alistair could return to the livery. She paused when she saw Mrs. Jameson, smiling with glee at her daughter. Sorcha slipped in between the café and a saloon so as to remain hidden and to overhear Mrs. Jameson's conversation with Helen.

"Isn't it wonderful news?" Mrs. Jameson crowed as she clung to her daughter's arm. "That man left town with that wicked woman, and now Mr. MacKinnon's free for you. Just as I planned."

When Helen paused in front of the café, it allowed Sorcha to over-hear the rest of their conversation. "What do you mean, you *planned* this?" An undercurrent of anger was woven through her voice.

"You need a chance to show that man your charms without the distraction of that shameless hussy. I did what I had to do to ensure she left town."

Sorcha stifled a gasp as she canted forward to better hear their furtive whispering.

"How, Mother?" A small stomp of a foot matched Helen's terse question. "I thought we agreed yesterday to cease pestering him and to leave her alone."

Mrs. Jameson patted her daughter on her cheek. "You are so innocent in the ways of the world. A man such as Mr. MacKinnon would never look to another while continuing to be tempted by that harlot."

Helen held her hands on her hips as she leaned toward her mother. "Have you heard nothing I've said the past few days?" At her mother's dismissive sniff, Helen said, "I'd prefer not to marry rather than trap a man who'd rather be with another."

"I merely gave fate a shove. Any mother would do what I did."

"What did you do?" Helen grabbed her mother's arm to prevent her from storming away in indignant glory.

"Your grandmother's pearls were only gathering dust. I pawned them to ensure that man had the funds he needed to leave with her."

Sorcha's eyes rounded as she heard Helen's horrified gasp.

"Those were mine—to wear on my wedding day!" Helen said.

"Mr. Finlay was reasonable in the price he gave me. He was most desirous of them for his wife," Mrs. Jameson said in dismissal. The town's banker, whose reputation as a miserly, miserable man, remained unchallenged. "You're beautiful enough you don't need pearls."

"And you're vicious enough that you'll never see what you've lost," Helen snapped as her footsteps sounded on the boardwalk.

Sorcha eased from her hiding place. Mrs. Jameson stood with her back to her, watching as Helen stormed away.

"Seems as though ye did no' plan that well," Sorcha murmured.

Mrs. Jameson spun, her glare intensifying as she saw Sorcha. "How dare you listen in on a private conversation."

Sorcha laughed. "I wouldna call it private if ye are discussin' it on the boardwalk for all to hear." She took a step closer until she was nearly nose to nose with her foe. "How dare ye force Leticia out of town? Ye had no right."

"I had every right to save this town from such a woman's presence. If I had the ability to rid us of the refuse at the Boudoir too, I would." She held her head high at her proclamation.

Sorcha's mocking laugh provoked an irate blush. "Yer son would lose his prime means of entertainment were ye to accomplish that."

"My son is none of your business," Mrs. Jameson rasped.

"Just as my brother is none of yers," Sorcha hissed. "Leave me and mine alone, an' we might get along. If ye do no', ye'll have to deal with our wrath, Mrs. Jameson, and it's no' pleasant." She waited a moment before she pushed past her. She stopped in at the butcher shop and the Merc before heading home.

She paused as she entered the kitchen area to find Alistair, sitting at the table. "Where's Hortence?" she asked.

"Playin' marbles." He pointed to the parlor across the hall and frowned when Sorcha pushed on his shoulders so he remained seated.

She set the basket of food on the floor with a loud *thunk* and sat across from him. "I have news."

"There's nothin' to say. She left. I was stupid to even consider chasin' after her." He gripped his fingers around a cup of coffee, his gaze as bleak as she had ever seen it. "She chose him rather than me. I shouldna have been surprised after Ewan told me that he saw her kissin' him Saturday night."

"No, I don't believe that is true. I think she was forced to leave. Or coerced. I don't believe she left of her own free will." She met his surprised gaze as she defended Leticia. Sorcha held up her hand and glared at her brother when he began to protest. "Ye ken I've never been supportive of Annabelle takin' her in. Never wanted to see Letitica have another chance at hurtin' ye." She took a deep breath and flushed. "But I think I was wrong."

Alistair frowned. "What changed yer mind?"

"I overheard Mrs. Jameson speaking with Helen today. The vicious woman pawned family jewelry meant for Helen to give to Leticia's husband so that he'd have funds to leave town. With Leticia."

Alistair shook his head. "I dinna understand what ye just said."

"Mrs. Jameson funded Leticia's husband. She is the reason that man had the money to leave with Leticia." She met Alistair's horrified stare. "Ye know that man had to have said or done something horrible for her to agree to leave Hortence behind." Her eyes gleamed with anger. "Even I would never criticize her as a mother. She's dedicated." Sorcha swallowed as panic replaced anger. "He must have threatened her with somethin' awful to convince her to leave wee Hortence."

Alistair nodded. "Aye." He closed his eyes, pinching the bridge of his nose. "I refuse to look a fool again."

Sorcha grabbed his hand and waited until he met her indignant gaze. "Would ye rather look a fool and be with Leticia? Or would ye rather hold on to yer mangled pride and be alone and separated forever from the woman ye love and be a greater fool?" She huffed out an agitated breath when he remained silent. "Would ye condemn her daughter to a life without her mother?" Her eyes held an echo of such an agony.

"Ye dinna ken what ye ask, Sorcha," he whispered. "I've already been …" He shook his head.

Her eyes filled as her grip on his hand turned into a gentle clasp. "I will never say I understand what ye went through. Witnessing it was horrible enough. But don't give up, Alistair. I ken ye love her, even through yer anger and rage and wounded pride." She relaxed when he nodded.

"Aye," he whispered. "I never stopped."

She smiled at his confession. "What will ye do?" They shared a long look before he rose and marched out the back door. She sat a moment before she stood to put the cold items in the icebox. After a deep breath, she pasted on a bright smile and joined Hortence in the parlor.

~

A listair burst into the livery. "I have to go."

Cailean leaned on his pitchfork as he waited for his brother to continue. He watched as Alistair paced the long hallway, stopping to kick at a stall door before turning around. "Where would you go?"

"They must have left on the train. I'll ask the stationmaster if he remembers their destination and follow them."

Cailean raised an eyebrow. "Seems a lot of effort for a woman you were determined never to forgive."

Alistair tugged out a stool and flopped onto it. "Don't, Cail."

His brother sighed and rubbed at his forehead. "I can't go with you. I need to stay here to run the livery." His gaze sharpened. "I know now is not the time to make such a decision, but what do you want to do about Jack's offer?"

Alistair shrugged. After a moment he closed his eyes and took a deep breath as though focusing on the pressing problem of money. "What did Warren say?"

"He can write up a contract that is favorable to us, although he agrees with me that $5,000 is excessive. He's concerned that, if we accept that much money, John will be the majority owner."

Alistair looked around the livery. "I dinna ken if it's even worth $5,000."

Cailean shrugged and nodded. "Exactly. Warren thinks we should accept part of it, and keep the rest in a fund for John, although Warren does agree that it should technically be in our name. Finlay will never do business with John, and that greedy banker would find a way to lose the money or rob John blind if possible."

Alistair grunted. "Why is it that bankers are always miserly bastards?"

Cailean laughed. "I don't know, but it's as true here as it was on Skye." He sobered as he watched his brother. "I'll speak with Jack, let him know what we've decided. However, you must focus on Leticia. We should see if Warren will travel with you. I have a feeling you'll need a lawyer before this is all over, and I'd rather you have a lawyer we trust by your side."

"We dinna have the money yet." He ducked his head in shame. "How am I to pay for travel, hotels, and food, never mind the presence of a lawyer?"

Cailean waved away his brother's concern. "There's money. Go to the station, determine when you'll leave, and then return for a while so I can go to the bank."

Alistair frowned as he watched his calm older brother. "How can there be money when we are in arrears? It's why we're makin' a devil's bargain with Jack." He shook his head. "We're still paying off Sorcha's and Ewan's travel."

"Belle has money," Cailean whispered. "The bakery is profitable, and we haven't used any of it." He glared at Alistair, silencing his protest. "Your happiness, Leticia's safety, and her daughter's future are more important than any money in the bank, Al. And now I know I can repay Belle with what we'll receive from our new partnership."

Alistair nodded and cleared his throat. "Aye. Ye'll be takin' it out of my share." He rose, stopping when his eldest brother gripped his shoulder.

"You need never repay me," Cailean rasped. "You brought me back from the brink more times than I care to remember. It's what family does." They shared a long look of understanding before Alistair slapped him on his shoulder and slipped from the barn and headed to the train station on the edge of town.

After the short walk back to town from the station after purchasing two tickets for the following morning's train, he saw Helen crossing the road. "Miss Jameson!" he called out. He hurtled off the boardwalk and dodged a carriage and a horse rider as he approached her. "I hope ye and yer mother are happy."

She blanched at his caustic words. "She is. I am not. I would never wish anyone to be consigned to a loveless marriage."

He laughed as he shook his head, incredulous. "Except me. An'

137

yerself. For that's exactly what ye had planned for us." He took a deep breath. "I ken what ye hoped, but it willna come to pass."

She grabbed his arm as he attempted to storm past her. "Mr. MacKinnon, I was a fool. I realized that, after we spoke the other evening. I tried to convince my mother that I no longer agreed with her. But she would not be persuaded."

Alistair looked at Helen with a mixture of pity and loathing. "I hope ye learned this lesson well, Miss Jameson. Yer mother isn't one to take advice. If ye want something in yer life, ye'd better act afore she can mangle yer dreams." He nodded once before he walked away.

CHAPTER 12

*L*eticia scooted next to the window on the train, intent on keeping as much distance as possible between her and her dissolute husband. He snickered at her movement, spreading his legs wider and keeping one thigh in contact with her leg. Her position placed her closer to the open window and the thick coal smoke puffing from the steam engine. She swiped at her cheek, grimacing when her finger came away blackened from the soot.

The train slowed to stop, and she looked out the window for any sign that they were approaching Helena. Instead a small hamlet appeared with a wooden water tower. She sighed with frustration as the train had stopped numerous times to reload water for the steam engine. She watched as men called out to those on the train, sharing gossip and snippets of information about track conditions as the tank was efficiently filled. Soon the men waved goodbye, and the train lumbered into motion again. She turned her face from the window as a fresh blast of coal smoke billowed back from the engine.

"You can't escape me, Lorena," Josiah breathed, his eyes closed as he rested his head against the back of the seat. "You've made your choice, and you must accept what you've done."

She gripped her hands together, jerking when he reached to hold one of them. She yanked until she was free from his touch. His chuckle made her shiver.

"You always were a naive, stupid woman to believe what you were told." He relaxed further in the private compartment he had reserved for them. "Even when we were first married, you were dumb enough to believe the tales I spun."

"Why did you want to marry me?"

He shrugged, his hand now on her knee. "I saw you and watched you. It was unfortunate you were not easily led astray as you demanded marriage before I could partake of any … pleasure from you." He smiled as he felt her shudder at the word *pleasure*.

"Why me?" she rasped, unsuccessful in her attempt to force her knee from his clasp.

"I needed a woman to aid in my endeavors. Your beauty and inno-cence were perfect foils for what I had planned." He turned his head and looked at her. "And you were malleable. Pathetic little orphan, desperate for love, with only an ancient aunt peddling her favors to aged gentlemen." He raised a mocking eyebrow.

"I was not malleable!" she protested.

He laughed. "Lorena, by the time you realized what I was doing, you were in so deep, you had no option but to continue your lying ways."

"I am not a liar or a thief," she snapped. "And my name is Leticia." She gasped and struggled but lost the battle to free herself when he slung an arm over her shoulder and hauled her next to him.

His fingers dug into her shoulder, stilling her squirming as the pain slowly intensified. "You are what I tell you that you are. You are of my making." His grip on her shoulder increased until she gasped in pain, and he turned her to the side so she faced him. "You ran once. You drugged me." He leaned forward, his fetid breath fanning over her face. "You won't have a second chance."

"Who really attacked you the night I left?" she asked.

He snorted and laid his free hand over his abdomen. "You remember that bastard Mitchell?" He turned and met her gaze, nodding when he saw recollection in her gaze. "He must have figured out my scheme wasn't all I'd made it out to be. And I miscalculated because he was attempting a scam on me."

She shook her head in confusion. "I don't understand."

"You and I worked as a pair. We had a pattern, and we followed it. We never hurt anyone."

"Except for robbing them of all their money," she said sardonically.

He ignored her sarcasm and said, "Mitchell had a gang of men working with him. When he realized I was the same man who had robbed one of his men a few months before, he was displeased." Josiah shuddered this time. "*Displeased* was his favorite word. It's what he said as he had his men carve me up."

Leticia trembled.

Josiah smiled at her. "It's nice to know you still care." His voice lowered, as though unable to speak of such evildoings in a normal voice. "Be thankful you weren't home. They had plans for you too. As for me, they wanted me to bleed to death slowly."

"Why didn't you?" She jumped as he gripped her arm.

"So you don't care for me? You wish I had died?"

She stared at him blankly, refusing to answer.

"I didn't die because they got bored and left while I still bled. I managed to bind my wounds and ride a horse to a doc in a neighboring town."

She shook her head and frowned in disgust. "Sounds like another story you've made up in an attempt to swindle me into caring for you again."

When he lowered his lips to kiss her, she jerked her head to the side so his lips brushed against her cheek.

"Don't touch me!" she pleaded as she wriggled in his arms.

He threw her away from him with such force that her head *thwacked* against the window. "One day, when that bastard of a liveryman has faded from your memory, you'll beg me for my touch." He traced a finger over her quivering cheek, seeming to take delight in the tears coursing down it. "You'll have to hope I'm still in a receptive mood." He smiled as she shook at his words.

His hand dropped as he noted the train slowing again. "Dry your tears, Lorena. We're arriving in Helena, and I refuse to have our arrival remarked upon because of your hysterics."

Leticia scrubbed at her cheeks as she took deep breaths, swallowing her sorrow and despair. When the train shuddered to a halt, she followed him, grabbing her meager bag. She clambered down the stairs unassisted and trotted after him.

Although a warm summer day, she pulled her shawl around herself at the lascivious, curious stares of many of the men as she walked behind Josiah. As they departed the depot, he reached backward and grabbed her arm, looping it through his. Men who had been on the verge of approaching her stepped back, disappointment evident in their expressions.

"Don't even think about finding a new protector," he muttered as he tugged her alongside him. "I know enough about your past to ruin you and put you in jail for years."

She shivered and matched his long strides. He helped her onto a raised boardwalk, and they walked at a more measured pace past numerous saloons, gambling halls, and hotels. The streets were filled with delivery wagons and carts, horses and buggies. Coachmen yelled at one another to clear a path as parked wagons impeded the movement of those riding through town. Horses dozed outside businesses, while the water in their troughs sparkled in the bright sunlight.

She glanced up a side street and saw a row of elegant brick houses away from the bustle of town. Josiah tugged on her arm as she had slowed to stare at the idyllic street. Now she focused on the chaos around her. Music blared from saloon entrances, as though to entice patrons to enter. The scent of fresh baked bread wafted from a bakery, and she fought tears as she thought of Annabelle and her friendship. Women loitered outside one saloon, soliciting customers. They ignored Leticia as they cooed over Josiah and flashed their petticoats.

After a few blocks, he turned her into a hotel whose charm had been chipped away over the years. The dark, dank foyer gave little hope that the upstairs rooms were in any better condition.

After acquiring a room, Josiah ordered Leticia to follow him upstairs to the back of the hotel. Once inside, she let out a huff of surprise and relief that the window let in light and that the room appeared to have been recently cleaned. After setting her bag on the floor near the closet, she stood near the window.

"You are to remain here. I will escort you to all your meals. Otherwise you are not to leave this room. If I find that you have, I will be most *displeased*." He watched her as she frowned at him. "You never caused me to show you my displeasure when we were married. Don't force me to now." He nodded with satisfaction as she shuddered with understanding. He looked around the room and sighed. "The only reason to leave this room if I'm not here is to use the bathroom." He relaxed when she nodded her head in understanding.

"Where are you going?" she blurted out in a quivering breath as he turned to leave.

"Where do you think? I'm looking for our next mark. Shouldn't be too hard in a town like this." He studied her a moment. "I'll let you know when I need your help." He shut the door behind him.

After he left, Leticia stood rooted in place for many minutes. Finally, when she realized he wouldn't return, she rushed to the door and locked it. Then she moved to the bureau, relieved to find water in the ewer. After a quick sponge bath and then changing out of her travel clothes, she laid on top of the bed.

The noises filtering inside were similar to the ones from Bear Grass Springs, only magnified tenfold. Gunshots sounded; men argued, and horses whinnied. She hugged a pillow to her chest, attempting to banish thoughts of Hortence and home as she willed herself to sleep.

A listair sat next to Warren on the train, his gaze unfocused on the passing landscape. Rolling burnished-gold hills dipped and rose to one side of the train while, on the other, a river sparkled in the afternoon sun with mountains looming above it. After a few minutes, the train veered from the riverbank and chugged uphill, spewing a cloud of coal smoke as it made slow progress.

The train was filled with immigrants from the East Coast and abroad, traveling to Montana to seek their fortune in mining or ranching. A couple with three children were crammed into a row of seats, their clothes travel worn. Men in rags stared out the window in a stupor at the passing scenery. A smattering of businessmen in fine suits sat along aisle seats to avoid dirtying their clothes with the coal smoke seeping in through the open windows. Most read newspapers and avoided the other occupants of the train car.

Red velvet tufted seats for two sat next to each window with an aisle down the middle. Ornately carved wooden paneling lined the walls and ceiling while overhead lamps down the middle of the car were dormant, awaiting nightfall. Train travel remained a relatively new, and expensive, mode of transportation for most living in Montana, as the transcontinental railroad traveling through the state had just arrived in 1883.

Warren lowered his paper. He had taken the aisle seat, and he frowned as Alistair's white shirt had a sheen of blackened soot on it. "What is your plan once we reach Helena?"

Alistair shook his head. "I havena really thought up a plan. I thought I'd arrive, find her, and then figure out what to do."

Warren snorted, incredulous. "Well, that's no strategy. Do you expect her to divorce the man? Do you hope to marry her? Should we secure three rooms or two?"

Alistair raised a hand to his forehead and shook his head. "I dinna ken, Warren. I dinna ken what should be done." He raised confused, worried eyes to Warren.

"You have to know that you need a plan more than go to Helena, get your woman, and return to Bear Grass Springs." He raised an eyebrow as he watched Alistair with sardonic humor. "Here is what I suggest. First, when we arrive, I will secure rooms. We do not want to alert that man that you are in town, and I doubt he remembers much about me. I will make subtle inquiries while you lay low. Once we know where she is, then we can determine what we should do." He studied Alistair a moment. "What is your ultimate goal? Do you still wish to marry her?"

Alistair shifted in his seat and then nodded. "Aye. I want her as my wife."

Warren tapped his friend's knee. "Then we'll have to secure a divorce first. They aren't as hard to obtain here in Montana, but they still aren't a pleasant experience." He met Alistair's worried gaze. "She'll have to speak in front of a judge, and anything she says will become public record. It will trickle back to Bear Grass Springs."

Alistair nodded again. "I can only give thanks we dinna have a reporter yet."

Warren stared at Alistair cryptically. "Our reporter should arrive by the end of summer. I imagine it will be a shock to all those in town to have their dirty laundry on the verge of exposure." He sighed with exasperation as the train slowed to pick up a passenger. The engineers used the stop to refill the water tank for the steam engine before the train slowly lumbered into motion again.

"'Twill be good to have a newspaper in town. If it keeps those like the Jamesons in line, I willna complain," Alistair muttered as the train gained speed. He watched his friend curiously as Warren shifted uncomfortably in his seat. "Why do ye act like that when the Jamesons are mentioned?"

Warren shrugged. "I think you don't understand all that Miss Jameson has suffered."

Alistair snorted out a laugh. "I ken a conniving little witch when I meet one." He flushed. "She attempted to convince Leticia that I was courtin' her. The wee fool."

Warren studied him. "You never were interested in Helen? Even after you were seen with her in private in the woods?"

"Ye ken I wasna," Alistair snapped. "An' she trapped me in those woods!" He flushed after he spoke. "She lives in a world of fabricated half-truths and hopes for what she wants to happen. Not what will truly happen."

Warren chuckled. "So what I heard was true? That she ruined your favorite thinking place?" He laughed harder when Alistair speared him with a fierce glare.

"Ye can laugh until ye've lost one of the few places ye sought as a quiet space for refuge." He shook his head. "I love my family, but sometimes I need to escape them, if only for a few minutes. And then to have that wee woman there, attempting to entice me to marry her …" Alistair closed his eyes, missing the panic and flash of pain in Warren's eyes. "I couldna escape fast enough."

Warren forced a chuckle. "I'd think Mrs. Jameson would prove incentive enough so that no man would ever look twice at one such as Miss Jameson."

Alistair opened his eyes and studied Warren. "Ye are too interested in Helen." He smiled as Warren flushed. "I always wondered what was between ye when she stomped on yer foot and chose to dance with a miner at the Founders' Day party last year." He shook his head. "I'd think ye smart enough not to pine for a woman like that."

Warren let out a breath, barely swallowing the sound of a growl. "And what sort of woman is she?"

Alistair studied the man he was quickly considering his friend. "A woman who isna intelligent enough to ken she should look to ye for marriage, rather than the MacKinnon brothers."

Warren flushed and shook his head. "You don't understand. Helen has her reasons."

He chuckled. "*Helen*, is it? Aye, there's always more to the story than the rest of us understand. I hope ye dinna pine for a woman who has no regard for ye for too long, Warren. Ye deserve better than that."

Warren shrugged his shoulders and stared out the window. After a few moments he changed the subject. "We are about to arrive in Helena. We are only one day behind them, but we still must find them before they move on."

"Aye, assumin' he used his real name when he checked into a hotel," Alistair whispered.

Warren nodded. "You have the picture?"

Alistair nodded.

"Good. It will make my search easier." He rose as the train slowed. After they exited the train and the station, they emerged onto the street.

Alistair paused and took a deep breath as he was jostled by those walking past him. "I'd forgotten what it's like in a bigger city." He grunted as Warren laughed.

"This is nothing. Try a city like Chicago. Or Philadelphia." They worked their way through a throng of men who had congregated near a saloon to watch two men fight and walked to a nearby hotel. "I always stay here when I come to Helena."

The main floor had a large reception area at the front with royal-blue carpets and white wainscoting. The man standing behind the highly polished pine reception desk welcomed Warren as though he were an old friend. "Always a pleasure to see you, Mr. Clark." He extracted two keys from the boxes behind him before he focused on Alistair and his less refined clothing. "As this is your first time in the hotel, sir, you will find the restaurant to the rear, a smoking room behind reception, and two parlors across the hall. The bathrooms are at the end of the upstairs hall."

Alistair nodded. "Ye're too kind." He snatched the keys from the man and turned away. He led Warren upstairs. "Puffed up bag o' air," he muttered.

"You should have let him show us to our rooms," Warren murmured around a chuckle.

"So he could swindle us out of more coin?" Alistair made a disagreeing noise in his throat.

Warren laughed as he pushed open his door. "God save me from thrifty Scots."

They walked into one of the rooms, and Alistair roamed about it. "Two rooms is an extravagance, but, once Leticia is with you, you will want a room for her."

Alistair watched his friend. "I hate to disappoint ye, but, when Leticia is here with me, I'll be with her. Even if I'm sleepin' on the floor. Until I ken she's safe from that bastard, I willna leave her vulnerable." He wandered to the curtained window and stared down at the street scene from Warren's room. "What an ugly city."

"Most towns based on mining are." He sighed at the racket coming from outside. "I hope we aren't here too long."

Alistair's voice was distant, as though lost in memory. "I've spent more time than I'd like in cities since I arrived in America. I never had a desire to see a city when I lived in Scotland. Nothing bigger than Portree, which was no' much more than a wee town. Skye is like a dream to me now, with its lochs and glens and heather-covered fields." He leaned his shoulder against the wall. "Bear Grass Springs was the perfect size after all that time in the large cities of New York and Chicago." He turned and faced Warren. "Where are ye from, Warren?"

"Philadelphia." He met Alistair's surprised glance. "You can rail all you want about the large cities, but they have luxuries we will never experience here in Montana. And anonymity can be a wonderful thing."

Alistair studied Warren as he perched on the windowsill. "I doubt a man such as yerself was anonymous. Ye had to have come from wealthy folk."

"My family was well-off. But, when a city is large enough, there will always be those who don't know you." He shook his head. "For now, all we must hope is that you remain hidden long enough for us to keep surprise on our side. Mr. Fry cannot know you are in town, or he may leave with Leticia, and we'll never be the wiser. No station-master will remember their leaving, nor will he be as inclined to speak with us as we are strangers here."

Alistair nodded. "I understood ye in the train, Warren. I'm to remain concealed here until ye've determined where she is. After that I will seek her out." He roamed the room. "I hope ye find her quickly. I hate havin' nothin' to do."

Warren laughed. "I wish I could have you do my paperwork, but that would defeat the purpose. I must review it to know if it is valid or not." He set a bulging briefcase on the desk in the room. "For now, let me venture out to ensure they aren't staying here. This hotel is one of the nicer ones in town, and I doubt Josiah would spend the money on such a place."

"I'll be in my room when ye return," Alistair murmured, hefting his bag as he left Warren to go snooping.

When Alistair entered his room, he nodded with satisfaction to see that it was toward the rear of the hotel and thus marginally quieter than Warren's room. He dropped his bag by the bureau and wandered to the window, looking out over an alleyway and rooftops of nearby buildings. A thin layer of smoke hung in the air and darkened the sky so it felt like twilight even though it was early afternoon. The summer day had a gloomy feel to it as though its bright promise was never to be met.

He kicked off his boots, pulled out a book from his bag, and laid on the bed. After staring at the first page for ten minutes, he rested it on his stomach and glared at the ceiling. He imagined Warren scouring the city as he searched for Leticia and her husband, and Alistair's mind shied away from envisioning any suffering Leticia had endured at the hands of her husband. Instead he took a deep breath and remembered first meeting her.

A half smile spread as he recalled little Hortence toddling into the livery, intent on petting a horse.

Alistair looked up at the squeal, his head cocked in the direction of that unusual sound in the livery. After a moment's hesitation, he moved from the tack area, bursting into a run as he saw a child about to crawl into a stall with an ornery horse. Even as he reached for the girl, the horse's hoof stamped the ground in warning. "Nae, little one," he rasped as he tugged her into his arms. "Ye dinna meet a horse that way."

She turned cheerful, innocent eyes to meet his and giggled. Red hair slipped from a braid, and she bounced in his arms. "Horsey!"

"Aye, I'll show ye a horse," he said as he grinned at her. He was distracted as a breathless woman with hair the color of spun gold burst into the livery. "Ye might want to keep a better eye on yer charge."

"My daughter," the woman breathed, a tear leaking out. "Oh, thank you, sir, for keeping her safe." She reached for her daughter, frowning when she clung to the man like a bur.

Alistair chuckled. "She's intent on seein' a horse. Come," he murmured, walking down the central part of the livery to a large stall. He made a clicking noise, and a brindle-colored horse whinnied, poking her head out. "This lovely lady is my horse," Alistair said. He took hold of one of the child's hands and held it out for the horse to snuffle, his smile widening when she giggled at the tickling feeling. *"Aye, she likes ye."* Still holding her hand, he showed her how to stroke the horse's nose and then behind its ears.

"I want a horse, Mama!" the girl said before giggling again as the horse sneezed.

"Oh, Hortence," the woman whispered, meeting Alistair's gaze with embarrassment for a moment.

"Horses are a lot of work," Alistair said to the toddler. *"I need a helper now and then. Come visit me, and I'll introduce ye to more of them."*

Alistair sighed as that particular memory faded, his mind jumping from one moment to another with Leticia and Hortence. "Thank God for wee Hortence," he muttered to himself.

A few hours later, he jerked awake at a loud rap on the door, having fallen asleep as he dreamed about his reunion with Leticia. He groaned and rose, flinging the door open.

Warren raised an eyebrow at his friend's unkempt hair and sleepy eyes and shut the door behind him. "I have news."

Alistair froze and focused on Warren. "Aye?"

"Seems that husband of hers is known by many names. The reason no one heard of him after he disappeared is because he's a chameleon. He perpetrates scams against innocent people, swindles them out of their money, and then leaves before he's caught. Each town he goes to, he adopts a new name."

Alistair paced as Warren settled into one of two chairs in the room. "Why does he want Leticia?"

Warren shook his head. "I'm uncertain, but many of the best scams work when there is a distraction, and many peddlers work in pairs. I imagine he used her beauty and grace to distract and legitimize himself."

"Where is she?" Alistair asked.

"In a hotel a few blocks from here." Warren jumped up and grabbed hold of Alistair before he could run out the door. "You don't even know the name of the hotel or the room number. Stop and think, Alistair!" When he saw Alistair take a deep breath and relax his fisted hands, Warren released him.

"I canna allow her to remain with him. He'll hurt her spirit if nothin' else," Alistair whispered. "I've failed her for too long, Warren. I canna continue to fail her now."

Warren nodded. "I understand. That's why I'm joining a high-stakes poker match in an hour where I will keep your Josiah Fry entertained. I will act as his next mark. If it goes to plan, you will have time to get her out. Don't dawdle, as I have to hope he doesn't remember me."

Alistair nodded. "I willna. She'll be here, safe, tonight."

CHAPTER 13

*L*eticia attempted to ignore the knocking on the door. However, when it turned into an unremitting pounding, she spun away from the window and opened the hotel room door a fraction. "I'm certain you have the wrong room—" Her voice trailed away as she beheld Alistair, breathing heavily, cheeks flushed, and his intent gaze zeroed in on her.

"What are you doing here?" Leticia whispered as she attempted to close the hotel room door. She stepped back as Alistair pushed his way inside.

"Looking for ye." His gaze roved over her as though assessing her for injuries, and it sharpened as he noted the drawn and devastated look in her eyes.

"You must leave." Her gaze darted to the closed door and then back to Alistair.

"He's not returnin' anytime soon. He's havin' too much fun with Warren at one of the saloons near Last Chance Gulch." He shifted from foot to foot and then exhaled when she remained silent. "Ye deserve better than a man like him."

She glared at Alistair. "I thought I did, but I learned differently."

When she moved to spin away from him, he grabbed her. "Dammit, I'm sorry. I let my pride an' anger an' hurt blind me." His touch gentled as she began to tremble. "I never thought ye'd leave." He tugged her forward, pulling her into his arms. She remained stiff as a board for a few moments, but he ran his hands over her shoulders and back, and she eventually relaxed into his caresses.

"How is she?" she breathed.

"Scared. Determined to be brave." He took a step away and traced her hairline with his thumbs. "Hopeful ye will return to her."

Tears poured down her cheeks, and she pulled from Alistair's embrace, sitting on the lone chair in the room. "Why have you come? There is no reason for you to be here, except to tease me with what I can never have."

He watched her with passionate intensity. "An' what is that, Leticia? What do you believe ye can never have?"

"A family. A husband who loves me." She closed her eyes as she scrubbed at her cheeks. "I'm married to Josiah Fry. I am Mrs. Fry." She shuddered at the words. "I must accept who I am."

"Nae," Alistair rasped. "Ye are Leticia Browne. The woman I love. The woman I will marry."

"I lied to you." She met his wounded gaze, her eyes dulled with disillusionment and grief.

"Aye, ye did. An' I failed to listen to ye when ye tried to explain to me why." He perched on the edge of the bed in front of her. He studied her and understood she would not yet leave with him. "I'm ready to listen now."

She wrung her hands together, her gaze lowered as she spoke in a barely audible voice. "We married in Kansas in 1877. I thought he was worldly and wise, and I couldn't believe he wanted someone like me." She gave a huff of humorless laughter and gripped her fingers tighter together. "I should have understood at the time that I was an easy mark with an elderly aunt as my only relative. We married two months after we met."

At the long silence, Alistair asked, "Was he cruel?"

She closed her eyes. "No. But he was a schemer and wanted more than a wife who was happy to remain home and keep a house." She sniffled. "Soon I was helping him with his schemes. Charming his so-called friends out of money as he talked about investments that he never planned on making."

Alistair leaned away from her. "Why? That's not who ye are. Ye're a good, honorable woman."

She half smiled. "At first I believed his far-fetched ideas. By the time I understood I was helping him swindle money from unsuspecting families, I was his accomplice. However, he convinced me that I would spend the rest of my life in jail if I ever spoke up and that my only recourse was to continue as I was." She shook her head. "I had no reason to believe him, but I could see no way free of him. I had colluded with him and helped him steal hundreds, if not thousands, of dollars." She shivered. "Words can be more powerful than a fist."

"What happened to make ye flee to Montana?" He reached forward and traced a hand down her arm until he clasped her hand.

"We had moved around a lot, and I wanted to settle down. I dreamed of a home with a piece of land. Someplace stable to raise our child." She sighed as she swiped at her cheek. "He was irate I was with child. At first he encouraged me to visit an herbalist." At the look of horror on Alistair's face, she said, "But I refused, and, as my condition became more obvious, he was more distant. I suffered terrible bouts of nausea, and I clung to that as my reason to refuse to aid him in his schemes."

She picked at a button. "It's as though my pregnancy gave me the strength to stand up to him and his scams. I wasn't only speaking for myself but for my child too." She finally raised her gaze to meet Alistair's. "We had a terrible fight after he failed to trick a man, and he returned to our rented house in a rage. He railed at me for my pregnancy, for denying him his rights as a husband to command me to do what he wished, that I needed to get rid of the brat as soon as possible because he needed my help."

"What?" Alistair asked, his hand tightening over hers.

She paled. "He wanted me to leave my baby, my Hortense, at an orphanage." She swallowed and barreled on. "I'd been having trouble sleeping with the pregnancy, and the doctor had given me something to help. I'm not sure what it was, but it was strong. The next night, when he came home, I gave him a glass of whiskey laced with the sleeping draught." Her gaze was filled with guilt, hope, and resignation as she stared at Alistair. "A part of me feared I'd killed him. That I was in fact a widow. But I dared not seek out any information about him for fear he'd find Hortense and me."

"Ye would have been lucky had he died."

She shook her head. "No. I'm so relieved to know I didn't kill him. That I'm not a murderer." She gripped her hands together. "I slipped away while he slept and hid near the train station that night, waiting until dawn, when I stole away on a train and traveled to Saint Louis. It was hot and humid, and I knew no one. I knew the small amount of money I'd taken from our sock drawer would quickly disappear." She let out a stuttering breath.

"What did you do?" he whispered.

"I found a desperately sad widower with five children and became his governess. He thought I was fat, and, by the time he realized I was to have a child, he was half in love with me." She bowed her head as though in shame. "He supported me through the rest of my pregnancy, through the birth, and wanted to marry me." She met Alistair's jealous gaze.

"Why didn't ye?"

"I feared I wasn't free." She blinked away a tear. "And no matter his kindness in the beginning, I didn't love him. I don't know if I could have loved any man at that point. After my husband." She continued to fidget with her hands in her lap. "And then the widower's sister visited and became irate at my presence. Called me words worse than those bandied about the women at the Boudoir. His perception of me changed, and he no longer saw me with much esteem. I was little more than a drudge, caring for his children."

After a moment's silence, Alistair whispered, "Did he hurt ye?"

She shook her head. "No, but I feared he would ignore any further denials to my bed. He had begun to doubt that I had been married. And felt that any deference I had been given had been in error."

"What did ye do?"

She took a deep breath and sniffled. "I read an advertisement seeking a teacher in a small town in Montana. I thought I'd be safe there. No one would think to look for me there." She swiped at her cheek. "And I wanted a new start for my child and me." She met his gaze. "I answered the advertisement and was shocked when I received a letter a few months later, asking me to arrive by the first part of August that year." Her gaze was distant as though imagining past scenes. "Hortence and I slipped away when the widower's family was at a private function I had not been invited to."

"That was courageous," Alistair said.

"Courage has very little to do with anything when you have a child to support," Leticia said. "You discover what you will do to ensure your child is cared for. And hopefully thrives."

"So you did have some training with children," Alistair murmured. At her absent shrug, he frowned. "What is it?"

"All I've done since I married Josiah is lie and deceive and hurt those who would be good to me."

He rubbed away her tears that fell. "I do no' agree. I think ye've learned how to survive, which is admirable." He shook his head. "I'll never understand why ye did no' tell me all this before."

"How could I? You're honorable and truthful, and I stole. I stole and cheated and lied. I forged letters of recommendation to obtain my teaching position." She swiped at her cheeks.

He sat in silence a few minutes. Sounds from the street filtered up, with wagons rolling past and men calling out to each other. "Why didn't ye want to marry me?"

"I wasn't divorced. I was uncertain I was a widow. And I dared not confirm that for fear he could track me down. A part of me hoped he had died at the hands of some irate man after one of his schemes failed." Her defiant gaze met his. "I'm not sorry for saying that." She turned her hand over and laced her fingers with his. "I feared using my real name. Would our marriage be legal if I didn't use my real name?"

"Ye should have talked with me. All this could have been resolved." He frowned. "I wouldna have been happy, but I would have wanted ye, no matter what. Widowed or divorced, it wouldna have mattered."

"I couldn't divorce him in Kansas. There was no abuse. He provided for me. He didn't abandon me." She shivered. "I abandoned him."

Alistair smiled. "It's not as difficult here, love. In Montana, ye can divorce because ye want to marry the man who will give ye a better life."

She failed to smile at his teasing. "I can't divorce. And I can't marry you." When she attempted to free herself from his touch, he firmed his grip.

"What are ye talkin' about?" His eyes flashed. "It's why we're spendin' a fortune havin' Warren travel with me. Although I think he's enjoyin' himself."

"If I divorce Josiah, he'll fight to have custody of Hortence." She blinked. "I can't let a man such as him raise her. If I am with him, I can't have her with me. She'll have the best chance of a good life with a family like yours."

Alistair groaned as he tugged her closer to him on the bed until their foreheads almost touched. "That's hogwash, an' ye know it. She'll have the best life with her mother." He backed away and traced a finger down her cheek. "Ye can't let him control ye with fear, with his lying words. I can imagine all he threatened ye with. Jail time. Living on the streets. Living the life of a whore. Sending Hortence to a faraway orphanage. Never seeing Hortence again." He paused as he saw the truth of his words echoed in her eyes. "Ye can fight him an' win."

"I've only ever bested him when I've run away."

"Ye're not runnin' this time," Alistair growled. "Except for right now. Gather yer things, an' come with me. I dinna want ye spendin' one more night under the same roof as him."

"I can't stay with you. We aren't married."

"I refuse to leave ye at the mercy of such a man. I failed to protect ye from him when he came back. I willna abandon ye now. Besides, we are to marry. If ye'll have me." He rose and held out a hand for her, frowning as he saw her on the verge of sobbing. "Leticia?"

She took his hand and stood, moving with alacrity to the small wardrobe to pull out her traveling bag and the few clothes she had stuffed inside when she left Bear Grass Springs. After only a moment, she turned and nodded. He opened the door and ushered her outside.

Dusk was falling when they emerged onto the boardwalk. Leticia clung to Alistair's arm as few respectable women walked along the boardwalk at this hour, and the men had become rowdier with the passage of time and the consumption of drink. The breeze had stilled, and the scents of manure, wood smoke, and rotting food permeated the air as they passed an alley.

They arrived at a grander hotel a few blocks away. Alistair grabbed her hand and led her upstairs, the clerk unperturbed at the arrival of another guest. Alistair opened the door to his room and waited for her to precede him inside. Its location at the back of the hotel prevented the loud din from the street to penetrate the room. Two sitting chairs, a bureau, and an armoire filled the large room, with the bed along the far wall. He flicked the lock after he entered.

She spun to face him, her eyes rounded at the soft *click*. "Alistair?"

"In case yer husband tries to find ye, I dinna want him waltzing in. He's no' a dumb man, and he will eventually remember Warren." He half smiled. "When the whiskey wears off."

"How can you afford such a place?" Her gaze flitted over the elegant furnishings, the thick curtains, and the fine bedding.

"Warren always stays here when in Helena. I needed his help, and I will stay where he likes, to ensure his aid." He shrugged. "There's money."

"I hate that you are going into arrears for me," she whispered.

"I'm not. But, even if I were, ye're worth any debt." He met her watery gaze. "Annabelle has money. She's helping us. And Cailean and I are going into a partnership with another soon. But that's a tale for another day."

Leticia seemed to deflate. "Annabelle," she whispered. "I'll never be out of her debt."

"Aye, I fear that's true. I owe her more than I could ever repay her." He watched as Leticia studied him in confusion. "For granting ye a haven an' keepin' ye safe. Ye an' wee Hortence." He cleared his throat. "The money will be repaid, Lettie." He watched her move with the restless energy of an unbroken colt as he sat in one of the chairs.

She nodded and looked around the room as though searching for another topic. "Why the grimace?" She flushed after she asked the question.

"These chairs look comfortable, but they're hard. I dinna look forward to a night spent sleeping in it."

Her flush deepened. "I thought you'd sleep beside me."

His eyes gleamed, but he shook his head. "I will no' dishonor ye. Nor make ye feel as though ye have no choice in what ye want."

Her face shone with gratitude. "Thank you." She paused as she cleared her throat after her voice broke as she fought tears. "I can't seem to stop crying. I'm sorry."

"I can only imagine what ye've been through the past few days. I've been frantic, and I did no' leave Bear Grass Springs believin' I'd never return." He shifted around in the chair, grimacing as no movement made it more comfortable.

"You can't sleep on that chair, Alistair," she said as she sat on the edge of the bed. She flushed as her stomach gurgled.

"Ye're hungry." He rose and met her startled gaze. "Wait here. I'll bring food back. I'll knock and talk to ye through the door. Dinna open it unless ye hear my voice." When she nodded, he strode through the door.

She shut the door and locked it after him and then spun to her bag. She raced behind the privacy screen and shucked her dress, donning a nightdress and wrap. She then sat in one of the chairs and removed the pins from her hair, rapidly freeing it and finger-combing it. After pulling it back in a loose braid, she tied it with a string and then sat as she awaited Alistair's return.

She jumped at the loud knock on the door and tiptoed to it.

"'Tis me, Lettie. I've food. Ye can let me in."

She unlocked the door and peered out before she fully opened it to him.

"Smart lass," he said with a wry smile. "I come bearing gifts." He held up two plates and winked at her as he entered. He set them on the bureau and then frowned as he looked around the room. "We have no real table."

She locked the door and then followed him. "It's fine, Alistair. I can eat with a plate propped on my lap." She pulled back a napkin to discover a plate of fried chicken, mashed potatoes, and creamed corn. "Smells delicious," she whispered.

Alistair frowned as Leticia moved to a chair and ate with gusto. "Did he no' feed ye?"

"He said he'd be back with food. But I think, once he started gambling or working on his next scheme, he forgot about me and any promise he had made." She wolfed down a piece of chicken, then attacked the mashed potatoes before she realized Alistair wasn't eating. Her fork hit the plate with a *clang*, and she flushed. "I beg your pardon. You must think I'm no better than a wild animal."

"No," Alistair rasped. "I'm sittin' here, attempting to fight my anger that ye've been starved since ye left Bear Grass Springs. That ye were no' cared for as ye should have been." He watched as one of her fingers traced the edge of her plate. "For God's sake, Lettie, eat."

She shook her head. "Why won't you eat?"

"I'm waitin' to see if ye are still hungry when ye are done with yer plate of food. If ye are, ye can have some of mine. Or all of it."

She fought and lost her battle with tears. "But you're always hungry. You should eat."

He set aside his plate and knelt in front of her. "Nae. I'll no' eat until I ken ye're full." He swiped at her tears. "I failed ye in the past, Lettie, but I mean to prove to ye that I am honorable. That ye can count on me."

She reached out a trembling hand and touched his cheek. "I still can't believe you are here. That you want to be here with me. That you are concerned about my welfare."

"I hope ye can accustom yerself to it, as I have no plans to cease."

His wry statement wrought a strangled sob from her. He set aside her plate and pulled her to him, enfolding her in his arms. "I dinna mean to make ye cry. I want ye to eat and to eat yer fill. Then I want ye to rest, as I ken ye havena rested since ye left Hortence behind. Ye are no' alone, Lettie. I'm here. Warren's here. The MacKinnons are behind ye. We will support ye as ye free yerself from yer husband."

He held her as she sobbed, running soothing hands over her back. "*Shh*, love, ye'll make yerself sick."

"I never thought you'd want to hold me again," she gasped. "I hoped. I prayed, but, after I left with him, I thought you'd forget about me. Find another to love."

"Never. Ye are my love. Ye and Hortence are my family." He leaned back and bracketed her face between his large hands. "I've acted as a wounded, miserable bear because I missed ye so badly. Forgive me for being an ass." He held her as her sobs quieted. "Come, my love. Eat and then rest."

He helped her to her seat, where she ate with more restraint. However, by the time she finished her plate of food, she was full, and she motioned for Alistair to eat. He ate most of the food, although he saved a large piece of chicken in case she woke hungry in the middle of the night. After she completed her evening ablutions, he tucked her into bed.

"Join me," she murmured as she battled sleep.

"No, Leticia." He kissed her softly on the lips. "When I join ye in bed, I hope it's for somethin' other than sleepin' next to ye." He pulled the blankets up around her. "Sleep well, my love."

❧

Alistair woke from a fitful doze. He groaned as he sat up in the uncomfortable chair and listened for what had interrupted his sleep. Moonlight streamed in through the windows, illuminating the bed. A whimper emerged from there, and he frowned as Leticia shifted as though in distress. He rose, tiptoeing to the bed. His fingers stroked her head, and he reared back as a hand emerged from the blankets to smack him in the throat and jaw.

"Stay away from me!" she said in a sleepy voice. "Don't touch me."

"Leticia, 'tis Alistair," he murmured. "Ye are no' with that man any longer." He watched as the tension left her and heard a quiet sob emerge. After settling a hip near hers, he touched her shoulder. "Ye're safe, Lettie."

"Alistair?" she asked, turning to face him. "You're really here?"

"Aye, my love." He lay down atop the bedding next to her and pulled her head onto his shoulder, his arms stroking down her back. "He willna harm ye again."

She shuddered in Alistair's arms. "But he might hurt you. I couldn't bear that." She hiccupped. "I should never have agreed to leave with you. I've put you in danger."

"That's rubbish, an' ye know it," he said as he kissed her head. "He's the only one causing mischief." He sighed and held her closer. "Let me enjoy the moment, love. I'm finally holding ye in my arms."

She huffed out a laugh. "You're sleeping next to me."

"Aye, an' I'm a fool," he muttered, pulling her closer. "But I want to wait 'til our weddin' day." He kissed her head. "Do ye mind?"

She rubbed her face against his chest. "Not as long as it is soon." She heard the rumble of his groan as her head rested on his chest. "I hate that you slept in that chair, Alistair."

"I wouldna dishonor ye."

"I dishonored myself," she whispered, her fingers drawing a circle over the biceps of one of his arms.

"Ye did no such thing," he rasped. "Now sleep, love. Let me hold ye as we sleep."

She snuggled into his embrace and fell asleep. He remained awake for some time, a quiet contentment filling him.

CHAPTER 14

The following morning, Alistair lay on the bed with Leticia snuggled next to him. They were both dressed, awaiting Warren's arrival. "It is scandalous to just lie about all day," Leticia murmured.

"It would be scandalous if we were naked," Alistair muttered. "As it is, we are merely passing the time." He jerked as a fist slammed against the door. He motioned for her to remain where she was and moved to the door. "Aye?" he called out.

"For God's sake, Alistair, open the door," Warren half shouted.

Alistair unlocked it and let Warren in. Alistair raised his eyebrows in surprise to find his friend disheveled with red-rimmed eyes. "Ye look awful."

"I feel worse than I look. I'm too old for this intrigue." He yawned, and his whole body shook. "Did you find her?"

"Hello, Mr. Clark," Leticia said, now sitting on the edge of the bed.

"Miss Browne, lovely to see you, healthy and well." Warren ran a hand over his hair that stood on end and then scratched at his growing beard. "I should have tidied up before coming to see you."

"No, we need to ken what happened." Alistair pushed Warren into a chair and thrust a cup of lukewarm coffee in his hands.

"Aah, elixir," Warren muttered as his eyes closed a moment while he took a sip. "That man is a card shark, but I suspect he's a cheat. I don't have proof, because I'm not nearly of his caliber, but there is no statistically sound way a man can continue to win with his rate of success unless he cheats."

Leticia snorted. "Of course he cheats. He cheats at everything."

Warren stretched his legs in front of him. "If he keeps it up here, I suspect you won't have to worry about him much longer. Someone will gladly put a bullet in him and save you the expense and infamy of a divorce."

"I don't want him dead. I just want him out of my life," Leticia whispered.

Warren rested his head against the back of the chair. "Then you're more generous than I am. After a few hours in his presence, I was ready to commit murder." He huffed out a laugh. "I think he's a raving lunatic."

Alistair sighed. "What does he ken about ye?"

"He thinks I'm an easy mark," Warren murmured, closing his eyes again, yet continuing to speak. "I lost some at the tables but mainly sat and watched them play. He is an inveterate liar, but it can be hard to discern truth from fiction." He opened his eyes to watch Alistair and Leticia. "He went on and on about his beautiful wife, Lorena. He'll be irate to find you missing, Leticia."

Alistair moved to her and put a hand on her shoulder as she shuddered. "Ye don't have to be afraid of him any longer. We will keep ye safe."

"He'll find me. He always does." She took shallow breaths and lowered her head as though she were fighting panic and about to faint.

Warren nodded. "Yes, he'll find you." Warren turned to Alistair. "I doubt you attempted to hide Miss Browne as you brought her in here." At Alistair's silent glare, Warren shrugged. "I have a meeting arranged with a judge in two days' time. The papers are to be delivered today to your husband, summoning him to the hearing and informing him of your wish for divorce." He met Leticia's panic-stricken gaze with an implacable one. "If this is not the course of action you desire, if you do in fact wish to remain married to such a man, I will cancel the hearing, and the summons will not be delivered."

Leticia shook her head. "No, I desire a divorce. It just seems that this is all happening so quickly. I don't know …"

Alistair crouched in front of her. "It will all turn out well. I promise. We must free ye from that man." He turned to stare at Warren. "How did ye arrange the meeting with the judge so quickly? I thought there was at least a month's backlog."

Warren shrugged. "He knew my father in Philadelphia. It helps to have connections." He met Leticia's gaze. "It also helps to have a lawyer with a family of very high standing representing you. There is no way we can discount your illicit behavior in Kansas, but we can highlight your years as an upstanding citizen in Bear Grass Springs."

"No one will believe me. I'm a woman, and I lied," she whispered.

"They will believe you if you believe it," Warren said. "And I will give credence to it as your lawyer. Few will doubt the word of a Clark from Philadelphia."

Alistair snorted. "That sort of thing doesna matter in a place like Montana."

Warren smiled slyly. "As you know, Montana is still a territory and not a state. The US Congress has no desire to accept our petition for statehood, despite our overwhelming desire by popular vote last November. We have not yet swayed those in Congress desperate to hold onto their power." He watched as Alistair fought impatience. "This means that our judges are not from Montana but appointed by someone in Washington, DC. These judges don't know our ways, and most don't care about our ways. They see this as a post to suffer through and survive until a better position becomes available."

"Warren, what does this have to do with how ye will help Leticia?" Alistair glared at his friend. "It willna matter that ye are a Clark from Philadelphia. It doesna mean anything here."

Warren smiled. "It does to some DC judges. And I picked the judge it would impress the most. He knew my father and is predisposed to like me simply because I am my father's son." His smile turned self-deprecating. "I learned some worthwhile things from my father." Warren rose. "I need to wash up and rest. Should we meet for a meal in the restaurant here around one?"

Alistair nodded and locked the door behind Warren. He sat beside Leticia and slung an arm over her shoulder. "It will turn out well. I know it seems odd, but Cailean told me that Warren has the credentials of a big-city lawyer."

She snuggled into his side. "Why did he decide to settle in a small town in Montana?"

"I dinna ken. I doubt Cailean does either. Warren is a man to know everyone else's secrets but to guard his own."

~

As they relaxed at the table after a delicious meal, Warren noted a disturbance at the front of the hotel. He rose, motioning for Alistair and Leticia to remain and finish their coffee. A few moments later, he returned, his forced air of serenity increasing Leticia's anxiety.

"Come. We must go to the back parlor." His smile failed to reach his eyes. "Your husband is here, demanding to see you."

"I take it he didna like the summons," Alistair muttered. He rose, and Leticia slipped her hand through his. "Ye are no' alone, love. Never forget that."

Just before they entered the parlor, Warren whispered into Alistair's ear, "Keep Leticia behind me, and keep her quiet. No matter what that man says." His intense gaze met Alistair's, and he nodded his approval when Alistair blinked his agreement.

They followed Warren into the private parlor to find Josiah Fry pacing like a caged animal. His spit-polished shoes gleamed in the early afternoon sun, while his trousers, shirt, and jacket were new. He stalked toward Leticia, only stopping when Warren and Alistair blocked his path.

His gaze flitted from Warren to Alistair, and then he shook his head in disbelief. "And to think I had selected you as my next mark. I thought Lorena could coax you out of your father's money."

Warren matched his glare and blocked his attempt to circumvent him. "You're small potatoes compared to who raised me." His low gravelly voice laden with bitterness hinted at a deeper betrayal. "You know nothing about a successful con."

Josiah laughed. "You might have your pretty words and your fancy education, but I have right on my side. She's a thief and a liar, and she attempted to murder me! She won't see her daughter again because I have the right to her in a divorce as I'm her father. I've been unjustly separated from my child."

Warren ignored Leticia's gasp of dismay, trusting that Alistair would hold her back and ensure she remained quiet. "Is that so? I have written testimony from at least ten townsfolk about your proclamation that Leticia played you for a fool while you were married to her. That the child isn't yours and that you would never accept responsibility for her." He met Josiah's irate gaze. "Seeing as you've proclaimed that you aren't her parent, and you've publically accused your wife of having an affair on at least four occasions that I am aware of, I believe your argument is futile."

Warren took a step forward, forcing Josiah backward. "As for your claim that she is a liar and a thief, I have written testimony, that has been notarized, from three couples in Kansas from the first year of your marriage. It will show that she was miserable and acting at your behest. There is mention of bruises on her arms, and one man said he would not treat a dog as badly as you treated your wife."

Josiah straightened his shoulders. "Lies. All of them lies. I'm a respectable man. Trying to make my way in the world."

Warren nodded as though considering Josiah's claim. "Which would explain why those such as the Mitchell gang continue to seek you out? Why they still want you dead?" He watched with satisfaction as Josiah paled.

Warren held up a hand to prevent Alistair from speaking. "Fry, you have two options open to you. You can accept this divorce. Accept that Leticia Browne will no longer be your wife and that you have legally disavowed Hortence as your child in two days' time. And give thanks that you can slink away into the shadows." Warren's voice deepened. "Or you can attempt to fight what will happen. And I will announce to the world who you are. Where you are. And everyone you've ever swindled will find you."

Josiah faltered as though he had been struck. He shook his head and swiped at his now-sweaty brow. "No. No, please. I'll agree. I'll divorce her. Give up rights to the kid."

Warren nodded. "You should have known better than to come back." His voice lowered. "You should have remained dead."

Josiah glared at Warren and then at Alistair who stood with an arm around Leticia's waist. "You may think you've won. But, at the end of the day, you're still stuck with a passionless woman and her brat. It will give me joy to know you'll be miserable." He stormed past them and slammed the door behind him.

Alistair led Leticia to a chair and sat beside her before staring at his friend in wonder. "How? When?"

"I've known this would happen at some point. Even though I said I wouldn't travel to Kansas to investigate didn't mean I wouldn't make inquiries. I have friends from law school there." He shrugged. "It was all worth it to see his reaction."

Alistair shook his head as though dumbstruck. "I've never seen ye in court, but it must be a magnificent sight to behold."

Warren laughed and shook his head. "It's what this case called for, and I'm merely glad the information arrived before we left Bear Grass Springs."

Leticia raised her wondrous, shocked gaze to him. "How will we ever repay you? How can we?"

Warren leaned against the mantel with a sigh. "Be happy. Let this time of discord go. That's all I want."

Leticia rose and stood on her toes to kiss his cheek. "That's not nearly enough. But I can promise you, if Hortence and I are with Alistair, I will be very happy."

CHAPTER 15

our days later Alistair paced in Warren's hotel room. He glared at the tapping on the door and continued pacing as Warren slipped inside.

"This isn't much different from your first wedding ceremony," Warren joked. "You seem to like to wander over ground you've already trod."

"I dinna usually, but I find, if I don't, I have all this energy burstin' to be free." He stopped and watched Warren, a man he now considered a good friend. "Is she all right?"

Warren chuckled. "She's better than all right. She's anxious to attend the ceremony."

"I worry that this is a mistake. We should marry in Bear Grass Springs. With our family around us and with the town as witness."

Warren shook his head. "I agree that it would be good to dispel rumors, but returning married with Leticia will help protect her reputation. You've shared a room with her for nearly a week." He met Alistair's glare. "You know I won't speak of it, but that information has a way of leaking out."

Alistair grumbled about interfering busybodies and continued walking back and forth across the room. "Will ye escort her to the parlor? I dinna want her to make her way there alone."

Warren slapped him on the back. "Yes, I will. And I'll be there next to you when you wed her."

Alistair watched as Warren slipped from the room again. After a few moments, Alistair walked downstairs and entered the parlor. A few of the hotel's guests sat in the chairs as witnesses to the marriage, and the pastor stood at the front of the parlor, a Bible in his hands. Alistair shook his hand and then tried not to fidget as he waited for Leticia to arrive.

Someone cleared their throat, and he looked to the door. Leticia stood in a dove-colored dress, cut to enhance her figure. Her gold hair covered by a short veil was pulled in a soft chignon, and her blue eyes were lit with joy. She stood beside Warren, waiting to walk the few steps to join Alistair.

Alistair beamed at her as he watched her approach. Soon her hand was in his, and they turned to face the pastor. "At last," he murmured.

He saw her battle tears as she whispered, "At last."

When the pastor recited the portion of the ceremony where he asked if anyone had a just cause to oppose their union, Alistair held his breath. After a moment, when silence prevailed, the pastor continued. When he announced that they were husband and wife, Alistair gave her a gentle kiss and then smiled at those present.

Warren slapped him on the back and then kissed Leticia's cheek. "Congratulations. I'm delighted."

Alistair accepted congratulations from all present and then turned to sign the forms Warren had prepared and the registry the pastor had brought with him. He saw Leticia stiffen as she read the forms Warren gave to her to sign, but she signed them, and they were soon drawn into a surprise reception in the dining room.

After they had cut the cake, and all their wedding witnesses had become friends, Alistair swung Leticia into his arms as the small group of musicians played a slow tune reminiscent of a waltz. "Are ye all right?" he whispered.

She shook her head and then leaned her forehead against his shoulder. "I am overwhelmed."

"Do ye want to go upstairs?" He stroked a hand down her back, eliciting a shiver.

"And have everyone think we are eager for the wedding night?" she asked and then flushed at his gaze that agreed with her statement.

After he studied her a moment, he frowned. "Are ye sayin' ye are no' eager? That ye prefer to spend yer time with a bunch of drunken men ye dinna ken rather than with yer husband on yer wedding night?"

Leticia shook her head. "Of course not. I don't want to cause any more scandal than we already have."

He chuckled. "'Tis too late for that, love."

"Why did you do it?" Leticia whispered into his ear. "Why have Warren write up such a document?"

He eased her away and met her gaze. "It was already written up before our first wedding ceremony, Leticia. I need ye to understand that. I wanted Hortence to be considered my daughter then. For there to never be any doubt."

She nodded as she fought tears.

He stroked her cheek, even though no tears fell. "An' now we have scared that man away, and I'll continue to hope he willna bother us again. But knowin' she is mine, legally, will ease any worry."

Leticia swallowed a sob. "I thought we had to go in front of a judge."

"Aye, we will. But with that form showin' our intent, from the moment we wed, it dispels any doubt." He met her joyous gaze. "I love ye. I love our girl. Ye are my family." He pulled her into his arms as they continued to dance around the floor. He met Warren's gaze and frowned as Warren made a motion with his head for them to leave. Alistair nodded in understanding and then led Leticia to the side of the room where they slipped out the door, their departure unheralded by the celebrating guests.

~

A listair stood in the hotel room, his back to the door as he stared out the window. He listened as Leticia did her evening ablutions behind the privacy screen. At her grunt of distress, he sighed. "Are ye certain ye want no help from me?"

He heard her mutter to herself. Finally she spoke in a voice barely above a whisper. "I can't free myself from this dress."

He strode over to her, pushing the screen to one side. She stood with the dress half open down her back, and her long blond hair falling from its pins. "Come," he grunted. "I should free ye from yer clothes tonight." His touch provoked shivers as his fingers stroked her back as he liberated her from the confining dress. When she remained in front of him with her head lowered, he deftly unlaced her corset.

As the corset fell to the floor, she flailed an arm in front of her until she caught the edge of a small table, holding herself up as her breath flooded in. A soft flush covered her skin as he caressed flesh reddened from the confining corset.

"Must ye wear such a contraption?" he murmured.

"If I don't, I'll be seen as even less respectable than I am."

He spun her until she faced him, her thin shift the only linen covering her upper body. "Ye are respectable. Ye will be until the day ye die." His passionate gaze roved over her. "Ye are my wife, an' no one will speak to ye without respect." He frowned as he saw tears threaten. "What is it?"

"You speak as though you truly believe I am worthy of everyone's regard."

He growled as he tugged her into his arms. "Ye are, my Leticia. My beloved. Ye are." His callused hands traveled down her back and up again to play in her hair and fully free it from the pins. "I'm to blame for ye thinking ye are no' worthy. Forgive me. I never stopped loving ye, Leticia. I'll love ye until I die." He pushed her back, trapping her head between his large hands and holding her immobile so she had to meet his gaze. "I never courted another. No matter what the rumors were or who said what, I never did."

She bit her lip before blurting out, "But you visited the Boudoir. After our first wedding ceremony."

He flushed. "Aye, I did. I was angry and mortified and wanted to hurt ye." He lowered his gaze. "I willna say I'm proud of what I did, but I do regret it."

She stiffened in his hold. "I must have your promise that you will not return to the Boudoir again."

His gentle smile spread, his eyes glowing with delight. "I should never want to, now that we are married." He sobered as he saw his answer failed to placate her fears. "I would never dishonor ye in that way. I shouldn't have acted in such a way afore."

"Why did you?" she whispered, relaxing fractionally as the clasp of his fingers eased and he began to caress her.

He ducked his head. "When that man interrupted our first wedding ceremony and informed the town ye were already married, I felt like a cuckold." He grimaced as she shivered at the word. "I had an irrational need to prove to myself and others in the town that I was a man."

She scoffed as she ran a hand down a strong bicep. "Anyone looking at you knows that."

His chagrined gaze met hers. "Never discount how ye can make a man feel. Ye stripped me of my pride that day, Leticia."

"I'm sorry," she said softly as her voice wavered. "I'm so sorry."

"Hush," he murmured, tugging her to him. After a minute, he whispered in her ear, "Where is your nightgown?"

"Slung over the hook in the closet." She grabbed his arm as he moved away. "Are you certain I need one tonight?" She flushed to her toes as he stilled, his intense gaze roving over her scantily clad body.

"No, ye're overdressed as it is." His smile widened as she reddened further and boldly met his gaze.

She took a deep breath and gripped the corset cover. She tugged it up and over her head, leaving her naked from the waist up. "If you want me ..."

He had her in his arms before she could finish the statement. His mouth collided with hers in a hungry, passionate kiss as he spun her around, knocking over the privacy curtain. He gave little thought to it as he tugged her to the bed, stripping her of her drawers before coaxing her to lay down. He watched as she shivered, awaiting him as he freed himself from his wedding day finery. When he joined her on the bed, he tugged her into his arms and sighed with pleasure as she curled into him. "Ye've the softest skin I've ever felt." He paused as he held himself over her. "Are ye sure?"

"Yes," she whispered. She leaned up and kissed him. "Please don't be disappointed in me," she blurted out as his head stilled over her shoulder on the verge of raining a trail of kisses over her.

"Why should I be disappointed?" He lowered his mouth, smiling as he felt her shiver in response. "I've the woman I love in my bed."

"I'm not as experienced as you think," she said.

He leaned over her and kissed the furrow between her brows. "I want ye, Leticia, as ye are. We'll learn together what we like."

～

Alistair lay on the bed with Leticia curled next to him, her head pillowed on his shoulder. She had feigned sleep since they had made love, and a restlessness pervaded him as each moment passed. His hand idly stroked her back as he relived the past hour. Their demanding caresses and kisses. Their passionate coming together. With a groan, he eased away from her and rose from the bed.

He walked to the window, staring blindly out it, his naked body concealed in the long shadows. A horse whinnied as raucous laughter emerged from a nearby saloon. A thick layer of smoke covered the burgeoning city, preventing him from staring at the stars. A long sigh from the bed had him turning, and he frowned as he met Leticia's sober gaze. "I'm sorry," he whispered.

She pulled the sheets up, covering her breasts as she sat against the headboard. "Why?"

He shook his head and clenched his fists. "It's obvious I did no' please ye." His voice emerged as though tortured, and his eyes flashed with agony. He clamped his jaw shut and glared at her startled laugh.

"You think you didn't please me?" she whispered. "Why would you ever come to that conclusion?" She kept one hand on the sheet at her breast and held the other out to him for him to join her on the bed. After a moment she relaxed as he moved toward her, sitting beside her and taking her hand.

"When a woman cries in my arms after I love her and then feigns sleep, I ken she's disappointed in me." He flushed at his harsh, rash words.

She moved, forgetting the sheet as she knelt beside him. She clasped his cheeks between her palms, stroking her fingers over his whiskers. "I cried because ..." She flushed and ducked her head. "Because I never realized I could feel this way. I thought ..." She broke off, her gaze falling to the sheet now around her waist.

"Ye thought," he murmured, his fingers stroking her jaw, exerting a subtle pressure to raise her head so their gazes met again.

"I thought ... I thought only a man found pleasure," she stammered. "I never knew, I never realized I could feel so much." Her eyes filled with tears. "It was overwhelming."

He swooped forward and kissed her. "I only ever want ye to feel joy and pleasure, Leticia." His thumb swiped away the tear that clung to her eyelash. "Was it too much? Did I hurt ye?"

"No, God, no," she murmured, hitching herself forward until she crawled onto his lap. "I feared you'd be repulsed by my exuberance." She flushed as she met his gaze. "By my desire to make love again."

He chuckled as his hold on her tightened. "Never. 'Tis like a fantasy come true. Havin' ye in my arms, with ye desirous of my touch." He kissed her neck, smiling as she shivered from his kisses and the scrape of his whiskers over her sensitive flesh. "We can discover so much more, my love."

She arched back, her arms around his neck as his eyes warmed to the color of molten chocolate. "I don't want you to think of anyone else when I am in your arms."

He chuckled and ran a hand over her head. "I couldna. Ye fill my head, my heart, and my soul, so there's no room for anyone else." He leaned forward and kissed her. "Ever."

At her sigh of pleasure, he eased her backward, his momentary misgivings replaced with the joy of holding his willing wife in his arms.

◠

A listair sat next to Leticia on the train, while Warren was a few rows behind them. Alistair's finger continued to trace the band on her ring finger, and he smiled openly when he met her amused gaze. "I canna hide the fact I like that ye wear my ring."

She flushed. "I can't either. It doesn't seem real yet."

He lowered his head and whispered in her ear, "I would have thought last night would have made it real." He chuckled as she blushed a brighter red. "What worries ye, love?"

"I know the townsfolk won't have forgiven me. They're so angry at the deception."

Alistair nodded. "Aye, but there's nothing to be done now except move forward. They are angry, and they must be reminded of all the reasons they liked ye afore they had reason to suspect ye of any malice. Before that moment in the church, none would have spoken out against ye. None."

"Well, except for Mrs. Jameson," Leticia said with a wry smile.

"That termagant doesna count as she speaks out against everyone. What matters is what the rest of the town believes." He raised her hand and kissed it. "Ye'll prove to the town that who ye have been the past years in Bear Grass Springs is who ye truly are." He waited a moment. "What else bothers ye?"

"Will Hortence forgive me?" Leticia ducked her head. "I worry she'll never trust me again."

Alistair made a crooning sound to soothe his wife. "Ye left her with people who love and cherish her. Ye cared for her the best way ye could and prevented her from being sent away to an orphanage. When she understands that, she'll forgive ye."

"I don't want her to ever know that he threatened to send her away," Leticia breathed. "I don't want to give her nightmares about that."

He nodded. "Of course." He squeezed her hand. "All she cares about is that ye come home. That the lie I told her has turned into the truth." When she looked at him in confusion, he said, "I told her that ye had to go away for a few days but would be home soon."

"Thank you," she whispered as she lost her battle with tears. "Thank you for loving her as your own."

"She *is* my daughter," he growled. He held her a moment as he looked out the window at the golden fields. "I must ask a promise from ye." He took a deep breath. "Never lie to me again."

She met his serious gaze and nodded. "I won't. I promise." She sighed. "I know you are upset I lied about his treatment of me. I saw how you tried and failed to hide your shock when Warren mentioned the bruises on my arm."

He let out a shaky breath. "I canna stand the thought of anyone hurtin' ye." He hugged her, tightening his hold incrementally.

"Thank you," she whispered. "The bruises were nothing compared to the way he shattered my spirit."

"He didna shatter all of it, love. Ye had the strength to leave. If ye were truly shattered, ye would have stayed with him, an' I never would have met ye." He felt her shiver in his arms.

"What is the partnership you mentioned days ago?" She traced patterns on his palm.

"Cailean and I will maintain majority ownership of the livery, but one-third will be owned by John Renfrew." He met Leticia's gaze. "His father's dyin', an' we couldna pass up the opportunity for experienced help and a large cash infusion in the business." He squeezed her hand. "It means we willna be in arrears with Warren, that we can repay Annabelle, and that all the money owed for Sorcha's and Ewan's travel will be paid."

"Isn't it a risk taking on an unknown partner?" She fought a frown and failed.

"Aye, but we already ken John. Also Warren wrote up the contract, and he's honest and honorable." Alistair stared at the bright blue sky's cloudless perfection through the window. "There is risk in livin', Lettie. This seems a risk worth taking."

"Why?" she whispered.

"John's as good, or better, with horses than I am. His presence at the livery will allow me to have more time with ye and Hortence." He met her gaze. "With any bairns we might have."

He smiled as she flushed. "I dinna like that we had to rush reviewin' the contracts, but we wanted everythin' signed afore I left for Helena, takin' the lawyer with me. Thus, the afternoon ye left town, the partnership was finalized." He sighed. "I fear Old Jack might have already died by the time we return."

She gripped Alistair's hand. "We will be good to his son."

He smiled and, after a few moments of silence, focused on her again. "There is a part of yer story I dinna understand. Why did ye no' go with yer aged aunt?"

Leticia shuddered and bowed her head. "She didn't want me."

Alistair shifted in his seat so he could better see her. After cupping her face and stroking her cheek with his thumbs, he murmured, "What?"

"She had just begun a relationship with a gentleman of some standing and feared that the arrival of her disgraced, dissolute great-niece would interrupt her chances with such a man. She was the one who suggested I find a protector."

Alistair frowned. "But ye're her family."

Her bitter smile turned down the corners on her lips. "Not everyone has a family like yours, Alistair. When a woman is all alone and is determined to survive, determined to find a way for herself in this world, she will often sacrifice all those around her. Including her family." She shrugged. "I was seen as expendable."

"Why do ye still write her?" He continued to caress her cheek in an effort to give her some comfort.

"I needed the illusion of family. I wanted Hortence to believe someone else in this world would care for her if I weren't here." She reached up and cupped his cheek. "Before I met you and the MacKinnons and was accepted."

"Did she ever apologize?" Alistair asked.

Leticia laughed, a bitter bark that caused Alistair to shiver. "Heavens, no. Great-Aunt Maude believed I was delusional to turn my nose up at such a man as the widower in Saint Louis. She thought I had too many scruples and that I shouldn't allow my concern that I might still be married to prevent me from marrying another." Leticia shuddered as she fought tears. "It took me a long time to realize that she was little more than a well-paid courtesan."

"Aye, an' one clingin' to her looks couldna have one as beautiful as ye around to distract her gentlemen friends," Alistair said. "Ye have to know that was her real concern."

Leticia nodded. "I do now. At the time I was hurt and confused and terrified."

"An' how is the old bat now?" Alistair growled.

"Living in luxury as her last man left her a sizeable income even though he never married her. She is not that healthy, and I'm certain I'll never see her again." She sighed. "For some reason, that saddens me."

Alistair grunted as he settled into his seat with Leticia cradled in one arm. "There is little I would deny ye. But havin' her visit would be more than I could handle." He let out a breath. "I couldna be kind to a woman who failed to show you the support ye needed for so many years."

Leticia chuckled. "Montana is the last place she'd travel. She enjoys her modern luxuries, and Montana won't have those in her lifetime."

"Thank God for small mercies," he muttered, kissing the top of Leticia's head as he felt the tension drain from her as she laughed in his arms.

CHAPTER 16

*A*listair held her hand as they stood at the back door to Cailean's house. The train had arrived an hour ago, and Leticia had spent the time pacing in the livery. John had seen them and retreated into the tack room without a word to give them privacy. Now Alistair had coaxed her to nearly enter the door. "They're yer family. I thought ye'd want to see Hortence." Alistair squeezed her hand as he dragged her forward.

"I don't want to face Sorcha. Or Ewan," she whispered. "But I can't wait to hold Hortence in my arms again."

He cupped her face, his gentle strokes easing some of her tension. "Ewan badgered me to speak with ye. To find out the truth. Then Sorcha discovered Mrs. Jameson's deception. Sorcha encouraged me to travel to Helena to save ye. Annabelle gave ye refuge, then money to pay for our travels. Cailean attempted to warn that worthless ba ... man away." Alistair broke off before swearing in front of her. "My family loves ye, Leticia. Let them rejoice with us." At her subtle nod, he gripped her hand, leading her across the small porch.

As the door opened, the raucous dinner conversation halted, all eyes turned toward the intruders. After a moment's shocked silence,

Cailean leaped up, grasping Alistair in a hug. He let him go as he saw Leticia. "Leticia, what a wonderful surprise," he said, pulling her close.

Hortence jumped down from her chair, pushing her way through the adults until she threw herself against her mother's skirts. "Mama," she cried.

Leticia fell to her knees, holding her daughter close. "My little love," she whispered in her daughter's ear. "I'm home."

Hortence clung to her like a bur as her mother attempted to stand. Leticia shared a look with Alistair and gave in, sitting on the floor, holding Hortence in her lap. "I'm not leaving ever again, my darling. Not without you."

Her daughter pushed away, tears pouring down her cheeks. "Did you make that bad man go away?"

Leticia smiled as she swiped at her daughter's tears. "Yes, I did. With your papa's and Mr. Clark's help. The bad man's gone forever."

Hortence looked at Alistair and glared. "Are you going to be my papa?"

Alistair smiled, kneeling next to Leticia. He ran a hand over Hortence's braids before reaching down and picking her up. He held her on one of his hips, allowing their gazes to be even. "Aye, I want to be yer papa." He cast a quick glance at his siblings, uncustomarily quiet as they allowed Hortence to have her reunion with them. "I'm married to yer mother. I'd be honored to be yer father."

Hortence let out a small sob, throwing her arms around his neck and holding him tight. "Yes, please," she sobbed.

"Ah, my Little Bug, dinna cry so," he crooned to her, and she soon calmed in his arms. He glanced up to meet the stares of his siblings and Annabelle. "We're home."

Ewan laughed. "We can see that. What took ye so long?" He nodded to Hortence who now rested in Alistair's arms. "She was beginning to fret."

"We had a few … legal concerns to clear up." Alistair shared a long stare, first with Cailean and then with Ewan. "Warren was a tremendous help. I dinna ken who I would have found to trust in Helena."

Annabelle moved to Leticia and helped her stand before pulling her into a tight hug. "Are you truly married?" she asked as she backed away to stare at both of them.

Leticia nodded, unable to hide her contented smile. "He convinced me that we should wed before returning to town."

Cailean motioned for them to join them at the table while Annabelle and Sorcha pulled out plates and silverware for them. Soon they were all seated together, eating dinner. "'Tis how it always should have been, eating dinner as family." His eyes glowed as his brother gripped Leticia's hand.

Hortence remained curled into her mother's side, and she picked at her food. "Mrs. Jameson'll be as mad as a wet cat. That's what Mr. T says."

Leticia couldn't stifle her groan. "That woman was born angry." She ran a soothing hand over her daughter's head. "I wouldn't worry about her. We'll be fine."

Sorcha spoke at last. "I wouldna move into yer home tonight. Stay here. Ye dinna want to alert the townsfolk of yer return and ruin yer first night back with unwanted visitors." She grimaced. "An' I fear Hortence is correct. Mrs. Jameson will be worse than a cornered bear. She still believes ye are to marry her daughter."

"Never mind that her daughter has given no indication of her wish to wed you in recent days," Annabelle said with a wry lift of her eyebrow.

Ewan choked and Sorcha giggled. Alistair looked at his siblings. "What's occurred?"

"Seems that Helen is a fickle lass," Sorcha said as she fought her laughter. "She's already makin' eyes at Ewan."

Alistair shared a chagrined smile with Ewan. "I fear Mrs. Jameson willna give up on me so easily. I should have put an end to such specu-lation afore I left." He looked at Leticia. "But I was too eager to follow ye. I did no' want to waste time arguin' with that woman." He faced his siblings. "What has happened since we've been away?"

Cailean sobered a moment. "Jack died nearly a week ago. John's been with us since then." His jaw tightened a moment. "Barclay wouldn't even wait until the funeral before he evicted John."

Alistair frowned. "And the business?"

"Steady. We are the only livery in town, and those with any sense know John is talented with horses. They mutter about paying the same prices when he cares for them as when you do, but I insist that those are livery rates and not dependent on who does the work."

Alistair bit back a growl. "Good. *Bluidy* fools," he muttered. After a moment, he looked around the table. "What else occurred while we were away?"

Sorcha laughed. "What happens in this town? Little of interest and little to be commented on."

"Except a new store has opened. Another general store to compete with Tobias." Annabelle could not hide the delight from her eyes.

Alistair chuckled. "I bet he's none pleased."

"Madder than a hornet's nest, but he's dropping his prices or risk losing all his customers. Few would swear loyalty to such a cantankerous man." Annabelle smiled at her family. "And, yes, I know there's no need to gloat, Cailean."

"She's taking an inordinate amount of pleasure at the disruption the new store owner has wrought." Cailean smiled and shook his head at his wife.

Ewan tapped at his plate with the tines of his fork. "A newspaper reporter has been hired and is headed this way. A Mr. J. P. McMahon. He's supposed to be a hard-nosed Eastern reporter. We'll have to see what scandals he digs up."

Cailean speared him with an intense stare. "I'll remain hopeful the MacKinnons are spared such infamy."

Ewan shrugged. "I've done little to cause you concern, Cail." His easygoing smile failed to soothe Cailean's tension.

Annabelle gripped Cailean's hand and looked at everyone in turn. "There is family news. We are to be fortunate, in the new year." When they gaped at her with blank stares, she flushed. "You will all soon be aunts and uncles again, and Hortence will have a cousin." She flushed as Ewan hooted, and Alistair grinned. Sorcha jumped up to hug her, and Leticia beamed at her.

"Can I name the baby?" Hortence asked, looking around.

Cailean laughed. "No, wee Hortence. That's for Belle and me to do. But you will have a little cousin to play with."

"But when will she arrive?" she asked.

Annabelle flushed. "Not until January or early February. And your cousin may be a little boy."

Hortence shook her head. "Then why are you celebrating now? Seems you'd wait until the baby arrived. Did the stork get lost?" She looked at her family as they burst out laughing at her question.

Cailean ran a hand over her braids. "I fear he must have, little one. But, soon enough, you'll meet your cousin."

Hortence looked at everyone and frowned as she shook her head. "I'd think you'd have the baby arrive some other way. Would be faster." She glanced around the table at her aunts and uncles who tried not to laugh. She hugged her mother once before she jumped down from her chair to go to the parlor to play.

Annabelle rose to carry the dishes to the sink. She was joined by Leticia and Sorcha, and they huddled around the sink, chatting.

Alistair watched the women as they laughed and spoke while working. "How have things been?" he asked Cailean.

"It's always a challenge when you aren't here." He smiled wryly at his brother. "The horses miss you. They don't take to my crooning the way they do to yours."

Ewan snickered. "'Tis because ye're tone deaf." He laughed as Cailean threw his napkin at him. "Not much has occurred. There's been rampant speculation at the saloons about what was occurin' in Helena."

Alistair sighed. "What were the most popular bets?"

Ewan scratched at his head as he ticked them off on his fingers. "That ye'd kill the husband in a duel and be sent to jail. That ye'd bed her but not wed her. That ye'd not find her."

"Few believed you'd truly wed her," Cailean said. "Not after the last fiasco of a wedding ceremony. Although some hoped you would."

Alistair frowned. "Why?"

His eldest brother rolled his eyes. "They want the celebration that was denied them when the first wedding ceremony was interrupted."

"An' the chance to eat Annabelle's cake without havin' to pay for it," Ewan said.

Alistair relaxed into his chair. He smiled at Leticia as she served him a cup of coffee. "I never realized the town was filled with fools until all this happened."

"Aye, ye did. Ye just did no' do anything that led ye to care." Ewan slurped down a few sips of coffee, rose, slapped Alistair on the back, and headed to the door. "Glad ye're home."

Cailean frowned as his youngest brother headed out the front door. "He thinks that his gambling poses no threat to the family now because Leticia's former husband is no longer here."

"He'll learn soon enough it's a danger to himself and to all of us. But only he can learn that lesson," Alistair said around a sip of coffee.

That evening he lay in his bed in his old room at his brother's house, waiting for Leticia to arrive. She was tucking Hortence in for the night. When the door creaked open, he roused himself from a half-dozing state. "Come to bed, love."

She slipped out of her clothes, washed, and donned her nightgown. He held the bed covers up for her, and she cuddled next to him.

His contented sigh escaped. "I love holdin' ye," he murmured. "Why a nightgown?"

She burrowed farther into his embrace. "I'll have to wear a nightgown from now on. If Hortence needs me, I can't run to her with nothing on."

Alistair chuckled. "No, ye couldna." He groaned. "Does this mean I must wear my underclothes to bed?"

She propped herself up on her elbow to look down at him. Her fingers traced the curve of his lips as he teased her. "Only if you want to."

His loving stare met hers. "I want to be a good papa. Of course I will." He coaxed her down to rest beside him. "Let me hold my wife."

His arms closed around her as she fitted her back to his front. "How is wee Hortence?"

"Delighted to have a sleepover in her aunt Sorcha's room. I fear they won't sleep much tonight. When I left, Sorcha was teaching her how to spin yarn." Leticia traced a hand over the arm curled around her waist. "I think Hortence forgives me for leaving her."

"Of course she does. Because ye came back." Alistair kissed the top of her head. "Ye've raised a wonderful girl."

She sniffled. "Thank you, Alistair. Even after you came to Helena and insisted I leave him, I didn't allow myself to imagine my reunion with Hortence. I feared something would happen, and it would never come true." She rolled until she hugged him. "Thank you."

"We all love wee Hortence," Alistair rasped. "We'd no' allow anything to happen to her."

She shook her head. "Thank you for ensuring she did not live with the self-doubt of why her mother didn't love her enough to stay." She kissed his chest.

"Aye, an' now she has two parents who love her." He ran a hand over her back. "Does she understand that the man she calls 'the bad man' was her father?"

Leticia shook her head. "No. I never told her. He never truly planned on claiming her so I didn't see the point."

Alistair pulled her close. "It doesna matter now. She has us and aunts and uncles. She'll never worry if she is loved." He held Leticia close as a few of her tears leaked onto his chest. "Rest, my love. For tomorrow we must face the townsfolk." He waited until she had slipped into sleep before he relaxed and followed her into slumber.

CHAPTER 17

The following morning, Alistair set aside his pitchfork as the livery door burst open. He walked down the aisle to shut the door behind the tiny woman who marched inside. As they walked down the center of the livery, they moved from patches of sunlight to shadow. He stopped in the shadows, while the woman remained in the sun, her expression readily visible.

"You've played my daughter false, and I will see you pay!" Mrs. Jameson screeched. Her reddened cheeks shone with a thin layer of perspiration. "I've just learned from the stationmaster that you were seen last night, escorting that doxy from the train station."

Alistair fought anger as the tic in his jaw increased. "There was never any agreement between Helen and me, ye daft woman."

"You were seen in the woods. Any kind of compromising activity could have occurred." She stood with her bosom out and her hands on her hips as she dared him to defy her.

"Ask yer daughter. Nothing happened."

"She has made no such denial."

"An' no such accusation!" Alistair roared.

"If you do not do the decent thing and marry my daughter, you will live with the infamy in this town as a defiler, a … a debaucher of innocents." She glared triumphantly at him as she waited with expectant hope that he would act as she wished.

Alistair took a deep breath and pinched his nose. "I canna marry her, Mrs. Jameson."

"Don't give me that hogwash about love and respect. I've heard enough of that from Helen these past few weeks." She tapped Alistair on his chest. "Plain and simple, you and my daughter would suit."

He chuckled. "Ye mean it would suit you. Ye want me as yer son-in-law, not for what I would provide yer daughter but what ye hope to gain from me."

"How dare you believe me so mercenary."

Alistair's amused expression transformed into a glower. "Were ye no' the one determined to defame and destroy Leticia, even to the point of giving her ex-husband money to help him leave town with her? Were ye no' the one willing to bankrupt me in your vendetta against Leticia? Were ye no' the woman with no regard for wee Hortence, ripped from her mother's side?" He glared at Mrs. Jameson. "*Mercenary* isn't a harsh-enough word for a woman like you."

Mrs. Jameson lifted her chin higher, no sign of contrition in her countenance. "A mother must do what she has to so as to ensure her children are well cared for."

"A mother should instill honor and loyalty and justice. Somethin' ye fail, daily, to do."

"Enough with your attempts to delay your marriage to my daughter." Her jaws snapped shut. "I want the announcement made by tomorrow, and I expect you to be wed by September."

Alistair cleared his throat and half smiled, his eyes lit with wicked mischief. "Well, that would pose a problem for yer daughter. I can only have one wife at a time." He waited a moment as she continued to glare at him. "My wife, Leticia, would object. As would I."

Mrs. Jameson gasped and nearly fell over due to her shock and tightly bound corset. "You can't have married that lying harlot! Not after all I did ..." She broke off, paling as she belatedly saw the air of contentment around him.

"I expect ye to speak about my wife with more respect from now on. And I married her in Helena." His smile bloomed. "We plan to hold a reception here in a week or so."

"It's an abomination!" she sputtered.

He leaned forward, his face inches from hers as he met her startled gaze. "Dinna test me, Mrs. Jameson. Word is spreading as we speak about the role ye played in Leticia's misery. Dinna make it worse for yerself."

Leticia walked through town, one arm slung through Alistair's elbow, the other gripping Hortence's hand. She raised her chin as she met the curious gazes of those they passed. Blatant animosity was soon well concealed as few desired to anger Alistair. Leticia smiled at those who moved out of their way, allowing them to walk down the boardwalk with little impediment.

When they turned down a small street toward their new home, she heaved a sigh of relief. "That's over," she muttered.

"'Tis only beginning. Ye braved that walk, but ye must brave it many more times afore ye'll feel comfortable," Alistair murmured. They arrived at their house, and he extracted the key. He ushered Leticia and Hortence in before him and hung his hat on a peg by the front door. "Home."

She smiled at him at his whispered word. "Yes, home." She held out a hand for Hortence. "Come, darling. Let me show you to your room." She led her upstairs to a square-shaped room. On top of the bed was a small knitted throw blanket, in varying shades of red. "Look what your aunt Sorcha made for you."

Hortence traced the soft wool with her fingers and smiled with wonder at her mother. "It's beautiful but why red, Mama?"

Leticia sat on the bed and draped one arm over her daughter's shoulders. "She wanted colors that matched the beauty of your hair."

Hortence's hand immediately went to her hair, and she shook her head. "It's ugly. A 'bomnation."

Leticia frowned. "Who told you that the color of your hair was an abomination?" When Hortence shrugged, Leticia asked, "One of the children you know from school?"

"Yes. He repeated what he was told after church when my aunts and uncles chatted and I played with the other kids," Hortence mumbled, looking at her feet.

"Well, I fear your aunt heard of the ridiculous mutterings being repeated by those who are too young to know better." She lifted her daughter's head with two fingers under her chin. "Your aunt wants you to realize how beautiful you are. Your hair is beautiful too. Soon those in this town will be jealous that you are so blessed."

"I have red hair, Mama. It's the work of the devil."

Leticia clamped her jaw shut a moment rather than give voice to her anger. "It is not." She traced her daughter's cheek.

"You didn't leave me because you worried I was evil?" Hortence whispered.

Leticia groaned and pulled her onto her lap. "No, my darling, no. You are wonderful and brave and kind. You are the furthest from evil as anyone could be." She hugged her close. "This is advice for both of us, my most precious daughter. We must each ignore the horrible, mean, spiteful words said by those who are jealous of us or who wish us ill." She swiped at her daughter's tears. "We are brave, strong, and honorable. We have a family who loves us. We will never be alone or abandoned again. I promise you."

She held Hortence in her arms as her daughter cried. When she had gone limp after having fallen asleep in her mother's arms, Leticia laid her down on her bed, pulling the throw blanket around her. She tiptoed from the room, leaving the door ajar.

She walked downstairs, smiling as she saw Alistair pouring boiling water into a teakettle. "I never realized you could make tea."

Alistair's answering smile faded when he saw the residual torment and anger in her eyes. "What happened?"

She sat at the table and reached for his hand, ignoring the steeping tea and cookies. "Hortence suffered more than I realized. She cried herself to sleep." She took a deep breath. "I should have known that the townsfolk's venom would extend to her, but I had hoped that they would show more decency than to attack a child."

"What did they say?" Alistair asked, his grip tightening on hers.

"That she was not lovable because of her red hair. That it was ugly. That she came from the devil and was evil and that was why I did not want her as my daughter." She held a hand to her mouth as she bit back further words and a sob.

"Idiots," Alistair rasped. "Can they no' ken what such words will do to a child?" His tormented gaze met hers. "I'm sorry."

She looked at him helplessly. "It's all my fault. If I'd had the strength to divorce him, to ensure he could never be in our lives, then this would never have happened."

He swiped at her cheeks and smiled at her tenderly. "Ye must forgive yerself, Lettie. Ye did what ye thought was best. Ye couldna have kent what would happen." He paused. "Hortence will only know love and acceptance from now on. Ye do ken that?"

She nodded. "Yes. Somehow your sister heard the rumors. She must have, because she made the most beautiful afghan for Hortence." At Alistair's quizzical frown, she said, "It's in all the colors of red that shine in Hortence's hair when lit by the sun. She made a masterpiece to show Hortence how beautiful red can be."

Alistair smiled. "How lovely of her. She's taken a shine to our Hortence. An' Sorcha can be fierce. I fear for anyone who's caught speakin' against my Little Bug."

Leticia smiled and took a deep breath. "I should prepare supper and unpack."

He rose with her and shook his head. "No need to cook tonight. Annabelle is coming by with supper for us. She thought ye'd not have time to travel to the Merc and purchase supplies." He held out his hand. "I'll help ye settle in upstairs."

She followed him upstairs, pausing as she entered their room. "What?" she gasped. On their bed was a beautiful quilt, made of scraps of cloth from old clothes she had thought lost. She spun to stare at Alistair. "Who made us such a quilt?" she whispered.

"I thought these were destroyed in the wash," Alistair whispered as he fingered a piece of cloth from a shirt and then another.

"This was a nearly threadbare dress. It went missing one day when out on the line. I thought it had blown away," Leticia murmured about the faded blue cloth she traced. "Would Sorcha have done this?"

"Aye, and Annabelle. She mightn't be good at sewin', but ye can see where she attempted to help." He fingered uneven stitches and shared a smile with his wife. "This is the surprise Sorcha teased me about."

"Didn't Ewan say he had left us a surprise?" she murmured as she entered the room, and Alistair shut the door behind them.

Alistair chuckled. "Aye. He'd decorated the room in flowers and candles, with rose petals on the bed. Seems he'd read about such things in a novel." He smiled as Leticia sighed. "He cleaned it all away the day after the first wedding ceremony. Cailean told me what he had done last night when we were chatting."

"Oh, poor Ewan. To have gone to all that trouble for no reason." She ducked her head.

"I ken he doesna mind, no' now that we're married."

"I had a surprise for you too," she whispered as she blushed red. At his inquisitive stare, she dropped her gaze before taking a deep breath and meeting his gaze. "I had bought something special for our wedding night. A special nightdress."

He groaned and kissed her. "I hope ye did no' toss it in the rubbish." When her flush intensified, he gave a satisfied grunt. "Surprise me some night, wife." They shared a long smile.

After a moment Leticia ran a hand over his shoulder before she moved to unpack her small bag. She opened the closet and stood still. "I'd forgotten," she whispered.

He lounged on the bed with his legs stretched out, feet dangling over the side so as not to dirty the new quilt. "What, love?"

"All the clothes I'd already moved here. I'd forgotten they were here, waiting for me." She rubbed at a tear as she looked at a new dress Sorcha had made her before the wedding. "I was to wear this on our honeymoon."

Alistair laughed. "We've already had all the time away we can afford while in Helena." He saw her running her fingertips over her clothes. "Why did ye no' come here to get the clothes that were right-fully yers?"

She shrugged and moved to empty her bag. "I did. Once. A few days after I moved in at Annabelle's." She took a deep breath, and she faced away from him as she worked. "I was advised by Sheriff Sampson that, if I entered your house, anything I removed could constitute theft. I never came back here again. Not until that night you found me here, trying to let go of my dreams for us."

He rolled until he was on the other side of the bed and nearer to her. He gripped her hand and tugged until she faced him. "I canna lie an' say I wouldna have acted like a fool and railed at ye for enterin' the house. I didna enter it again until today. I couldna." His eyes gleamed with regret. "I couldna return here without ye." He shook his head. "I hate I was such a fool. I didna consider what my pride cost ye."

She shook her head as a few tears fell. "We hurt each other, Alistair. I will not deny that you hurt me. Your absence hurt Hortence." She sat and faced him. "I don't want the past to continue to intrude on our present and future. We are together again. Josiah will never come between us because you had enough faith in me to hire Warren." She attempted a watery smile. "Can we agree that we both were hurt, but that we will try not to focus on it?"

He nodded, leaning forward to kiss her. "Aye, my love. Aye. But nothin' ye say or do will take away my regret for actin' like a jealous fool."

She smiled, her fingers tracing the grooves of his face. "I love you, Alistair MacKinnon."

Her words lifted the concern in his eyes, and he smiled fully. "And I love ye, my beloved wife, Leticia MacKinnon." He settled back against the pillows as Leticia rose to continue her work.

The following morning, Leticia left Hortence with Annabelle and Sorcha at the bakery and walked to the General Store. She had waved off everyone's concerns about her venturing to the store alone, although she suspected Annabelle saw through Leticia's forced calm. However, Leticia was determined to face one of Bear Grass Springs's worst gossips and critics head-on.

The bell over the door sang, and she squared her shoulders as a group of women congregated near the linens turned to see who had entered. Their glares before they spurned any form of greeting from her signaled she was far from forgiven. She walked to the glass counter and met Tobias's derisive gaze.

"Hello, Mr. Sutton," she murmured as she set her empty basket on the floor and placed her list on the countertop. After a few moments, where he merely raised an eyebrow and refused to respond to her greeting, she said, "I would like to have this order filled."

He glanced at the other women in the room and shook his head. "I have no reason to serve a woman like you."

Leticia stiffened. "Is that so? Would you prefer if I took my custom to the new upstart setting up shop across the street from the Boudoir? Would you prefer if I spoke with Annabelle, advising her that the MacKinnons should no longer shop here? I'm certain your aunt and uncle would be interested to know how you treat a returning customer and to see if they would obtain better rates at the new business."

"Quiet your jabberin'," he snapped as the gaggle of women leaned in their direction to overhear their conversation. "I offer the best prices in town. Everyone knows that."

Leticia laughed at his boast. "That is what you proclaim. However, I find it remarkable how the rate you charge depends upon the standing of each particular woman's husband in town. Or the lack of a husband." Her gaze turned flinty as she glared at him. "My husband, Alistair MacKinnon, will be disappointed to hear of your treatment of me today."

"Now no need to be hasty," Tobias said as he slapped his hand over her list before she could grab it and depart. "I'm certain this is a minor disagreement."

Leticia took a deep breath as she stared at him. "Is it minor when you exclude my daughter from the half-penny treat, informing her that little girls like her should know better than to enter your store?" She raised her chin. "Is it minor when you spread false, hurtful rumors about me in an attempt to force me from town?" She leaned forward, ignoring the fact that the group of women had sidled closer to them. "Is it minor when you join together with Mrs. Jameson in an attempt to force Alistair to marry her daughter?"

He held up his hands to ward off her verbal barrage. "Now there's no proof to anything you say."

"Actually there is, Tobias," one of the women in the group said, her mouth turned down in displeasure. "My daughter was there when you treated Hortence abominably."

"And we all heard the rumors. We knew they couldn't have come solely from Mrs. Jameson," another said.

A third leaned forward and tapped a finger on the countertop. "Do you really change your prices depending on who places the order?"

"Ladies, ladies," he sputtered, "this is nonsense invented by a spiteful woman we all know to be a liar. Her failed wedding proved it of her."

The mother shook her head. "No, that ceremony only showed she had bad judgment. And that she'd been foolish not to divorce the man."

The women talked among themselves, although, from the snippets Leticia heard, they condemned Tobias and saw her in a new light. While she might not yet be absolved of all her misdeeds, these influential women would speak of her in a more positive light after leaving the store.

"She's probably lying about being married!" Tobias sputtered.

Leticia laughed as the women looked at her. "Not that a wedding ring proves anything, but Alistair MacKinnon and I were properly married by a preacher in Helena. Mr. Clark witnessed the ceremony."

"Seems unusual to have the wedding away from his family," a woman muttered.

"We wanted there to be no doubt when we returned to Bear Grass Springs." She smiled at the women who studied her.

"She has that contented look," one muttered, provoking Leticia to flush fiercely.

Leticia turned to Tobias. "I hope you will fill my order?" Her gaze flicked to the list under his hand. She smiled as he glowered at her.

"Don't think a reception will make the townsfolk forgive you," he snapped as he lifted the list to examine it.

"A reception!" the women exclaimed. "Oh, we love any reason to celebrate and dance."

"And we hope that Annabelle will bake a cake. We were rudely denied your cake at your first ceremony."

Leticia sputtered out a laugh. "I believe that was because there was no wedding." She shook her head at the women. "I hope you understand I meant no harm. I taught your children with all the expertise available to me. And I've loved being a part of this community."

The mother patted Leticia's hand. "I know. Hopefully all will come to understand why you acted as you did and have their faith restored in you. You did what you had to in order to survive and to keep your daughter safe. As mothers, we can commiserate."

After a few more moments, the women left, and Leticia remained with Tobias.

"You believe yourself to be so cunning," he rasped.

She shook her head. "No, I don't. I merely want the people in this town to know the truth. And not just about me. About everyone here." She leaned forward as though imparting a great secret. "You preside over your store like a little king, and you believe you have the right to pass judgment on those who enter it. Either by your treatment or by the prices you charge." She paused and took a deep breath. "But you don't. You have no idea what each patron is struggling with."

"You will never understand me."

She laughed. "You're right. I won't, and I must admit that does not sadden me. However, I fear that someday your misdeeds will come back to haunt you." She met his irate gaze. "I'll return in a few hours to collect my items." She spun on her heel and walked with her head high out of the store.

CHAPTER 18

*A*listair stood inside the livery, his hands hung over a stall as he watched John work. By the time Alistair had arrived this morning, water had been hauled in to each stall and over half the stalls had been mucked out. For the first time since opening the livery with Cailean four years ago, Alistair had spare time. Cailean had gone to speak with Warren, so Alistair was alone with John in the livery.

He frowned as John sweet-talked his horse, Brindle. "Dinna fall in love with her. She's mine, lad."

John looked up, his black eyes fathomless and impossible to read. He gave Brindle a final pat and moved to enter another stall.

"Nae, come here," Alistair said, pointing to the stools he and Cailean always sat on for their chats. "Seems we'll need a third." He watched as John sat, his body ready to bound up and away at a moment's notice. "Relax," Alistair said with a shake of his head "'Tis my second day back. We should discuss this partnership a little."

John remained silent, waiting for Alistair to speak.

Alistair picked up a piece of hay and ran it through his fingers. "I dinna ken what ye think working with us means, but ye are no' our drudge. Ye dinna need to have all the work done afore I or Cail arrive." He shrugged. "'Twas nice not to have to muck out stalls or carry water, but 'tis part of livery work, aye?"

He frowned when John remained quiet. "I'd hoped with yer arrival we could consider expandin' our animal husbandry business. I'm a decent farrier, but it takes time. With three of us here, there should be time now."

His frown turned into a glower as John continued to stare at him. "Do ye never speak? Do ye have no opinions of yer own?"

His black eyes gleamed. "I hate bookwork."

"Aye. Cailean does that." He waited for John to speak again.

"My name is Bears or Runs from Bears. Not John." His defiant gaze was challenging, but he relaxed when he saw Alistair nod. "I like soothing the horse that is deemed untamable."

Alistair smiled. "Ye should have a go with Mr. Tompkins's cantankerous beast, Brutus. He's the reason the man's pantaloons are all patched." He chuckled as a glimmer of humor shone in Bears's eyes.

Alistair sobered after a moment. "I'm sorry about yer father's death. He was a good man."

Bears nodded.

After a prolonged silence, Alistair cleared his throat. "There is one thing neither I nor Cailean will tolerate." He spit out the piece of hay between his teeth. "We willna accept others treatin' ye poorly. If they disrespect ye, we want to ken about it."

Bears frowned as he cocked his head to one side to study Alistair. "Why? I'll always be treated differently."

"In here, ye're our partner. An' we stick together." He nodded as Bears blinked his agreement.

They rose and moved to a stall where Bears had been nursing a sickly horse back to health. Soon they were lost in the world of the livery and horses.

∽

L eticia hummed to herself as she washed dishes after a busy day at the bakery, looking forward to heading home to Alistair and Hortence. Leticia had received word from Alistair that he would collect the supplies from the Merc and then Hortence from Sorcha's care. Although Leticia had feared that the locals would shun Annabelle due to Leticia's presence—even after word had leaked of her marriage to Alistair—business had been brisk at the bakery. Leticia smiled as the back door opened, expecting to see Annabelle returning from her deliveries. Her smile transformed into a frown as Fidelia shut the door behind her. "Annabelle's not here." The cold, crisp words were as unwelcoming as she felt.

Fidelia paused a moment before walking to the counter and pulling out a stool to sit. She was drawn and looked thinner than the few times she had spent Sunday dinner with the family a year ago. "I'll wait."

Leticia shrugged, although her hands tightly gripped the cloth she had used to dry the bowls. She put away the plates, bowls, and other cooking instruments, ignoring Annabelle's sister.

"You succeeded," Fidelia whispered, her voice laced with bitterness. "You escaped your fate."

Leticia met Fidelia's outraged gaze. "I don't understand what you mean. I'm living my fate."

Fidelia flushed red with her anger. "No, Leticia. You are no better than me. A liar and a cheat and a woman without a reputation. There's no reason you are here, living with a man who loves you, while I'm stuck in a place like the Boudoir."

Leticia grasped the dishcloth in an attempt to hide her shaking hands. "I'm sorry your life hasn't gone as you planned ..." Her voice broke as Fidelia grabbed the cloth from her and tugged it away.

"Stop with the meaningless inanities!" She panted out a breath. "I hate you. I will always hate you."

Leticia stood frozen, her gaze fixed on Fidelia's. The spell was broken when the back door slammed shut.

"What is this about hate?" Annabelle asked in a soft voice. She grabbed her sister's arm, preventing her from leaving. "Hello, Dee. I've missed you. It's been too long since I've seen you."

Leticia lowered her head and scurried from the room.

"Yes, run away. Although you can't hide from the truth!" Fidelia yelled after her.

"Fidelia!" Annabelle snapped. "Although I wish you to visit me again, if you are going to treat Leticia poorly, I will ask you not to return."

Fidelia stilled, the anger in her gaze replaced by disillusionment for a moment. "Of course. You'll always choose someone else other than me."

Annabelle stood in front of her sister, blocking her easy escape from the room. "That's not true. I hope someday you'll know that's not true." Her astute gaze roved over her sister. "You look terrible. You're at least ten pounds too thin, and your makeup is too heavy again." She raised a hand, stilling her movement when Fidelia flinched away from any possible contact to her face. Annabelle frowned. "He's visited you again, hasn't he? And he's abused you again."

Fidelia shrugged. "Of course. I knew the Madam's promise was worthless in the face of her greed." She reached behind her and sat on the stool. She watched as Annabelle fought tears. "I'm not worth crying over."

Annabelle sniffled. "I am the one who determines your worth to me, and, as my sister, you are precious." She moved to the icebox and pulled out milk. She extracted a cake and cut a thick slice. "Eat."

She watched, the worry evident in her gaze as Fidelia gobbled down the cake. "Aren't they feeding you there?"

Fidelia shrugged. "The Madam has read that men like thinner women. She's decided to cut the food budget."

"Then who eats the buns I bring every day?" Annabelle demanded.

"She and her henchmen. She has three now. It's only on the days you give the basket to one of us that we get any of it." Fidelia rubbed at her forehead. "I should never have told you that."

"If she has three henchmen, why don't they prevent anyone from harming you?" Annabelle frowned as her gaze took in her sister's protective posture on the stool.

"They do from everyone but that one man. The Madam wants his money, and she will do whatever he wants to ensure she receives it. She believes she can always find another whore if the worst happens." She met her sister's shocked, irate gaze. "She knows few would mourn the death of a whore."

Annabelle took a deep, rasping breath. "I would. I would mourn forever."

Fidelia looked at her empty plate, ignoring the terror in her sister's gaze. "She's hoping for a virgin auction soon."

"A what?" Annabelle gasped.

"An auction where she sells a virgin to the highest bidder." Fidelia stooped lower onto the stool. "Only a desperate woman would want one of those men ..." She shook her head. "I beg your pardon. I should never discuss such things with you."

Annabelle pulled out a stool and sat down. "I like to believe I am not so naive. After all I'm a married woman. I lost my first child, suffering the miscarriage alone. I understand the cruel realities of the world. But I never considered such a thing." Her hand shook as she set it on the countertop.

Fidelia reached forward and clasped her hand. "Life is harsh. And unjust. And mean." She looked around the bakery. "It's not all cakes and cookies and sweetness." She blinked as though clearing away tears. "Although the reminder that such things exist is a balm."

Annabelle squeezed her sister's hand, frowning when her sister freed herself from any further contact with her. "Speaking of sweet things"—she raised the knife over the cake as well as her eyebrow—"another piece?" She watched hunger war with fear in Fidelia's gaze, finally making the decision for her and cutting her a smaller slice. "Here. Eat. I refuse to watch you starve while also suffering beatings so that woman can prosper."

"Who was the cake for?" Fidelia asked around a mouthful of chocolate cake.

Annabelle flushed. "For me. For the family." She looked down and shrugged. "I'm to have a child. I have tremendous cravings."

Fidelia's fork clattered to the plate, and she stared openmouthed at her sister. "You're expecting?" Her gaze flitted over her sister, and she sighed. "I should have paid more attention. The signs are there, but I didn't notice."

"We're just beginning to tell family and friends," Annabelle whispered.

Fidelia bit her lip and pushed her plate away. "I fear I will be a useless aunt."

Annabelle grabbed her sister's hand. "No, you will be a wonderful aunt. I will want my baby to know you. To know Aunt Fidelia."

She scoffed. "Yes, let's visit auntie in the whorehouse. I'm sure that's what your husband's always wanted for his child." She stood, knocking over the stool behind her. "I wish you well, Anna. You've found happiness."

Annabelle jumped up, racing after her sister. "Dee," she rasped, grabbing her arm. "You don't have to return there. You never have to return there. We would help you."

Her sister turned a deadened gaze to Annabelle. "Your desire to help is six years too late, Anna. Thanks for the cake." She wrenched her arm free and slammed the door shut behind her.

~

Alistair entered the General Store and waited as Tobias attended to another patron. He listened for the door to close behind the customer before he focused on Tobias. He smiled with grim satisfaction as he saw his glower caused Tobias to pale. "I'm most displeased with how I heard ye treated my wife today."

Tobias raised his chin in defiance. "She got the treatment she deserved."

Alistair slapped his hands onto the counter, causing the glass to rattle in the case. "No, she didna. She got the scorn and derision of a bitter, angry man. Ye be careful, Tobias. Ye are no' the only mercantile in town any longer. We have other options where we can purchase our goods from."

Tobias gave a derisive snort. "Your wife said much the same. I'm not worried."

"Ye should be. Yer aunt and uncle help keep ye afloat with their bulk purchases for the café. 'Tis no great secret. However, even their patience for how ye are treating the townsfolk is runnin' thin." He smiled with satisfaction as he saw Tobias grimace.

"They are loyal to family." He swiped at a sweaty brow.

"Ye'd better hope they remain so." Alistair stood tall. "I have no regard for a man who preys on the weak, who bullies women, and harasses those he knows have no one to champion them." He leaned forward as though imparting a secret. "It doesna make ye a man. Nor does it prove ye strong."

"What do you want?"

"The order my wife placed. And for ye to ken I'll be paying close attention, Tobias. As will all the MacKinnon men." He watched as Tobias hefted boxes of supplies from the back of the store and dropped them on the ground near the counter. "Would ye have helped my wife had she come alone?"

When Tobias shrugged, Alistair shook his head in disgust as he lifted a heavy box and walked out the door to a waiting wagon. He repeated the trip three times before paying the bill and leaving the Merc, stopping by the family home to pick up Hortence, and then heading to his new home.

Leticia stormed out of the bakery, intent on returning home. She walked down the back alley behind the main street buildings, with few lingering outside in the midafternoon heat. She stopped short when a man blocked her path. "If you would excuse me, sir," she said.

He matched her sidestepping movements and laughed as she flushed with aggravation. His brown eyes gleamed with malice as he saw her discomfort. "I thought you would soon join the beauties at the Boudoir, rather than run away with that useless scoundrel."

She shivered at his words. "I'll never go to the Boudoir." She stiffened her spine and raised her head. "I'm a married woman. Alistair MacKinnon will be displeased to hear of your mistreatment of me."

He laughed. "Speaking with a lovely woman is not a crime." He reached forward as though to stroke a finger down her arm, and she jerked away from his touch. "Jittery. That can soon be ... worked out of you."

She shuddered at the word *worked*. "You have no reason to be upset with me, Mr. Jameson. Your sister would never have success with my husband."

He laughed as he loomed over her, lowering his face so his whiskey- and coffee-tinged breath wafted over her. "My sister will never have success with any man. I hope my mother realizes that and allows her to earn money for us some other way."

Leticia blanched at Walter Jameson's blatant disregard for his only sibling. "I would think you'd protect your sister."

"She's a stupid, fat woman. She's none of my concern." His lascivious gaze roved over Leticia's body. "Whereas you, ... you are quite fascinating."

She glared at him, hating the quiver of fear that raced through her at his look. "I am nothing to you, sir."

He nodded. "Not yet," he murmured. "Not yet." He moved to stand in the shadows, and Leticia wasted no time racing past him as she rushed for home.

When she arrived there, she went upstairs and slammed the door shut to the room she shared with Alistair. She shrugged out of her dress and moved to the ewer, pouring out cold water to wash. Her hands shook as she scrubbed clean before donning another dress. She set the day's dress to be washed and then collapsed on the bed.

A while later she woke to Alistair caressing her cheek. "Love," he whispered as he bent to kiss her forehead. She gasped and wrenched away from him. He froze, watching her with confused, guarded eyes. "Leticia? What's the matter?"

She shook her head, her gaze wild as she panted in an attempt to catch her breath after waking in a panic. She watched as he departed, and she collapsed back onto the bed, crying into her pillow. A moment later, she heard the door open and close, soft boot steps, and then the bed dipping near her hip.

"Leticia"—he softly stroked her arm—"I made sure wee Hortence is settled for now. Will ye tell me what is the matter?"

"I … Will you hold me?" she whispered, holding up an arm as she lay on her side. She heard him kick off his boots as he settled onto the bed. Soon she was hauled up against him, nestled in his arms. After a few minutes, the quaking receded, and she relaxed in his arms. "I thought I had begun to be accepted in town today. Women at the Merc stood up for me against Tobias." She sniffled. "I'm such a fool."

"Ye're the furthest I've ever seen from a fool," he soothed. He rocked her back and forth.

She was silent for many minutes, silent tears coursing down her cheeks as her fingers played with a button on his shirtsleeve cuff. "I never encouraged him."

He stiffened underneath her, although his caresses to her back and arms remained gentle. "Did someone hurt ye?" he rasped.

"With words," she murmured. "Walter Jameson was in the alley behind the bakery today. He said he was disappointed I hadn't been forced to the Boudoir for survival. That he would have enjoyed seeing me there."

"Bastard," Alistair hissed. "No one has the right to speak to ye in such a manner, my love."

She curled into him. "I fear many will doubt the legitimacy of our marriage for some time. Too many disapprove of divorce, and others are eager to believe the worst of me."

He kissed her. "Nothing can be done except give them time. We know the truth. Our family accepts the truth. That is what matters." He kissed her nose. "Hortence is happy."

Leticia curled into him as she fought a sob. "Yes, she is." She took a deep breath. "I saw Annabelle's sister. She too believed I belonged in the Boudoir. Said she would always hate me for escaping my fate."

Alistair made a deep noise in his throat and tugged her closer. "She's a jealous, spiteful woman who canna see the good fortune of having her sister move to this town and attempt to help her escape her miserable reality at the Boudoir. She's intent on making everyone else around her wretched. Don't give her the satisfaction, Lettie."

Leticia let out a deep breath. "I couldn't help but wonder at all we don't know about her, my love." She raised her head and met his worried gaze. "At the root of it all, I think she is jealous of me. Of the life I have, and she can't stand that I have this life when she doesn't."

Alistair kissed her head. "The thought of ye at the Boudoir is more than I can handle." He leaned into her palm as she stroked his cheek. "I ken she's jealous and that it makes her mean, but she doesna have the right to upset ye. Or Anna."

Leticia rested her head on his chest. "I fell asleep and dreamed of life in the Boudoir. I thought you were a man come to pay for his time," she whispered.

He groaned as he tugged her closer. "I promise ye that ye will never live there. Ye've family now. We will always care for ye." The tension in his hold eased as she relaxed again in his embrace, only to be interrupted when his stomach rumbled loudly.

"I didn't make supper," she whispered.

He laughed as he eased her out from under him and rose, reaching a hand down for her. "I know. I picked up the supplies from the Merc, and they await sorting in the kitchen." He traced a finger down her cheek. "Although I did put the things away in the icebox." He grinned as his stomach grumbled again. "Come. Let's go to the café. We can have our first home-cooked meal tomorrow."

He linked their hands and walked with her downstairs, calling for Hortence who played in her room. Leticia fixed her hair and smiled as Alistair hefted Hortence to his hip as they departed for the café.

"Are you better, Mama?" Hortence whispered. "Papa told me that I needed to play quietly while he soothed you."

"Oh, I'm all better, little love," Leticia said. "I needed a little rest and then to speak with your papa."

Hortence reached her hand out to her mother, shifting from Alistair's hold to her mother's. "Remember what you told me, Mama. Words only have power if you give it to them."

Leticia shared a long look with Alistair and then kissed her daughter's head. "We all need to be reminded of that lesson, my little darling."

They arrived at the café, and Alistair followed his wife and daughter inside. He smiled at Irene who fussed over Leticia and then whisked Hortence away to the kitchen.

Harold winked at them as he filled their water glasses. "We can't do much by way of a wedding present, but we can give you a dinner for the two of you."

Leticia flushed. "I spent plenty of time separated from her, and Alistair and I had time alone in Helena. Once she's had her visit with Irene, I'd like for her to have dinner with us."

Harold nodded. "Of course." He pointed to the board propped against the wall. "You have two options for this evening." He waited as they read them before he whispered, "I'd recommend the trout." After Leticia and Alistair agreed with his suggestion, he wandered away to speak with other customers before delivering their order to Irene in the kitchen.

Alistair played with his wife's fingers. "All is well, love. Eating dinner at the café only helps the townsfolk accustom themselves to seeing ye with me again."

She smiled and traced his thumb with one of her fingers. "School starts soon. The new teacher is to arrive any day." She bit her lip. "Do you think he will truly bar Hortence from attending?"

Alistair heaved out a deep breath. "No' if I have anythin' to say about it. But it would help if some of the parents were friendly toward ye."

Leticia shrugged. "I don't know what we can do."

Alistair's smile was wry as he flushed. "I had a run-in yesterday with Mrs. Jameson. She was irate we had tricked her and that I had used her daughter so shamelessly." His eyes flashed with anger. "It took all I had not to do her bodily harm when I think about how she gave that man money so he'd leave town with ye." He took a deep breath as he closed his eyes and tried to relax.

She stroked his hand. "She's a mean, bitter woman, who wants to hurt us because we escaped her net. Just as Cailean did with Annabelle."

"Aye, but she can still harm wee Hortence, and that I canna allow." His brown eyes were molten with their fury. "I advised her that we'd have a reception in a few weeks' time. To thank the town. I think that would be a way to reestablish ye here."

She flushed before giggling. "I promised the same to the women in the Mercantile." Her eyes shone with mischief. "Although I'd said it would be in a week."

"The timing isna what is important. What matters is that we have the reception and invite everyone. Including the Jamesons."

She shuddered. "Why should we invite them?"

Alistair's gaze was cunning. "To show we are above their pettiness. And to make it known, through stories and whispers in the right ears, all that she did in her attempt to separate ye from yer daughter. And from me."

Her smile broadened. "You want to use the town's inherent addiction to gossip against her?"

"Aye, why no'?" He shrugged. "She shouldna be the only one capable of manipulatin' the feelings of those in this town. We should have a say." He squeezed her hand. "With any luck, the new teacher will be here, and he will see how you are esteemed by those in this town. At the very least, he'll doubt any nasty rumors he hears about ye."

Leticia sighed with relief. "I know Anna will make us a cake. Let's say two weeks from Saturday. All we must do is post a flyer at the livery, café, and bakery, and the whole town will know within a day."

CHAPTER 19

Two weeks later Leticia arrived at the bakery earlier than usual. She entered the back door, dragging a sleepy Hortence alongside her. After tucking her into the cot in the back room, Leticia joined Annabelle in the kitchen. "I don't know why I insisted on coming in early. There isn't much I can do to help you."

Annabelle laughed. "I disagree. Stir this for me while I start on another cake batter. My mother always said it had to be stirred at least one hundred times to ensure it rose properly." She grinned. "You can have the arm exercise today!"

"How many cakes are you making?" Leticia asked.

Annabelle shrugged. "I like to believe everything I make will turn out perfectly. However, I'm not that conceited. I'll make an extra layer cake in case one of them sticks to the pan."

Leticia paused as she swiped at her sweaty forehead. "I always thought, if a cake fell apart, you fixed it with icing."

Her friend laughed. "I refuse to have you make do with an iced-together cake. This is your wedding party!" She took the bowl Leticia had just stirred and handed her another with an impish smile and a nod to start stirring. She giggled as Leticia groaned. After pouring the cakes into tins, Annabelle set them aside a moment before putting them in the oven. "I'll wait until you're done and then bake them all at the same time."

"Aren't you opening today?" Leticia asked.

Annabelle shook her head. "No. I put a sign up yesterday, announcing that I was closed for regular business today, but that I would see everyone at the reception." She rolled her eyes. "Irene told me, when I delivered her basket, that the café was humming with excitement. Her patrons couldn't stop talking about the fact they'd eat their fill of my goodies without having to pay for them."

"It would serve them right if we arrived with nothing."

"No, Leticia," she said in a mildly scolding voice. "It's not about them. It's about celebrating you and Alistair. And I'm bound and determined to show how proud I am to have you as part of the family." She swiped at her forehead.

Leticia flushed and smiled her thanks. "Are you still making your baskets for the café, hotel, and Boudoir?"

Annabelle shook her head. "No, I'm not today. I informed them of the same yesterday." She rubbed at her belly before arching her back. "I'm more tired than I would like."

"Each pregnancy affects every woman differently." Leticia paused and moved to the sink to wash a few bowls. "Perhaps Cailean is correct, and you should close the bakery for a while."

Annabelle shook her head. "Absolutely not." She groaned as she sat on a stool for a moment and took a break. "I used to never need breaks," she muttered.

"Why are you opposed to closing the bakery?" Leticia wiped her hands and leaned against the counter as she watched her friend who looked more exhausted than usual.

Annabelle sighed and rested her head on her palm. "You see what's happening to Tobias. The new store owner is cutting into his profits after less than two months in business. I wouldn't be surprised if Tobias ends up closing." She rubbed at silky flour on the butcher block as she thought. "If I close, someone will start a bakery. I've shown there is a demand for one."

"I highly doubt they will bake as well as you do," Leticia said.

Annabelle shrugged. "That's because you're my friend and now my sister and loyal to me. Many excellent bakers live here who haven't had the opportunity to shine as I have." She took a deep breath. "I know you understand. You had to give up teaching when you married. I don't want to give this up yet."

Leticia sat on a stool next to Annabelle.

"I want to save a nest egg. In case ..."

"Because of me. Because you worry something else could happen," she whispered. She saw the answer in Annabelle's eyes. "There's nothing I can do to pay back what the MacKinnons have lost helping me. The need to enter the partnership. The loss of full control of the livery."

Annabelle grabbed her friend's wrist, preventing Leticia from rising and rushing from the room to her daughter. "I want you to understand one thing, if you understand nothing else," Annabelle said in a low, serious voice. "We lost nothing in helping you. We gained everything." Their gazes met for many moments. "We would have spent any amount of money to see Alistair happy, with the woman he loves, and the child of his heart."

"I hate how they felt compelled to accept the partnership because of me," Leticia whispered.

"It's as much for them too as for you. Cailean wants more free time with me, as Alistair does with you. Did you know, after you married, they were to draw straws every Saturday afternoon to see who got to sleep in with his wife the next morning and who had to work?" She raised an eyebrow as Leticia sputtered out a laugh. "I told Cailean they should have it be every other week as makes sense to me, but they thought such a routine would kill any hope of romance."

She and Leticia shared a long look before bursting into laughter.

Annabelle swiped at her cheeks. "Now with you helping me full time in the bakery so I'm not so tired and Jo ... Bears helping at the livery, we will have more time for our families. I think they would have accepted the partnership, without the threat of financial ruin."

"You've helped me so much. I shouldn't accept a salary. Especially not for these past weeks."

"Of course you should, and you will. Your help is essential for me to remain open." She met Leticia's gaze. "I understand a woman wanting money that is not solely from her husband."

"He provides well for me," Leticia protested.

"Of course he does. But that doesn't mean that you don't want to have a little something that is yours. Or to purchase him a gift from your own money, rather than money that he gave you. Or to have some set aside in case of an emergency." She shrugged. "I learned from my mother that, if possible, a woman should always have a little set aside that was her own. Fate isn't always kind."

After a somber moment, Annabelle forced a smile. "However, it has been kind to you and to me. We married wonderful men, and today we will celebrate." She rose and accepted a dried bowl from Leticia. "What kind of cookies do you prefer?"

"Anything but snickerdoodle." She poked her head into the back room to see Hortence still asleep on the cot. "I hope she rests up as tonight could be a late night for her."

"No matter how much she sleeps now, I'm sure she'll run around so much that she'll be worn out at her usual bedtime." Annabelle smiled as she thought about Hortence and her youthful exuberance.

"Should I go by the Hall and help with decorations?" She frowned as Annabelle burst out laughing.

"Absolutely not. Sorcha and Ewan are in charge, and I want to see what they deem acceptable for decorations. I also know they'll nag and bicker until they're blue in the face, and I have no desire to bear witness to it."

"Thank God I have the excuse of helping you in the bakery!" They shared a laugh as they continued to chatter as they prepared for the reception.

E wan loitered on the side of the reception hall, leaning against the wall and watching the festivities. Tables with pristine white cloths and bouquets of wildflowers filled the majority of the space. A small area had been left open for dancing later, although Ewan knew the townsfolk would move tables if needed. A long table, filled to bursting with food, was set along one wall with Annabelle's cake in a place of honor on a nearby small round table. He smiled as he saw Alistair hoist Hortence up, holding her against his shoulder as he and Leticia walked around the room, accepting the well-wishes of all those present. Ewan grimaced. Well, of most of those present as Mrs. Jameson, Helen, and Tobias appeared to have come for the food and drink as they took no delight in the party.

Ewan took a sip of his drink and eyed an unknown woman wandering among the townsfolk. Her flame-red hair shone like a beacon, and she appeared to have forgotten that she had a pencil stuck behind one of her ears. Her demure brown dress did little to conceal her lush figure. Ewan frowned as he realized she stood behind one group, listening to their conversation. When he saw her smile at something that was said, his frown transformed into a glower.

Gripping his glass of beer, he wandered over to her. She failed to see him approach as she now seemed focused on listening in on the conversation behind her. "Enjoyin' yer eavesdroppin'?" he asked and smiled with wicked delight when she jumped next to him, splashing the front of her dress with water.

"I beg your pardon," she hissed, her cognac-colored eyes snapping with ire. "I see no reason for you to accost me."

"Ye mean, you see no reason for me to interrupt yer bit of snoopin'," he snapped. "Who are ye? Why are ye at my brother's reception? This is a gathering for townsfolk only. We dinna know ye."

She stood as tall as her five-foot-two-tall frame allowed and met his glare with an equally defiant expression. "I'm the reporter hired to take over the floundering newspaper. I'm getting my bearings."

Ewan's mouth gaped open as he stared at the hand she held out to him. "That was to be a *Mr.* J. P. McMahon," he stammered. "A man."

A delighted smile lit her eyes with mischief. "I never said I was a man. It's not my fault if the townsfolk assumed J.P. stood for a man's name."

He glowered at her. "Ye kent ye were trickin' us! Ye kent what we expected and dinna care that we are disappointed."

She sniffed. "It's not my fault that you built up unrealistic expectations." She glared at him as he grabbed her wrist to prevent her from walking away.

"It's no' an unrealistic expectation that the reporter hired for the town be a man. It's a man's job!" Ewan snapped.

She straightened her shoulders and stood on her toes as she leaned forward, refusing to back down. "You only believe it to be a man's job because, up to this point, you've only seen a man do it. I will show you how successful a woman can be as a reporter."

Ewan and J.P. backed away from each other, and Ewan released her wrist at Warren's cajoling laugh as he joined them. "I feared some in town would be shocked." He smiled at J.P. "It's always a pleasure to see you, Miss McMahon."

Ewan gaped at Warren. "Ye kent she was a woman!"

Warren chuckled. "Of course I did. I wrote up the contract. And it's not my fault if everyone assumed J.P. stood for something other than Jessamine Phyllis." He pulled at Ewan's arm and tugged him away from the reporter. He smiled to those around them and nudged at Ewan. "Smile," he muttered.

Ewan lifted his lips in a horrible mockery of a smile. Warren rolled his eyes as Cailean joined them. "What has you up in arms?" Cailean asked as he surveyed the crowd. "I know it's not your usual group, but you'll be at the Stumble-Out soon enough."

"Dinna start," Ewan said, as he continued to track the reporter's movement through the room. Cailean followed his gaze and watched him curiously. "That woman's our new reporter," Ewan muttered.

Cailean choked on his drink and then laughed with such vigor that Mrs. Jameson stared at them. When he realized Ewan was serious, Cailean had trouble sobering. After a moment, he swiped at his eyes and looked at Warren. "I suppose you knew all about it." He shook his head as Warren shrugged. "Well, I hope no one will be upset with you and believe that you willingly tricked us."

Warren sighed. "The fact is, I did mislead those in town. However,

I know I'll never be popular with most of the townsfolk. Too may are unwilling to forget my wild antics three years ago. I'm tolerated because they need me. Nothing more." His gaze followed Helen as she obtained a glass of punch and then returned to stand beside her mother. He then watched Ewan again. "You're the only free MacKinnon brother now. I'd watch out for Mrs. Jameson and her daughter."

Cailean laughed and slapped his youngest brother on the back. "Ewan will never marry. He's even more of a free spirit than Sorcha."

~

A listair set Hortence down, and she raced to the side of the room to play with a few of her friends. He gripped Leticia's hand before kissing it. "Are ye well, my love?" he whispered.

"Ecstatic," she said as she squeezed his hand. "This gathering is like a dream to me. I can't believe we are being feted by those in town."

He paused, facing her and ignoring all those around her. "I want ye to never doubt how valued ye are. How much ye are esteemed by the townsfolk." He brushed at her cheek. "Just because ye are no longer the schoolteacher doesna mean that ye are no' deserving of respect."

She nodded and then stiffened as the new schoolteacher approached. "Hello, Mr. Danforth," she said as she gripped Alistair's arm. "I hope you are finding everything to be satisfactory."

He nodded at her and then Alistair. "I am. This is a most charming town." He pushed a pair of wire-rimmed glasses up his nose and peered at her, his chestnut-brown eyes inquisitive. "However, I do have a few questions about the children. I have heard from many parents that you were an exceptional teacher, and they were sorry to see you retire to wed. I was hoping I could meet with you someday soon to discuss the students with you." He paused. "Congratulations, by the way." He raised his glass of punch, nearly sloshing it onto Leticia's sky-blue dress.

She smiled as she swallowed a giggle at his clumsiness. "How gratifying to hear that I will be missed." She shared a grin with Alistair. "Of course I'd be pleased to help you as you plan for the new school year.

Why don't you come for dinner on Wednesday?" After he agreed, he moved on to meet others present.

Her hand tightened on Alistair's arm as she fought a giggling fit. "Oh my. The children will eat him alive."

"He looks like he belongs in a library, not a schoolroom," Alistair murmured. "I shouldna think we'll have any trouble with Hortence attending."

She and Alistair moved on to speak with others present who waited to wish them well. While she spoke with a pair of parents, Alistair excused himself. He approached the food and drink area, picking up a glass of water rather than the sweet punch and munched on a cookie.

He wandered from the refreshment table and slipped into the shadows along one wall. "Enjoyin' yerself?" He smiled with satisfaction as the man next to him stiffened in surprise. Alistair half noticed his brothers moving to stand in front of him, blocking him from view of the revelers in the room.

"I was," Walter Jameson hissed.

"Aye, as was I until I noticed ye had arrived." He turned to lean on a shoulder so as to better watch the room and to face Walter. "I understand ye spoke with my wife a few weeks ago."

Walter laughed. "No crime in a man congratulating a woman on her marriage."

"Nae," Alistair said in a low, lethal voice. "But there is one in threatenin' a woman with ruin. With disgrace. And finding joy in any fear ye provoke." His arm lashed out with such speed it was barely visible as he thrust Walter farther into the shadows against the wall, his hand around Walter's throat. "Ye are no' good enough to even speak my wife's name, never mind talk with her."

He met the anger and fear in Walter's eyes. "Ye think because ye have had success in the mines the past few months that it gives ye a right to treat those around ye with even less regard than usual. Never forget. I'm watching."

Walter sneered. "As though that scares me. You have no right to threaten me."

"I have the right of a husband." He met Walter's defiant stare. "These are large woods, Walter. 'Tis easy for a man to go missin' an' never be found again. Especially someone as forgettable as you." Alistair let him go, and Walter's head *thunk*ed against the wall. "Leave me an' mine alone."

Walter nodded as he emerged from the shadows as though he had shared a genial conversation with Alistair and walked away.

Alistair moved to join Leticia but was soon intercepted and surrounded by his brothers.

"Are ye all right, Al?" Ewan asked as he pasted on the smile that made him look like an easy mark at the poker tables.

"Did ye set things straight?" Cailean asked. He smiled at the mothers in town.

"Aye. I think he'll leave Leticia alone." Alistair let out a deep breath. "Thanks for helpin' me."

Cailean slapped him on the back. "Anytime, Alistair, you know that. Besides, that man's a menace. I hate to think how he treats his sister."

Their three gazes turned to watch Walter speaking with Helen, her face so pale it looked as though she had been gutted.

"I wonder if we should interfere," Ewan murmured.

Alistair shook his head. "I fear 'twould only make it worse. Bullies need to feel strong. This is how he regains his sense of superiority." Alistair shook his head as he saw that Helen, who he had seen as brave and resolute when she confronted her fears, shrank into herself as her brother continued to speak to her. "Poor lass."

"No wonder she dreams of escape from that house. From her mother and her brother," Ewan said.

"What worries me is that Fidelia told Belle that the Madam is hoping for a virgin auction," Cailean said. All three pairs of eyes turned to Helen, cowering in the corner.

"Ye'd have to be desperate to agree with such a harebrained idea," Ewan sputtered.

Alistair shivered. "Aye. I've seen what desperation can do to a woman. Poor lass," he whispered again. "Too bad there isna someone willin' to help her."

Ewan looked at his brothers with wide eyes. "Dinna look at me. I'm not marryin' her. I'm not savin' her. I'm not that sort of man."

Cailean laughed and squeezed Ewan's shoulder. "Aye, that I know well. We'll never attend your wedding as you have vowed to never marry."

Alistair sputtered out a laugh as Ewan relaxed with Cailean's teasing. "I must return to Leticia," he murmured. He slapped his brothers on their shoulders and rejoined his bride.

He frowned at the woman speaking with Leticia. "I beg yer pardon. I dinna ken ye."

She smiled and held out her hand as a man would. "I'm J. P. McMahon. The new reporter." When Alistair gaped at her and then her hand, she glowered at him. He belatedly shook her hand and smiled his welcome.

"Alistair runs the livery with his brother and their partner, Bears. If you ever have any trouble with your horse, he can help you," Leticia said, her pride glinting in her eyes.

"How fascinating to have a mixed-blood partner," J.P. murmured.

"Bears kens horses." Alistair shrugged dismissively as he met her curious stare. "Are ye certain ye're the new reporter? I ken Warren well, and he never said we were gettin' a woman." He frowned as he studied her from head to foot.

She held out her arm as though to help him peruse her with more ease. "As you can see, I am a woman. All my family members were in newspapers before me. I've learned the trade from the best. There can be no better profession for me than to follow in my family's footsteps."

Alistair nodded. "Aye, learning a trade early is important. But how do ye expect to learn what ye need to from the men in this town? They'll never open up the way ye'll want them to."

J.P. shook her head. "Men always believe that. However, what men don't like to admit is that they enjoy gossip as much as or more than women. And they love to tell stories as much as women. It's a matter of finding a way to entice them to speak."

Leticia bit her lip. "You'll ruin your reputation if you go into the saloons."

J.P. rolled her eyes. "Do you believe I was a hard-hitting reporter in Saint Louis and New York City without venturing into unsavory establishments?" She laughed. Her gaze focused on Leticia. "I wouldn't mind speaking about an acquaintance we share in Saint Louis."

Leticia paled, and her hand gripped Alistair's arm. "I have nothing to speak with a reporter about." She looked over at Annabelle. "If you will excuse us? Our sister-in-law would like us to cut the cake."

She tugged Alistair alongside her. Before they reached Annabelle and the three-tiered cake, he pulled her to a stop. "What has ye worried?"

"I don't want a reporter digging around into my life." She shook her head as she saw J.P. watching them with intense concentration. She pasted on a smile and watched as Alistair nodded his understanding. She walked with him to the small round table with the cake on it.

Alistair smiled at his sister-in-law. "I assume the middle layer is chocolate?" He saw her flush, as Cailean's favorite flavor was chocolate.

"Yes, although one is waiting for us at home in case the townsfolk gobble this one up," she whispered.

"Lucky Cailean," Alistair murmured.

"There's one for you too," Annabelle breathed. "I didn't want to disappoint Hortence. Not a second time." She smiled at the emotion glinting in Alistair's eyes. "Be happy," she murmured to them before she called for the crowd's attention. After a short speech and a few catcalls, Alistair cut a sliver of cake and handed it to Leticia. She did the same for him, and they ate their cake as the town applauded.

He leaned over and whispered in her ear, "I think the town is delighted for us."

She giggled. "Either that or they are ecstatic they can finally eat another of Annabelle's cakes."

He laughed and swung her into his arms as the music sounded. "Dance with me," he whispered, although they were already twirling around a small space, cleared by the townsfolk as they lined up for cake.

"Always," she whispered.

～

Sorcha danced with one of the men from Frederick Tompkins's ranch. The ranch hand maintained a respectful distance from her, although his hand around her waist was tighter than it needed to be. She squirmed, but it only made his hold on her tighten.

"Beggin' your pardon, ma'am," he said. "I'm not so good at dancin', and I fear, if I were to let go at all, you'd spin away from me like one of those little toys children play with." He shared a chagrined smile with her as she relaxed and laughed.

"I have no desire to be a spinnin' top!" She followed his lead and belatedly realized he danced with galloping steps rather than smooth, gliding movements.

"I don't have a chance to dance much, and I couldn't pass up a chance with a pretty girl like you." He blushed.

"What's it like working on the ranch?" she asked. "I didn't expect Mr. Tompkins's men to be here today."

"Not all of us could come of course. Some had to stay behind to work the ranch. But he's a fair man. He likes to give us a chance to go to town every once in a while." He nodded at his boss who stood tall, talking with his grandparents. Sorcha followed his gaze and bit back a smile as she saw Irene brush at the black hair falling into her grandson's eyes.

The music came to an end, and the ranch hand led her to the side of the small dance floor. He bowed, and she laughed at his chivalry. "Thank you, Mr. Dixon." She declined three other men's requests for a dance and moved to the refreshment stand.

She made a face as she took a sip of the punch and set it aside. After taking a gulp of water, she wandered the room. She stilled when she heard a woman whispering in a carrying voice about Leticia. The woman faced the other way and was so intent on her conversation that she failed to notice those around her.

"I tell you, Myrtle, that woman should be in the Boudoir. We shouldn't be forced to stand here as though we are delighted that she tricked a man like Alistair MacKinnon. She is a deceitful slut."

The woman named Myrtle patted the other woman on her arm as though in consolation. "There is such a lack of morals in a town like ours. What can we hope for when men are so readily taken in by any pretty face?" She sniffed in disdain as she looked at the happy couple enjoying another dance. "Shameful. Dancing more than once together. They set a horrible example for the youth of this town."

"To think she was a teacher!" The first woman shuddered. "To think she had the responsibility of instructing my precious grand-daughter. As though a woman like her understands the principles of right and wrong. I hate to think what my grandchild learned from such a woman."

Sorcha took a deep breath and finally spoke. "I think yer grand-daughter learned more about kindness, forgiveness, and decency from Leticia than she could ever have hoped to learn at home from two bitter women like yerselves." She met their appalled expressions with one of absolute derision and ire. "Ye do no' have the right to speak Leticia's name, never mind discuss her."

Sorcha leaned forward, cutting off their protests. "One day ye'll be thankful for what she did for this town. For how well she taught yer children. For her ability to care for all the children, independent of their parents' standing in town." She raised her chin. "I couldna be more proud to call her sister-in-law."

She pushed past the women and marched toward Harold and Irene. She ignored their grandson, who watched her with annoyance as she approached.

"Always a pleasure to see you, Sorcha," Irene murmured. "I'm not certain you've met our grandson, Frederick Tompkins." She beamed at her grandson and gripped his arm with pride. "We convinced him to come into town today for the celebration."

Sorcha met his appraising stare. "I'd begun to think ye more myth than reality, the way ye slipped in and out of town without ever bein' seen."

He chuckled. "I see no point wasting time on pleasantries with those who will have no influence on my life. Or the running of the ranch."

Sorcha raised an eyebrow and met Harold's delighted gaze before she glared at Frederick. "Ye certainly didna learn charm from yer grandparents."

Frederick stared at her, his blues eyes a flinty steel. "I learned all I needed to from them."

Irene grasped Sorcha's hand as Sorcha braced for a scathing come-back for Frederick. "Ignore this latest battle you could begin. I want to hear what happened with those two old biddies." Irene nodded in the direction of the two women Sorcha had upbraided. They had their heads together and whispered fervently as they glared ferociously at Sorcha.

"I heard them speakin' ill of Leticia. I advised them that they should be thankful for one such as Leticia and that one day they will be grateful she taught their children."

Irene sniffed with disgust and met the women's glare. "There are none blinder than those who will not see."

Sorcha tilted her head. "Is that from the Bible?"

Irene waved her hand. "Something I heard from the preacher. I swear, if he did any worse a job, we'd all kill each other and be done with it." She smiled as Frederick choked on a laugh. Irene looped her arm through Frederick's and led him toward Alistair and Leticia who now stood on the other side of the dance floor.

Sorcha stood next to Harold and watched the thinning crowd. "Now that the cake's served, many will leave."

"Oh, plenty are hopeful of a dance with a lovely woman, like your-self," Harold teased. "Frederick's men have spoken of little else since they arrived around noontime for a quick feed before the festivities began."

Sorcha shook her head. "I've danced with almost all of them. I don't have the energy to dance with many more," she protested as she shook her head again as another man motioned for her to join him on the floor.

"I noticed you haven't danced with Frederick yet." Harold took a sip of punch and smiled with pleasure.

"How is it ye drink that sickly sweet stuff and seem satisfied? The rest of us detest it." She huffed out a breath as he answered only with a mysterious smile. "I should think yer grandson wouldna need to dance with the likes of me. I'm one of those uninteresting people who adds little to his life or the running of his ranch."

Harold guffawed. "Don't get yer knickers in a knot. He's cantankerous at best on a good day. He has his reasons. As do most men. I think your opinion of him might change if you were to know him better."

Sorcha sniffed. "That's as likely as snow in August," she snapped.

Harold laughed. "Well, that has come to pass, so we'll see."

~

Warren pushed away from the wall he had been holding up and stood in line for cake behind Helen Jameson. He inhaled, breathing in her subtle gardenia scent. "Why do you allow him to speak to you as he does?" He frowned as she froze at the sound of his voice.

"I've asked you to cease speaking with me. It seems such a simple request," she snapped, although her voice was so low, he barely heard it.

He spoke into her ear. "The simple requests are often the most difficult to grant."

"He is my brother. He is allowed certain liberties in his treatment of me that others aren't."

"That's horse dung, and you know it." He saw a faint blush emerge on the skin of her nape. "It should mean that he treats you with even greater respect so that you understand the dignity and esteem you should receive from any man."

She huffed out a snort. "That's rich, coming from you." She stepped forward and accepted her plate of cake before hurrying to her mother's side.

Warren nodded his thanks for his slice and then joined Cailean and Ewan. He took a bite of the white cake and closed his eyes with appreciation. "Glorious," he murmured.

"Aye, it is," Cailean said. He smiled at his friend. "It's why I got two tiny pieces, one white and one chocolate. Come by the house tonight, and you can have a chocolate piece."

Warren stared at the quickly diminishing cake. "There won't be any left."

Ewan laughed with satisfaction. "'Tis wonderful to have the baker as a sister-in-law. We have a cake waiting for us at home." He nudged his brother with his elbow. "And it's chocolate, as the baker's partial to this man."

"Lucky man," Warren said with a chuckle.

"What did Helen say that put you in a sour mood?" Cailean asked in a low voice. "Seems she wasn't too pleased to have to speak with you."

Warren shook his head in frustration. "She allows her brother to treat her abominably, and I asked her why. She had no good defense."

Ewan shrugged. "Sometimes those who are meant to protect us treat us terribly. We dinna ken any better, because that's how it's always been. Ye have to learn yer worth by how others treat ye."

Cailean nodded. "Aye, and, if you're someone like Helen, the town only reinforces what she's learned because they treat her as badly as her mother."

"As her brother," Warren muttered.

Ewan sighed. "Aye. We saw it with Sorcha. She had to learn that love was stronger than anger and disappointment."

Warren frowned at that statement, but the brothers remained silent.

Cailean looked at Warren. "Don't treat Helen like she's on trial, Warren. Or make her feel like the town lawyer is speaking with her." He met his friend's shuttered gaze. "I believe she's a woman who needs a friend."

Warren grunted his agreement. "Where is Bears?"

"He refused to come, and he's watching the livery for us, although he knows we've left it for hours in the past." Cailean rolled his eyes. "It would have been good to have him here, but he's his own man. He can decide what he wants to do."

Warren nodded. "Coming to a town affair, even if to honor a MacKinnon, would be overwhelming." He took a bite of cake. "Where will he sleep when the weather turns to winter?"

Cailean looked to Ewan, and he nodded so Cailean continued. "For now, he's sleepin' on a cot in the tack room. But we do not want a stove or a flame in the barn." He shrugged. "Too great a risk for fire. So Ewan will build him a small place near the paddock."

Warren smiled. "Excellent. Jack would be pleased." He glanced around the room and focused on the reporter slinking through the crowd and nodded in her direction. "The fact she's here alone makes her rather remarkable."

He and Cailean laughed as Ewan sputtered about the new reporter and left to find another glass of beer.

Warren raised an eyebrow as he saw Ewan and J.P. glaring at each other again. "I shouldn't think he'd want the attention of such a reporter. She has a hell of a reputation."

Cailean groaned and then frowned. "Then why'd she come to Bear Grass Springs?"

Warren nodded at his friend. "That's the question that was never satisfactorily answered." He slapped Cailean on the shoulder as he snuck one last look in Helen's direction. "I'll see you tonight at your house. I'll slip out to work on a few things before I come by for cake."

Leticia excused herself from a few of the mothers wishing her well as she saw Hortence speaking with two unknown men. As she approached, she frowned because one man moved to keep Hortence separated from her. "Hello," she said in a friendly voice. "I hope you are enjoying the celebration."

One man—wearing only a single layer of dust, as compared to his companion with multiple layers, but with a thick brown beard and hair past his collar—eyed her appreciatively. "We are, Mrs. MacKinnon. Or should we say, Mrs. Fry?" He smiled when he saw her stiffen.

"Mama, these men want to know about the bad man," Hortence said. Her voice quivered, and she darted around them, evading their grasps until she was at her mother's side.

"I see," Leticia murmured. "Go find Papa," Leticia said to her daughter as she continued to watch the two men. She heard Hortence scamper away and saw their frustration as Hortence eluded them. "If you thought to use my daughter in some way, you were delusional."

"We want answers, missus," demanded the other man, shorter and stockier than the first. "Where is your husband?"

"Here," Alistair said in a deep, authoritative voice. He rested a hand on Leticia's shoulder and met their glowers. "If ye mean her former husband, Mr. Fry, we last saw him in Helena a few weeks ago. He was most interested in evading those from the Mitchell gang."

The men nodded. "You've had no contact with him?" the first man asked.

"None," Leticia said. "I avoided contact with him for nearly seven years. I never wanted to see him again. Why would I seek him out now that we are divorced and I've married a good man?"

They studied her closely as though looking for any signs of prevarication before relaxing as though finally believing her. "Thank you, ma'am. It seems our journey is not complete." They nodded to her and to Alistair before slipping from the Hall.

Leticia leaned into her husband's strong arms. "Thank you," she whispered.

"Ye know I'll support ye in any way I can. Always." He kissed her head. "Ye dinna have to fear him anymore. He has enough problems without time to bother ye again."

She laughed. "You don't have to sound so gleeful about it!"

"I canna help it. I'm here, with my wife in my arms, our daughter nearby, at our wedding reception. Life doesna get much better than this."

~

Alistair carried a sleeping Hortence against his shoulder as he and Leticia walked home. Although late for Hortence, she had been asleep at the reception for the past two hours. Few lights shone in businesses, other than the saloons and the Boudoir. A multitude of stars lit the sky, and a soft breeze blew, bringing the scent of fresh pine trees and clearing away any stench of the town. He followed Leticia as she opened the door and walked upstairs to set Hortence on her bed. "Should we change her into her nightclothes?" He ran a hand over Hortence's head, slipping his fingers into her loosened braids and freeing her hair.

"Yes," Leticia whispered. She reached under her daughter's pillow and pulled out her nightshirt. Alistair moved aside, slipping off Hortence's shoes as Leticia tugged off her party dress. Soon Hortence was tucked under her covers. First Leticia and then Alistair kissed their daughter on her forehead before they left.

"Come, love," Alistair murmured as he drew Leticia behind him. "Come frolic with yer husband." He kissed her in the hallway, swallowing her chuckle.

She pushed him, backing him into their room and shutting the door until he knocked into the bed and sat down. "Shall I undress you as I did Hortence?" She smiled with wicked intent as his eyes gleamed with love and passion. "I'll take that as a yes," she whispered as she clambered up, sitting astride his lap as she tugged at his tie. She pulled it loose, tossing it to the floor. At the first hint of flesh, she dropped her face, inhaling his musky scent. "I love how you smell."

"How odd. I stink of sweat and horse and leather." He raised a hand to tangle in her hair. "God, Lettie," he rasped as she rained kisses over his bared skin, "how I love ye."

She leaned back, her eyes gleaming with triumph. "Do you know how much I love you? Can you possibly understand?"

He nodded as he palmed her face. "Aye. I thought I loved ye before. Before our first weddin' ceremony. Now I ken what it is to lose ye.

And to regain yer love." He swooped forward and kissed her. "I'll do whatever I must do to never lose ye again."

She smiled through her tears. "It's only made my love for you stronger too."

He stared into her eyes. "I felt like the luckiest man alive today and pitied anyone who wasna me."

"What a nice change from our first wedding ceremony."

He chuckled as he leaned forward, kissing her deeply. He turned her, so she lay beneath him, and he methodically removed her clothes. "Let me love ye, wife," he whispered.

"As long as I can love you in equal measure." She arched up, helping him ease off her dress.

"I'd have it no other way."

L ater Alistair rubbed his stomach as it growled. "Do I remember correctly that cake is downstairs?" He heard Leticia giggle. "Come, love. Put on yer nightgown." He slipped out from underneath her and pulled on a nightshirt. He waited as Leticia wriggled from bed and into her nightgown, grabbing her hand as they walked downstairs.

He sighed with appreciation to see the two-layer cake on the dining room table. "Thank God." He extracted milk from the icebox and glasses from the cupboard while Leticia pulled out plates, a large knife, and forks. When she cut it, he grinned with pleasure. "One of each. She's a smart lass, is our Anna."

He sat next to Leticia at the table and wolfed down a piece of cake. For his second hefty slice, he ate more slowly and chatted with his wife. "How do ye think the reception went?"

"Better than I could have hoped. There are always those who will mutter and wonder about me. But the majority are more accepting of me than I would have expected." She gripped his hand. "I had thought it would take a year for so many to look upon me favorably."

"Never discount the effect of a formidable family. Or the benefits of a good cake." He sighed with pleasure as he ate another bite. "What do ye think of the new teacher?"

She giggled. "I can already imagine the stories Hortence will come home with. The frogs that will be released. The children glued to seats. The braids tied together. The privies overturned."

Alistair chuckled. "And those are the innocent possibilities. Imagine when the boys put their heads together. They'll wreak havoc."

"Is it right of me to warn him? I fear I'll frighten him away. What if there is no one to teach the town's schoolchildren?" Her worried gaze met his.

"If he had any training at all, he will know what's in store for him." He pushed away his now-empty plate, patting his belly, wiping away any milk on his lips. "I hope wee Hortence isna upset we started the cake without her."

"As long as we save her some, she'll be ecstatic," Leticia said. "She'll demand cake for breakfast."

He played with his wife's hands as his gaze turned somber. "Are ye all right? Ye have to know those men willna bother ye again. Wee Hortence is safe."

Leticia let out a deep breath. "I will believe it as time passes. Josiah tends to cast a long shadow, and I must wait for it to fade."

After a moment Alistair said, "Why did the reporter upset ye?" He frowned as he was lost in thought. "I've thought through the tale ye told me, an' there is nothin' about yer time in Saint Louis that should make ye embarrassed."

Leticia flushed. "Imagine how it would look to the townsfolk. She could write a sensationalized story about me. I flee my husband and find another man to protect me." She lowered her gaze. "Then I come here and entangle you in my web."

Alistair cocked his head to the side and frowned with confusion. "Is that how it was? It sounded to me that ye found a way to earn a living without having to resort to the kind of life the women of the Boudoir live. Ye cared for the man's children. It isna yer fault ye couldna love him." His eyes shone with pride. "Nothin' she could write would embarrass me."

Leticia shuddered. "I pray you remember those words. I fear she could conjure plenty that could humiliate me." She took a deep breath. "Now that I've finally begun to regain my standing in town, I can't imagine losing it again."

"Nothing matters except what we ken to be true," Alistair said as a smile bloomed. "An' I've enjoyed bein' *entangled in yer web*." He sighed with contentment as she giggled at his words.

CHAPTER 20

*L*eticia and Alistair joined the family at the larger MacKinnon house for Sunday dinner one week following the reception. After dinner, they sat around the table chatting while Hortence played in the parlor. Most drank coffee, although Annabelle sipped tea.

"I can't abide the bitter brew right now," she whispered to Leticia.

Leticia smiled. "How are you feeling?"

"Well enough, although I sleep more than I would like." She leaned into Cailean's shoulder.

Cailean squeezed his wife's hand. "She doesn't rest enough. If it were up to me, the bakery would close."

Annabelle ignored her husband. "How are things on the council, Alistair?"

"Fine, although we should meet soon." He shrugged. "The town's growin', and we need to find ways to fund what we need."

Ewan took a sip of coffee. "Do what all the other towns do and have a whore tax." He jolted as he was kicked by Cailean but motioned to the parlor where Hortence played with her marbles and dolls, away from their boring talk. "I'm serious. Ye'll make more money than ye thought possible."

Alistair frowned. "Wouldn't that give the impression we approve of the Boudoir?"

Cailean chuckled. "It's not as though it's going away. The town might as well benefit from its presence. I've heard of towns whose schools are funded through the taxes imposed on such places."

Annabelle bit her lip. "Won't that make life even harder on the women who live there? I hate to think of Fidelia suffering more than she already does." She squeezed Cailean's hand.

"The tax isna just on the Boudoir," Ewan continued. "It also dictates how the women from the Boudoir can act outside of the Boudoir. They canna meet the eyes of townsfolk or risk bein' taxed. They canna shop with other women or be taxed. They canna speak with townsfolk, unless placing an order at a business or be taxed." He shrugged. "I ken it sounds horrible. But they live outside of what society deems acceptable behavior."

Annabelle sputtered. "Why would such a law be acceptable? They are people. Women who have fallen on hard times."

Cailean glared at his brother before speaking with his wife in a soothing tone. "You know the majority of the townsfolk aren't as accepting of their presence as you are. That they would rather ignore its presence here than acknowledge it."

"Which is hypocritical as I doubt any man in town, except Mr. Tompkins, has failed to visit the Boudoir!" Annabelle snapped. "I heard you whispering about the minister's presence there last week." She glared at the MacKinnon brothers as they flushed red.

"Ye've already battled the town once by acceptin' yer sister," Sorcha said. "To most, she should have been dead to ye."

Annabelle shook her head. "She'll never be dead to me." She swiped at her cheeks.

"I hate to say I agree with Ewan," Alistair said, "but, with an influx of cash into the town's coffers, we could have a larger school and two teachers. Warren has all sorts of ideas for expansion. A windmill-powered water tower. A horse-drawn fire-fighting wagon. Starting a brick factory." He shrugged. "But it takes money, aye? Such a tax would be a boon for us."

"But a disaster for the Boudoir. The Madam barely ekes out a living as it is, cutting the food budget for the women." Annabelle watched her family with a panicked expression.

"Why is that?" Leticia asked. "Seems she has enough customers to keep her flush with money." She bowed her head as she blushed.

"The Madam has a terrible gamblin' habit," Ewan said, meeting his family's shocked stares. "And Lady Luck hasna been on the Madam's side of late."

"Who would gamble with a woman?" Cailean sputtered.

"Oh, the men in the private rooms at the Stumble-Out. Ye have no idea what goes on there." Ewan shrugged. "'Tis why Alistair saw a few of the whores from the Boudoir at the Stumble-Out last month. The Madam lost an' had trouble payin' her debts. She lent her girls to cover what she owed."

"I hate that the women working there are nothing more than pawns for her," Annabelle whispered. She rubbed at her belly.

"Word is that a poker match will soon be held to equal any in a large city." Ewan shrugged. "I canna imagine what she would barter were she to lose."

Cailean glared at his brother to cease speaking about the Boudoir as his wife shuddered. He pulled her closer to him and kissed her head. "Where's Warren? I thought he would join us for dinner."

Alistair shook his head. "He has a large case coming up. Something to do with mining rights and encroachment. I dinna ken it all but seems complicated. Warren looked delighted, although his eyes were red from lack of sleep, and I doubt the man's eaten a good meal in nearly a week."

"I'll make up a plate and bring it over later. He's been a good friend to us." Sorcha met her family's speculative glances. "I believe the word I used was 'friend,'" she snapped.

"Seems ye are no' that good at makin' them," Alistair teased. "Irene told me how ye annoyed her grandson when ye met him at the reception."

Sorcha made a low sound as though growling at the mention of

Frederick Tompkins. "He's a rude man. Refuses to even attempt the niceties of conversation."

Cailean laughed. "And you are always so polite." His laughter deepened as she tossed her napkin at him.

Leticia smiled. "He was quite handsome."

"If ye like cowboys," Alistair muttered.

Leticia rolled her eyes and clasped his hand and., in a low voice that only he could hear, murmured, "No need to be jealous." Her delighted gaze caught and held his until they were interrupted by Ewan's groan of distress.

"Did ye see what that woman wrote?" Ewan tapped at the paper he had pulled out as dessert was to be served. He ignored the plate of oatmeal raisin cookies and glasses of milk.

"What woman?" Alistair asked, his eyes gleaming with mischief at his brother's ire. He snatched away the paper and read aloud:

Word has arrived from Helena that a certain man of interest, who previously had ties to the now Mrs. Alistair MacKinnon, has met an unfortunate demise. Over a round of poker, the known liar was exposed as a cheat and was duly shot. As no one was inclined to run for a doctor, he expired. To nobody's surprise, as they moved the body, an ace of spades fell from his boot leg. Few will mourn his passing, although one wonders which of his traits will be passed on to his progeny.

Alistair slammed the paper onto the table. "I thought we were gettin' a proper journalist! Not some woman intent on fillin' the townsfolk's heads with gossip." His cheeks flushed with anger as his eyes flashed. He met his siblings' irate gazes. "She should ken maligning children is off-limits!"

Leticia stroked a hand down his arm. "Although I wish she had refrained from the last sentence and the rampant speculation that will cause among certain townsfolk, I hate to admit I am relieved Josiah can cause no more mischief in our lives." She battled tears. "I should not feel such relief at someone's death."

Alistair pulled her close as she cried against his chest. "Shh, ... love, ye suffered enough with the man. Now ye know 'tis truly over."

Sorcha sighed. "She could have written the first part of her *News and Noteworthy* segment without the last part. Seems she's intent in sensationalizing news to garner a greater readership."

Annabelle shook her head, frowning. "It's how things are done in the larger cities. The greater the scandal, the larger the sales. People love to read about others' foibles and failures." She shared a look with her family seated around the table. "We wouldn't be so upset if it weren't about our little Hortence."

Ewan tapped at the paper. "That's the point. It's always about us. Can ye think of one *News and Noteworthy* column we have yet to appear in?" He tilted his head, his eyebrows raised. "Somehow we have been in every single one the past week!"

"And she's only been printing the paper for a week," Cailean said drily. He nodded at Ewan. "I agree. For some reason, she's fixated on the MacKinnons and you in particular." He watched as Ewan fidgeted. "I have a feeling your welcome, or lack of one, at Alistair and Leticia's reception, has something to do with it."

"She was snoopin' on others' private conversations!" Ewan protested. "She canna believe that is normal or acceptable."

"Whatever ye did, ye angered the woman, and she has a printing press," Alistair said. "Ye need to find a way to calm her down as she seems intent on houndin' us—ye—on a daily basis."

Cailean nodded. "You don't want your business to suffer due to her, Ewan."

$\sim$

After dinner, Alistair and Leticia walked to the barn so that Hortence could visit Brindle. She had the scraps of carrots from the stew to give the horse as a treat, and she had informed her parents that she had a story to tell Brindle that could take some time. They stood at the stall next to Brindle's and listened to Hortence's soft murmur as she spoke to the horse, feeding her the vegetables and patting her on the nose.

"Would ye object if I bought wee Hortence a horse?" he whispered so that Hortence would not overhear. "I think she would love having one of her own, and she's a good age to learn to ride."

"Wouldn't it be too big for her?" Leticia asked. "I fear spending too much money. We should save what we have." She kissed his cheek as she shook her head. "I love that you want to do that for her. For now I think her frequent visits to see Brindle are enough."

He pulled her against his side. "How are ye, truly?" He nuzzled the side of her neck.

"Relieved. I cried in the kitchen, not out of grief but from a sense of overwhelming relief. I can't believe I am finally free of him." She wrapped her arms around her husband's waist. "I know I legally freed myself when I divorced him, but I didn't trust him enough to abide by that. I always feared he would return some day."

"An' now ye dinna have that fear," Alistair murmured. "I'm glad. I canna say I'm sorry." He sighed as he kissed her neck. "I ken I should as someone died. But he threatened ye. He threatened Hortence. An' I canna forgive that."

"I love you, Alistair, more than I can ever express," she whispered, tightening her arms around him. "I would be lost without you. Thank you for believing me. For overcoming your anger."

He chuckled. "An' thank ye for forgiving me for abandoning ye when ye needed me most." He leaned away and smiled at her. "This has only made us stronger, my love."

"You rekindled my faith in my dreams," she whispered as she arched up to kiss him.

"Aye, an' now it's time to make them all come true."

Want to read a bonus epilogue about Leticia and Alistair? Join my newsletter today to read a bonus epilogue!

SNEAK PEEK AT MONTANA MAVERICK!

Chapter One

Montana Territory, September 1885

*J*essamine Phyllis McMahon, Bear Grass Springs's recently arrived resident and reporter, nodded to a neighbor as she wiped down the windows of the newspaper office. The latest edition of her newspaper was on full display, and she wanted those passing by to easily read the headlines. However, *"Delinquent Cow Wanders Main Street"* proved of little interest. After another pair of townsfolk walked past with only a cursory glance at the paper in the window, she sighed. During her first week in town last month, she had published a newspaper daily to drum up interest. Now, a month after her arrival, she printed a twice-weekly paper, and this edition did little to elicit curiosity.

Her print shop, located next to the bank, was often overlooked as townsfolk rushed to complete a transaction at the neighboring business. Or, she mused, they were too eager to arrive at the Boudoir, the town's whorehouse, which stood just past the bank and at the edge of town. She glanced across the dusty main thoroughfare—apply named Main Street—to the town's most popular saloon, the Stumble-Out. The man she had coined the town's most disreputable gentleman was not among the men loitering outside, and she quickly lost interest in those wandering in and out of the saloon.

After a final swipe to polish away an imaginary streak, she reentered her print shop. When she had first arrived, a year's worth of old papers and notes had been stashed in corners and crannies of the one-story building. After collecting most of the excess paper, she decided to keep it on one side of the large room to use as fuel for her fire in the winter. She walked along the front of the shop, with its tall shelves and bookcases blocking the view of the back of the shop and forming a sense of a hallway. Her desk sat between two windows, and a large flat table sat opposite the press where she hand set the newspaper with metal letters.

To the far side of the room, near one window, the press stood on a small raised dais. A lamp hung over the press for dark days or when she wanted to work at night. Covered buckets filled with ink sat near the press, and reams of paper were piled on the floor to one side of her desk. Long rows of wires, like multiple clotheslines, hung across the room for drying the paper after printing. Currently no papers were there, as they were stacked by the door, ready for purchase.

She sat at her desk, pushing aside a stack of article ideas with corresponding research and pulled out a blank sheet of paper. On one side she made a column for what she considered a success in her newspaper so far, and in the other she wrote what she thought were challenges. For success, she wrote N&N. Her *News and Noteworthy* section that came out once a week garnered the most interest from the townsfolk. It made that edition of the newspaper outsell the others three to one.

Her articles about national affairs and global events were rarely remarked upon. However, she always received letters to the editor about the N&N section, along with suggestions for the next edition. "I'll expand that section to include it in every newspaper, and I'll make it longer in each paper. I should have known to play to the townsfolk's vanity and need for gossip," she muttered.

She tapped her pencil on the paper as she brainstormed other topics that would interest the townsfolk in a small Montana town, with a mining town in the mountains above and an expansive valley below filled with cattle and cattlemen. She left that thought for later and wrote it in the challenges column. *Little interest in nonlocal affairs. No distribution network. Questionable literacy of townsfolk.*

She dropped her pencil and jerked around as the door burst open. She met the irate gaze of the man she had termed the town's "most disreputable gentleman" since her arrival. "Hello, Mr. MacKinnon. It's lovely to see you today."

Ewan MacKinnon strolled into her office with the grace of a panther. His blond hair with hints of red in it hung to his shoulders, and he was in need of a shave. In his anger, he forgot to doff his hat to her, and he took it off, tracing the brim between his long fingers. Irate brown eyes met her cognac-colored gaze, and his glare intensified as he saw her poorly concealed amusement. "Must ye write about me in every damn edition of yer newspaper?" he demanded.

"You know as well as I do that an *N&N* isn't in this paper," she said with a triumphant smile.

"Oh, ye act all coy. I ken what ye're doin'. Ye're tryin' to make me out to be the town fool. But ye willna succeed. I promise ye that." He took a deep breath. "How can ye write that the cow got the better of me and that I'm lookin' for a rematch?"

She giggled and looked away. "Forgive me. I thought that was what truly occurred. Did you or did you not interact with the cow? And did you not end up in the middle of a cow pie after it … nudged you with its behind?"

He reddened. "Aye, that is what occurred. But ye dinna have to write about it and tell the entire world about it!"

She laughed. "I doubt the world is interested in the meaningless antics of a cow in our little town of Bear Grass Springs, Mr. MacKinnon. From what I've heard, the rest of the world is busy mourning the death of P. T. Barnum's giant elephant, Jumbo, in a train wreck. I'd be thankful you rate over the death of an elephant in the townsfolk's estimation."

"Ye are a daft woman," Ewan said as he rolled his eyes.

"That may be, but, from what I heard, you had quite a cotillion of women eager to aid you as you struggled to rise."

He flushed red as he turned away from her.

"It's such a pity you pulled Miss Jameson onto your lap rather than allowing her to help you up." She bit her lip as his back stiffened and his hold on his hat tightened. "I don't know as her dress will ever recover."

After a moment, he spun to face her. "Yer articles, an' the actions of women in this town who should ken better, willna force me to marry a woman I dinna like."

She smiled. "Then I suggest you be more careful about whose hand you accept for aid."

"I could barely see!"

She cleared her throat as though swallowing a chuckle. "Yes, I did hear about the unfortunate, uh, splatter that covered your face."

He ran a hand over his jaw but not before she saw a hint of a smile. "Ye enjoy this, do ye no'? The small-town antics that drive most of us insane?"

She shrugged. "It's what keeps a small town going and knits everyone together. I have to say, it was a difficult article to write as the Jamesons will not speak with me, and the cow was more interested in chewing her cud. And *you*, well, I know better than to ask you for an interview. So I listened to others describe what they saw as I ate my meals at the café."

Ewan rolled his eyes again. "Why should the Jamesons speak with ye when ye started speculatin' about Helen's respectability in one of yer first papers?" Any humor hidden in his gaze disappeared as he sobered. "Ye can write articles about me, an' I will no' be affected. I'm a man. But ye canna write about a lass. 'Tisn't right, Miss McMahon."

Jessamine shrugged. "If she is acting outside of the bounds of propriety, she is fair game for a reporter."

Ewan cocked his head to one side as he stared at her. The light glinting in through the windows cast a reddish tint to his dark blond hair. "Do ye no' care what ye could do to that girl? Do ye not ken how hard her life already is, livin' with her mother and brother?"

She rolled her eyes. "Life is hard, Mr. MacKinnon. It's the one truth we should all understand and accept."

He took a step toward her as his gaze hardened. "Aye, 'tis. But that means ye should no' go around attemptin' to make it harder for those who canna defend themselves. Yer cow story is entertainin' until the point ye make Helen a laughingstock. Then ye go too far. Ye always go too far."

His irate glare met her indignant, defiant stare, and then he spun on his heel and stormed away. The door rattled as it slammed shut behind him.

She dropped her pencil on her desk and sighed. "You're wrong, Mr. MacKinnon. I never go far enough."

~

Order Now to Read Montana Maverick Today!

ALSO BY RAMONA FLIGHTNER

The O'Rourke Family Montana Saga

Never fear, I am busy at work on the next book in the series! If you want to make sure you never miss a release, a special, a cover reveal, or a short story just for my fans, sign up for my newsletter!

Follow the O'Rourke Family as they settle in Fort Benton, Montana Territory in 1860's.

Sign up here to receive the prequel, *Pioneer Adventure* to the new Saga as a thank you for subscribing to my newsletter!

Pioneer Adventure (Prequel)

Pioneer Dream (OFMS, Book 1)- Kevin and Aileen

Pioneer Desire- (OFMS, Book 2)- Ardan and Deirdre

Pioneer Yearning- (OFMS, Book 3) Niamh and Cormac

Pioneer Longing (OFMS, Book 4)- Eamon and Phoebe

Pioneer Bliss (OFMS, Book 5) Declan and Lorena

Pioneer Devotion (OFMS, Book 6) Maggie and Dunmore-

Pioneer Ardor (OFMS, Book 7) Lucien and Samantha

Pioneer Redemption (OFMS, Book 8) Finn and Winnifred

Pioneer Delight (OFMS, Book 9) Coming August 2022!

Bear Grass Springs Series

Don't worry, I am busy at work on the next book in the series! If you want to make sure you never miss a release, a special, a cover reveal, or a short story just for my fans, sign up for my newsletter!

Immerse yourself in 1880's Montana as the MacKinnon siblings and their extended family find love!

Montana Untamed (BGS, Book 1) Cailean and Annabelle

Montana Grit (BGS, Book 2) Alistair and Leticia

Montana Maverick (BGS, Book 3) Ewan and Jessamine

Montana Renegade(BGS, Book 4) Warren and Helen

Jubilant Montana Christmas (BGS, Book 5) Leena and Karl

Montana Wrangler (BGS, Book 6) Sorcha and Frederick

Unbridled Montana Passion (BGS, Book 7) Fidelia and Bears

Montana Vagabond (BGS, Book 8) Jane and Ben

Exultant Montana Christmas (BGS, Book 9) Ewan and Jessamine

Lassoing a Montana Heart, (BGS, Book 10)- Slims and Davina

Healing Montana Love (BGS Book 11)- Dalton and Charlotte

Runaway Montana Groom (BGS, Book 12) Peter and Philomena-

Substitute Montana Bride (BGS Book 13) Tobias and Alvira

Enraptured Montana Bachelor (BGS Book 14) Cole and Wilhelmina

Fervent Montana Devotion (BGS, Book 15) Shorty and Rose

Reluctant Montana Husband (BGS, Book 16) Coming October 2022!

The Banished Saga

Follow the McLeod, Sullivan and Russell families as they find love, their
loyalties are tested, and they overcome the challenges of their time. A
sweeping saga set between Boston and Montana in early 1900's America.

The Banished Saga: (In Order)

Love's First Flames (Prequel)

Banished Love (Banished Saga, Book One)

Reclaimed Love (Banished Saga, Book Two)

Undaunted Love(Banished Saga, Book Three) (Part One)

Undaunted Love (Banished Saga, Book Three) (Part Two)

AFTERWORD

Thank you for reading, Montana Grit! I hope you are enjoying this new series as much as I am enjoying writing it. I love hearing from you, so please feel free to write me and let me know what you think! You can reach me at: ramona@ramonaflightner.com

Ramona

ABOUT THE AUTHOR

Ramona is a historical romance author who loves to immerse herself in research as much as she loves writing. A native of Montana, every day she marvels that she gets to live in such a beautiful place. When she's not writing, her favorite pastimes are fly fishing the cool clear streams of a Montana river, hiking in the mountains, and spending time with family and friends.

Ramona's heroines are strong, resilient women, the type of women you'd love to have as your best friend. Her heroes are loyal and honorable, men you'd love to meet or bring home to introduce to your family for Sunday dinner. She hopes her stories bring the past alive and allow you to forget the outside world for a while.